CENTRAL
FRIENDS

THE
VANISHING
SMILE

THE
VANISHING
SMILE

EARL EMERSON

BALLANTINE BOOKS
NEW YORK

Library of Congress Cataloging-in-Publication Data
Emerson, Earl W.
  The vanishing smile / by Earl Emerson.
    p.   cm.
  ISBN 0-345-38486-5 (alk. paper)
    1. Black, Thomas (Fictitious character)—Fiction.   2. Private investigators—
Washington (State)—Seattle—Fiction.   I. Title.
PS3555.M39V3   1995
813'.54—dc20   95-5594
                                                                               CIP

Manufactured in the United States of America
First Edition: November 1995
10 9 8 7 6 5 4 3 2 1

TO SANDY,
WHOSE SMILE NEVER VANISHES

"I do not draw a very sharp line between business and sex," she said evenly. "And you cannot humiliate me. Sex is a net with which I catch fools. Some of these fools are useful and generous. Occasionally one is dangerous."

—*Raymond Chandler*

A good detective never marries.

—*Raymond Chandler*

THE
VANISHING
SMILE

CHAPTER 1

We met purely by chance one evening at McCormick's. I was walking up Fourth Avenue in the rain and she was sitting inside at a small table in the bar area.

She was alone.

I stepped into the alcove entrance and shook my umbrella dry, then stood as dull and dumb as a new patient in a brain ward.

The hostess, a delicate-looking young woman with green eyes, smiled and told me my party had not yet arrived. The wait for a table would be forty-five minutes. Would I like to sit in the bar? "I guess so," I said. "Sure."

It was Friday night, showering in bursts, not quite cold enough for snow, and McCormick's, a fish house on Fourth, smelled of booze, wet wool, cigarette smoke, perfume, and broiled salmon. It was bustling with bonhomie and the rowdy, slightly fatuous jokes you're more likely to hear at the end of the week when people are off guard and feeling loose. A noisy backdrop of chitchat robbed my thoughts of the last strains of coherence.

Hands shoveled into the pockets of my slacks, I hesitated ten feet from Kathy Birchfield's table while a florid-faced man in a suit marched up to her and said something I couldn't catch over the hubbub. Perched on stools, two of his cronies sat at the bar sipping mai tais and eyeballing women. When the florid-faced man turned to leave, he saw me and said, "Don't bother, my friend. She's got a tongue like a jazzman's razor."

I took a couple of steps forward. For a moment or two she must have thought I was a waiter or another bumbling pickup artist. When she finally looked up from a section of the *New York Times*, she spoke without blinking.

"Shoot anybody lately?"

She might have spent weeks trying to come up with a crack that would have cut deeper, yet it had rolled off her tongue like a grape off a table. When I glanced around the room, the hostess caught my eye and smiled one of those institutional smiles designed to make sure you didn't catch her eye again.

"Meeting a client?" I asked.

"Actually, a man I've never seen. Connected loosely to something I'm working on. Sounded quite charming over the phone."

"How is the office these days?"

"About the same as when you decided to move out—what, five months ago?"

"If I remember, you waited until I was in the hospital and then threw my stuff into the hall."

"We put everything in boxes," she replied. "We didn't know where you were."

"Yeah? Well, somebody heisted my stuffed dog, Alfred. You going to have dinner with him?"

"Your stuffed dog?"

"This guy you're waiting for."

"Depends."

Her shiny black hair was pulled back tightly and knotted into a bun. Her skin had that pale winter look it took on so readily. Her bearing was so easy she might have owned the joint. She was prettier than I remembered, though lately I had been hard at the remembering.

"We haven't seen each other in a while," I said. "I thought you'd be friendlier."

"You should expect a person to get a little distant after you kill her fiancé."

"It was an accident. You know that."

"I'm afraid I no longer believe in accidents."

"Convenient."

"No, I don't think it is convenient. I think it's closer to the truth of the universe. I've been thinking a lot, trying to gather in truths, and I think this is one of them. There are no accidents."

"If I *could* take it back, I *would* take it back. You know that."

"Why? Because I walked out of your life?"

"That, yes. And the rest of it."

"We all do what we have to do. I did. You did."

"And Philip did."

"Yes. And Philip did."

"Mind if I sit down?"

"Of course not."

Laying my umbrella and raincoat on the bench seat along the wall, I dropped into a chair across from the woman I loved. I felt like a naughty child in a corner.

CHAPTER 2

Months ago our friendship had disintegrated, the intervening time filled with a groggy and, for me, depressing silence between us that made me feel like one of those wretches in a bad French novel kept alive only by the hope of dying.

At the end of last summer Kathy told me she was engaged to a man I considered a phony.

Because it was hard to remember a time when we hadn't been best friends, in the strictest brotherly/sisterly fashion, I reacted to the news of her engagement in a manner that surprised her.

I kissed her, and not the way you kiss a woman who has moments earlier announced her engagement to another man. Had she slapped my face, or laughed, or asked for an apology, I might have scampered off into a corner and licked my wounds, but she returned my ardor, tentatively at first, and then with a sort of hunger that confused me. It must have confused her too. I asked her to cancel her engagement to Philip and make a place in her life for me, to which she responded that we would always be friends, and to which I responded that friendship wasn't what I had in mind. Bewildered and surprised, she found it impossible to camouflage her delight at my actions. What I had found hard to camouflage was that my kiss and proposal had startled me as much as it had her. But all that had passed.

Sitting at the table in McCormick's, it was a long while before either of us spoke. When the waitress arrived, Kathy ordered a glass of wine. I asked for a soda. "Still a teetotaler?" she asked, knowing I hated the word.

"Some things don't change. Can I see you after your appointment?"

"It might take a while."

"I don't mind waiting."

"I'm not sure that's such a good idea."

"Kathy, I *need* to see you."

Her eyes widened slightly and I thought her voice wavered. "What about your date? You don't want to stand her up, do you?"

"I got no date. It's my father."

"You haven't been playing the field?"

"My last date was the one you fixed up for me last summer. The genius bus driver who almost broke my neck."

She smiled, and I thought for a moment she was going to let loose a laugh. "So you're having dinner with your father? All the way from Tacoma?"

"All the way from New Jersey."

"What? Your other father? You finally met up with your real dad?"

"My sister looked him up."

"What's he like?"

"Nigel means well, but he's the kind of guy who argues with bus drivers about their routes."

"You know, that's quite a coincidence. The man I'm supposed to meet is named Nigel."

"Yeah, well, it's probably not Nigel Reusser."

Kathy dug into her purse, unfolded a slip of paper. "Nigel Reusser is your father?"

"Oh, cripes."

"Your father—"

"He must have engineered this to get us together. He'll be fashionably late and then he'll pontificate about friendship and lost opportunities and—"

"But your last name is Black."

"My adopted father gave me his last name. My birth name was Reusser. I told you."

"So your father knows all about us?"

"*I* didn't tell him."

"Why didn't you tell him?"

"You are not a topic I discuss with Nigel."

We gazed at each other across the small table. I had forgotten how truly violet her eyes were. Had forgotten her flawless skin. The fullness of her lips. It seems I had been in the company of a great many thin-lipped women lately. I had forgotten the way she could look at me. I had forgotten her habit of squinting slightly, a friendly hint of coauthored amusement in her eyes, just before she burst into laughter. I hadn't heard her laugh in a long while, not that I was going to hear it tonight.

And then the look evaporated. It was hard to ignore our roles: I the reckless killer, she the wronged and grieving fiancée. It was hard to deny her the grief or bitterness I had caused. It had been my gun, my bullets, and my finger on the trigger that killed him. Philip Bacon had been a grade school teacher. I was a private investigator, an ex-cop, an experienced pistoleer. I should have been in control of the situation.

The bar was so raucous now we almost had to shout to be heard. "I'm sorry, Kathy. Nigel likes to think he's a page or two ahead of God."

"Nothing to be sorry about. But why something like this?"

"Somebody probably told him I'm going crazy without you."

She sat on that for a minute, fussing with her purse, then met my eyes. "Are you?"

"Yes."

Kathy sipped from her drink and looked me over. "I don't see any percentage in disappointing your father. Let's go have dinner."

Producing her institutional smile again, our hostess seated us at a booth in the restaurant. For thirty-five minutes we made small talk and waited for Nigel, and then, too hungry to care any longer, we ordered: Kathy the salmon, I the mussels. It was obviously a mercy dinner, but at this point, in order to stay close to her, I would have volunteered to clean out the used gum wrappers from the bottom of her coat pocket.

"Maybe he planned not to be here," she said.

"Nigel is not the sort to consciously miss an occasion to hold forth."

"Then we should have waited?"

"I don't think so. The last time Nigel was late for a dinner with me, he was two days late."

"I gather you don't get along."

"I don't know. He came out here for a two-week visit. Staying with my sister. So far, it's been two months."

"I'm sorry." The tone of her voice reminded me how much the legends of my battered youth affected her. The smart tactic here would be to recount a couple of bad Christmases I'd had as a kid and gain her sympathy, but the intrigue was too squalid even for me.

From our first meeting years earlier, Kathy and I had shared an effortless, albeit platonic grace, one filled with a jesting camaraderie more often shared by companions of the same sex than those of the opposite, a camaraderie that had puzzled our friends and infuriated our lovers. Despite our former closeness, I was not optimistic that we would ever be friends again, much less lovers, which we had never been. In fact, I was mildly perplexed over why she agreed to have dinner with me.

We managed to converse amicably enough, although our discussion was so orthodox and politic it would have made a cultural anthropologist guffaw. It was a bizarre feeling to feign indifference across the table from a woman I knew so well that I could point out the scar on the bottom of her left foot where she'd stepped on a nail in fifth grade. Or the slight imperfection on her upper lip where she had split it open in a game of tackle football with the older neighborhood toughs when she was thirteen.

As we gabbed, I mentally rehearsed a short speech of apology for murdering her fiancé, but each time I was on the verge of uttering it, I chickened out. The truth be known, there was no explanation that would exculpate me, nor any words I could devise that would do anything more than stir up nasty sediment—and sentiment. No revelation that would make her feel better or me feel blameless. The killing had been accidental. Sure, I hadn't liked the guy, but he hadn't liked me much either, and she already knew it was an accident.

After we had eaten, Kathy got a phone call. She returned a few minutes later with a dour look, then slid into the booth, picked up her fork, reached across the table and chipped off a corner of my carrot cake. It was the most intimate act she had engaged in all evening, and the multiple elements of desire it telegraphed through me were downright spooky. For a moment I was as giddy as a librarian with a brand-new tea bag.

"What's the matter?" she asked.

"Nothing. So who called?"

"It was the strangest conversation. I've got a client who needs to see me tonight. She's been under considerable pressure. She asked if I knew any 'hired muscle.' "

"How'd she find you?"

"My answering service."

"You tell her you were having dinner with a guy who has at least two muscles in each arm?"

"I believe she was thinking more along the lines of an ex–nose guard from the Green Bay Packers. Anyway, I've got to leave. The weather's bad and it's a long drive."

"Where is she?"

"Snoqualmie Falls. Wants to meet me at the lodge." Kathy picked up her purse and coat and began sliding out of the booth.

"Uh-uh," I said, signaling for the bill. "No way. Your client wants hired muscle and you're heading there alone at night in this rain? I'll go with you."

"I'm sure it's not anything. You don't have to tag along."

"I may not *have* to, Sister. But you know me. Any excuse to hang around a babe."

Though she never would have extended the invitation, I surmised from her expression that she was glad I was coming. She picked up her purse and coat and slid out of the booth, and for a single moment I thought everything was going to be all right between us, but then, walking out to her car as the rain made loud finger-taps on my umbrella, she grew impersonal again, as if the downpour and the night and our forced huddling under the umbrella had doused whatever intimacy we might have re-kindled, as if she had remembered how she was supposed to behave around me.

Climbing into her Firebird, I flashed back a year earlier to a football game in my backyard, thought about it on the drive out of Seattle.

Kathy had been quarterbacking a ragtag team made up mostly of her nephews when I tackled her, manhandled her over my shoulder, and carried her across our goal line, she laughing, trying to pass the football to Petey, her sister's ten-year-old. Later, Petey showed us how he could touch his nose with his tongue. We almost died laughing that afternoon, our jeans stained with grass and dirt and crushed crab apples from the tree in my yard. I could still remember the feel of Kathy's hips across my shoulder, the backs of her legs in my hands, her squirming body. I could remember the look of exhilaration in her eyes, too, when we rolled together in the damp grass after she and her nephews knocked me down.

We took the Fourth Avenue South ramp onto I-90 and crossed Lake Washington on the third and newest floating bridge. We were quiet for most of the drive. Thirty minutes out of Seattle we exited onto the Preston/Fall City Road and drove down into the valley, then followed Highway 202 toward Sno-qualmie and the falls. The closer we got to the foothills, the harder the rain fell. Here and there in the darkness we could see pastured horses, barns, and evergreens towering alongside the roadway.

At last Kathy broke the silence. "I'm sorry about that crack."

"Which crack?"

"When I first saw you? Back at McCormick's?"

" 'Shoot anybody lately?' "

"That's the one."

"I've heard worse."

"Not from me."

"Who is your client, anyway?"

"A woman named Marian. She was about the first client I ever had. I helped her with a divorce a few years ago. She said she's meeting somebody out here and feels as if she might be in danger. I was supposed to bring a man who was . . ."

"What?"

"Big and scary and ugly, she said." Kathy laughed. "Two out of three ain't bad."

"Two out of three? Which two?"

Kathy laughed louder this time and didn't reply.

It was raining so hard that when Kathy tapped the high beams, the glare against the raindrops edited our field of vision down to only a few feet. On low beam, the headlights pushed a narrow and inadequate cone of light in front of us. The wipers worked across the windshield. All four tires channeled noisy jets of water against the underside of the car. The radio was so low we almost couldn't hear it. I was still trying to think of something clever to say when a woman stepped out of nowhere and went over the top of the Firebird with a thunkity-thunk.

For a split second as the body passed inches over our heads, I thought I heard a strangled scream. Or perhaps it was only the sound of jewelry scratching the paint on the roof.

CHAPTER 3

One leg stiff on the brake pedal, Kathy wrestled the steering wheel trying to keep us in a straight line.

Part of her problem was the hay truck barreling down the hill several feet into our lane, headlights bleaching the inside of our car, blinding both her and me. The lights had burned Kathy's face to a fine frost, and for an instant I thought the whitewash of illumination was going to be the last thing either of us saw. We fishtailed, then skidded to a stop crossways in the road.

Brakes screeching, wheels shuddering, the hay truck halted farther down the hill, and as it did so the second trailer rolled slowly onto its side like a great beast lying down for a nap.

The truck and both trailers ended up blocking the highway, the cab tipped on two wheels and twisted at an angle so that, should the driver open his door, he would fall six vertical feet to the pavement. Dozens of exploded hay bales mulched the scene. The wheels on the upended trailer continued to spin. A hundred yards up the hill two cars braked carefully on the slick pavement. I glanced at my watch and wrote the time on my wrist.

Kathy's body was pulsating in a high fever of disbelief. I reached across, turned off the ignition, set the emergency brake, cupped her chin in my hands and whispered, "You all right?"

"I think I wet my pants."

"I think I did too. Don't worry about it."

"I can't believe what just happened. I can't believe it. Did I kill him?"

"I think it was a woman."

"Is there any chance?"

"I don't know. Listen, I'm going to see if I can give some first aid. Leave your lights on and stay in the car. Another accident isn't going to help anybody." Her body began quivering uncontrollably, and though I yearned to stay with her, somebody had to check the victim. There was the additional prospect that the driver of the hay rig was hurt.

When I got out of the car, rain pelted my face so that in seconds my hair was pasted to my skull. Gusts of wind brushed the roadway, spitting rain that felt like BBs.

I jogged down the highway, headlights from above spearing the showers so that individual droplets stood out like fast-falling snow. Douglas firs surrounded the road on both sides. A high bank on my left was spotty with low ferns. There were no streetlights, no ambient light from any nearby city. We might as well have been in the bowels of a national park. The big truck had been traveling too fast for this road under normal circumstances, yet tonight half an inch of rainwater gushed across the macadam.

When I reached her, I found myself overwhelmed with an incredible sadness, for, not only was she dead, but there was no doubt it would be a closed-coffin ceremony. In one respect she resembled any other roadkill, so much broken bone and gristle, yet she had been human only moments before, had been a daughter, a sister, a mother, a wife, maybe even a grandmother.

The victim had gone over the top of our car and had been lying on her back in the roadway when the rear duals of the tractor trailer rig passed over her.

It was while I was standing over the body that I noticed a car a hundred yards in front of Kathy's Firebird. The car, an older American sedan, pulled away from the right shoulder and accelerated up the hill away from us. The driver—who appeared to be male and large—was silhouetted briefly in a splash of headlights from the idling traffic above. He was situated toward the middle of the front seat instead of the driver's side. He spun his rear tires a couple of times, making a high-pitched whistling noise, and disappeared around the curve. Sixty seconds had elapsed from the time of impact. He might have been a turnaround, but I had a sense that he'd been there all the while. Somehow I'd missed him in the hurly-burly of lights and brakes and rain.

The victim had on a yellow anorak, which was pulled up awkwardly over her shoulders. She was also wearing blue jeans and one deck shoe. The other shoe was sitting upright in the road back at the point of impact. Next to the upright shoe on the other side of the dew line, a small foreign car was parked. Unbroken, a pair of spectacles was still on her face and in just about the right place. A gray-haired woman, she had a deep tan and the kind of wrinkles that come from decades of too much sun. To my horror, the situation reminded me of a bad joke. Why did the chicken cross the road? Because it wanted to show the possum it could be done. I wondered who she had been trying to show.

By the time I got to him, the driver of the hay truck had his door open and had dropped to the pavement. He wore cowboy boots, a black Garth Brooks T-shirt, and dirty jeans that were so tight he could hardly walk. He had veined arms, large hands, scruffy hair, and a tire iron in his fist. "You all right?" I asked.

"You the asshole was driving?"

"You didn't hit your head or chest or anything?"

"What the hell happened? You fuckers were all *over* the road. You know how much money this is going to cost me?"

"Not a lot we can do about it now. We'll have to sit tight until the State Patrol gets here."

"I oughta break your head."

"You're the one who put tire tracks on her. If you'll notice, she's in *our* lane."

"Tire tracks? What the hell you talking about?"

"The lady you ran over."

"You stupid fucker. I didn't run over no lady. What the hell you talking about?" He stepped closer and waved the tire iron. I nodded at the body. Rainwater, alfalfa fragments, and blood sluiced past his boots as the trucker walked over and stared at her. "Oh, shit," he said, trotting toward the soggy hillside to empty his stomach.

Kathy had piloted the Firebird around the curve, but because it was a curve, her headlights had allowed the woman and her parked car a certain amount of shadow in which to lie concealed. To make matters worse, there had been the hay truck careening down the hill in our lane with its lights on high beam.

There would be no skid marks, for we had all been motoring on a layer of rainwater, road oil, guesswork, and raw hope. Aside from our vehicles, the body, and the single deck shoe sitting at the point where we had struck her, I failed to spot any physical evidence.

A minute later two volunteer firefighters jogged down the hillside with a first aid kit, identifying themselves loudly and asking if everyone was all right. They stood over the dead woman for only a second. As they returned to their pickup truck I noticed there was a different hang to their jackets. When they passed the fogged windows of the Firebird, Kathy still had not budged.

I mulled over the situation as a noise began registering at the outer edges of my consciousness. It had been going on for some time, but now that I had a moment, I realized it was coming from the twenty-year-old Datsun B-210 parked alongside the roadway. Vapors exhaled off the hood in small puffs, so I knew it had been driven recently, that the engine was warm.

As I approached the vehicle, a small, white poodle leaped at the window and yapped at me from the backseat. A duplicate poodle sat calmly behind the steering wheel with the implacable veneer of a dog who thinks he's human, the kind that climbs behind the wheel the moment his owner gets out and then refuses to move when the owner comes back. My dog did the same thing, and I had only recently convinced the neighborhood kids that he possessed a driver's license to go with the attitude.

Even with the raincoat, I was sopping now, rain trickling down my hair and neck. My damp trousers caught on my legs when I walked.

A state trooper brought his car, blue lights flashing, slowly around the queue on the hill and parked above Kathy's Firebird. Another police car, this one county, parked at the curve to block traffic.

Wearing a long rain slicker and his World War I hat with a plastic cover, the trooper got out and walked to Kathy's window, said something, and then came toward me, walking carefully on the wet pavement in his spit-shined brogans. When he drew close, I nodded at the lump in the roadway. He went over to the dead woman and a few moments later made a call on his portable radio.

CHAPTER 4

After giving my version of the accident, I watched the trooper open the passenger door of the Datsun and go through the purse on the seat. The poodles sat without barking, as alert as racehorses at the starting gate. The one in the back kept up a little dance with his front paws, the way a cat being petted would knead a carpet.

The driver's license in the purse belonged to a woman named Rosemary Wright. Five feet six inches tall. A hundred fifteen pounds. Gray eyes. Brown hair. Born seventy-one years ago. The description, except for the brown hair, seemed to fit the woman on the highway. The trooper, who was tall and saturnine and looked as if he'd graduated from high school last week, crouched beside the open passenger door in the rain and penned notes that were so square and precise a machine might have stamped them out. As he did this, the truck driver strutted past with a fistful of unlit flares and a bloodless look on his face, boots tattooing a dull wooden noise on the pavement that contrasted oddly with the staccato pelting of the rain on the roof of the car.

The Datsun reeked of dog, its seats webbed with animal hair. Two cigarette butts had been snubbed out in the otherwise pristine ashtray. This woman either didn't smoke or scoured her ashtray with cleanser and metal polish after she did.

A note that looked as if it had been there a while was taped to the dashboard: THOU HAST BROKEN THE TEETH OF THE UNGODLY. The heating controls were set on defrost, which meant it had probably been raining when the car was last driven. No surprise, since it had been raining everywhere the past couple of days. A cluster of keys, a rabbit's foot, and a tiny canister of pepper spray dangled from the ignition. The driver's window was rolled down an inch, probably for the comfort of the dogs. Rain had spattered the interior.

"My second fatal tonight," said the trooper. "Just came from a bad one on I-90."

He made me recount the story, this time in the back of his car, moisture rising off me in visible whorls. He sat in the front and made finicky notes. When I concluded, he walked over and brought Kathy through the rain. Avoiding my eyes, she sat next to me and ran through her version in a faltering voice.

She was trembling, seemed on the verge of losing her coherence a couple of times. Our stories diverged slightly, as unrehearsed stories did in times of stress. She did not realize the hay truck had drifted into our lane. Nor was she as certain as I was that his brights had been on.

Afterward, Kathy and I went back to the Firebird, waiting for the accident investigation officers to wrap up their measurements and photography. I was in the driver's seat now, and after a while I turned over the motor and ran the heater to brush the fog off the windows. Using an index finger, Kathy wrote something on the side window where I couldn't see it.

"What about my client? I can't leave Mrs. Wright out here at this time of night thinking I'll be there any minute."

I began to get a vaguely electric feeling in the pit of my stomach. "Mrs. Wright? Did you say her name was Marian? Or was it Rosemary?"

"Rosemary Marian. She prefers her middle name, though. How did you know?"

"Seventy-one years old? Gray eyes? Gray hair? Rosemary Marian Wright?"

"What are you talking about?"

"Kathy, I'm sorry. I'm pretty sure she was the lady we hit."

She wrote on the window again. "This is a very bad joke, Thomas."

"She had poodles."

"Marian did. She took them everywhere."

"There are poodles in that car. The trooper went through her purse. I saw the license."

"Oh, Christ. I killed my own client."

"It was an accident, Kathy." She sulked in a stupor in the humid atmosphere of the car for a long while. It was bad enough to see one's universe shattered in the blink of an eye, but to have it altered twice in the space of twenty minutes was mind-boggling. I knew because I had gone through an identical cataclysm last autumn: shooting a man and five minutes later finding out he was Kathy's fiancé.

We watched the flashing blue lights and flares through the steam on the windows, the colors painting a Barnum and Bailey atmosphere over our plight. Finally, Kathy said, "Thomas? I feel sort of dizzy and tingly around my lips and the tips of my fingers . . . and I have the strangest sensation that I'm in a dream. Like none of this happened. It reminds me of when I was a kid and used to have headgear nightmares."

"You're hyperventilating."

"I didn't know anybody could feel this lousy without being dead."

I wanted to say welcome to the club. I wanted to say, you want to feel bad, try murdering the boyfriend of the woman you love. Try that on for half a year or so. But I kept my mouth shut. As much ruminating as she was bound to indulge in the next few weeks, she would discover the parallel for herself.

A second trooper rapped on Kathy's window and stood in the rain asking the same questions the first had. When Kathy mentioned the dead woman was a client, he gave us a look salted with mistrust, though you could see him trying to keep a facade of normality on his face. He moved from Kathy's window to the first trooper and they conferred, each making a point not to glance our way.

"I don't get it," Kathy said. "She was supposed to meet me up at the lodge. It's—what, three miles up the hill to the lodge?"

"It's more like a mile. We take a lot of Sunday club rides this way."

"So what was she doing here in the rain?"

"Coulda been a lot of things. Car trouble. Maybe she had been drinking."

"Marian didn't drink. And how did she get out in the road like that? So quickly?"

"I hate to ask this, but had she ever discussed suicide?"

"Marian was the last person on earth to think about suicide."

"She know what sort of car you drove?"

"I'd taken her to lunch once or twice. Sure. What do you mean by that? Are you saying she was waiting here to throw herself in front of my car?"

"I was thinking more along the lines of her car breaks down, she runs out of gas, whatever, she knows you'll be here any minute, she waits until she thinks she recognizes your car and steps into the road attempting to flag you down. Maybe she gets disoriented with the rain and the headlights. People lose their night vision when they get older. She misjudges and steps smack in front of you."

"Geez, Thomas. She has a son, but they're estranged. What am I going to tell him? I don't even know if I can find him." She began sobbing. After a moment's hesitation, I leaned across and draped an arm over her shoulders. We sat like that for a long while.

When they finally let us go, we took the poodles and I drove Kathy back to Seattle, to a house on Queen Anne Hill that had been converted into apartments. I knew the address because I had been past it a couple of times, but I let her give directions just the same, knowing it would force her to focus on something other than the minutiae of the accident. It was a grand old house on Aloha Street on the south side of Queen Anne Hill overlooking the Seattle Center and the Space Needle, downtown, and Elliott Bay. I parked in the graded gravel lot behind the building. At this time of night the Needle looked like a flying saucer on a spindle. "Want me to come in and sit with you for a while?"

"That's okay."

"You sure?"

"I'm only sure of one thing right now."

"What's that?"

"I don't want this car around."

"Why don't I take it and bring it back after the weekend?"

"Thank you. And thank you for offering to come in. I don't want to be alone, but I don't want to be with you either. Don't take that badly. It's just . . ."

"I know." I gave her a peck on the forehead and watched her climb out of the car and stagger across the gravel, followed by Marian Wright's wary poodles. They went along a walkway at the side of the brown-shingled house while I waited until I saw the lights in her upper apartment before heading home.

Four weeks ago, after months of silence, Kathy had phoned me and said hello, just that one word: hello. What made it eerie was that I could tell she wasn't sure I recognized her voice and I sensed her deliberating over whether to identify herself, for she had plainly dialed my number by mistake.

Finally, she said, "Oh, I'm sorry. I guess I got the wrong number."

"Kathy? Is that you?"

"Thomas?"

"I've been waiting for you to call. It's been a while."

"Yes, and I've been meaning to. I really have."

"Wait a minute. You dialed Donna, didn't you?"

"No, not really. Well, yes, I did. I dialed Donna and I got you. You know how close your numbers are. But I was going to call."

"No, you weren't."

"No. I was. I was just thinking about it tonight. I was going to telephone you. I just have a couple of other calls to make first. Believe me."

"You're not just saying this?"

"No. Of course not. You know me better than that."

"And you are going to call back?"

"For sure. So, hey, let me talk to Donna, 'cause I gotta get her before she leaves—she's going to the stock car races with her boyfriend, if you can believe that—and then I'll call you right back. You'll be home, right?"

"I'll be here."

It was the kind of cowardly stunt a man would pull, the kind that would get him talked about across the feminine universe, yet I could see how a woman—pushed to her limits— might pull it too, especially if she was a little flustered and a lot bitter.

The punch line was she never called back, and the coda to the punch line was, of course, that I stayed up past midnight waiting, even though I knew she wouldn't.

CHAPTER 5

Monday morning I bounded up the marble steps into the foyer of the Mutual Life Building at First and Yesler in Pioneer Square, thumbed a button, and rode the elevator to the top floor, trying to pretend the butterfly cotillion in my stomach was from the elevator and not from a battery of memories, impressions, and fantasies that were all zeroing in on Kathy Birchfield.

When Beulah, the receptionist, saw me, she let her mouth fall open and feigned a gagging sound. "You cut your hair," I said. "Looks terrific."

I knocked on Kathy's office door. She opened it and shot a look past my shoulder at the waiting room. "Come in," she said to me. "We'll be just a minute."

The last was spoken to two women on a couch against the wall, each leafing through a *Cosmopolitan*. After she closed the door behind us, Kathy said, "I'm glad you came." Her face was a smidgen puffy and I knew she had been crying. It was the same look she'd worn the weekend she got canned by Leech, Bemis, and Ott.

Across the room behind her desk stood a bear of a man, a black private investigator named Bruno Collins. I had seen him around the courthouse in double-breasted suits that scarcely buttoned around his torso and ties so splashy people asked where he got them—a question that invariably tickled him. The few times I had seen him working, it had been as a bodyguard for celebrities passing through Seattle. Somebody as ample and villainous-looking as Bruno dissuaded most troublemakers.

Although his bulk and somnolent mood dominated Kathy's office, Bruno eyeballed First Avenue throughout our chat as if we didn't exist.

"What's up?" I asked.

"Marian and those two out there were working with Bruno on a project. I need you to help explain the circumstances of . . . you know. The accident." Kathy was having trouble meeting my eyes, the way a rookie snake-oil salesman at a preacher's tea party had trouble pocketing that extra piece of silverware. I was beginning to get the sense she had called me here for this single petition and that afterward she would make no more mistakes with phone numbers. If not for the accident and its aftermath, Friday night, no doubt, would have been our last shot together, but then, I was in no position to guess at this, my recent months having been tempered with borderline bouts of paranoia where she was concerned. "I'm just wondering if you could help me."

"Sure. Bring them in."

She left me alone with Bruno Collins, who might as well have been a file cabinet. I assumed the strong odor of baby powder in the room was coming from him.

It wasn't until I heard one of them laughing and the other working herself out of a fit of giggles the way she might work herself out of a pair of tights that I realized this was going to be no lark.

When they came into the office, the laughter woke Bruno out of his trance. He marched across the room and shook hands with each of them, then me, then took up a post behind us by the door, folding his arms against his gargantuan chest until the sleeves of his suit looked as if they were going to rupture. He had a tiny mustache. The baby powder smell was stultifying up close. The two clients pulled up chairs.

I caught Kathy behind the desk while the women seated

themselves, and I whispered, "I thought you wanted me to explain how it happened, but they don't even know she's dead, do they? You want me to do the whole shebang? Kathy, I can't do this."

"They think she's out of town. I've had such a miserable weekend. I'm in no condition to tell them. Please? These are her best friends."

"Couldn't you have found some close relatives? What about grandchildren? I mean, best friends—that's not that much of a challenge."

"Please?"

I took a deep breath and turned to the two women.

Kathy introduced them as Susie Scudder and Juanita Raykovich. Susie was somewhere in her early twenties, looked as if she had been on a swim team since grade school. Blond and tan even in February, she wore a short bomber jacket with rabbit fur inside, a tight green skirt that left most of her brown legs bare, and tall, black Dr. Martens styled like marine combat boots. She was small-breasted, big-thighed, well-muscled, and wide across the shoulders. I had the sense that she liked herself a lot, which was not meant as an unfavorable comment, merely a comment. She did not seem a plausible candidate as best friend of a woman in her seventies. Women's best friends tend to come from their own generation, not from their grandchildren's.

Juanita Raykovich was fifteen years older, another kid compared to Wright, thin, with long auburn hair and bulging eyes. She wore an immaculate navy skirt and matching jacket. She didn't like herself quite as much as Susie, or at least it didn't show as much, but she imparted a self-confident air too, as if she knew what she was capable of and had demonstrated prowess in unguessed-at arenas.

"I have some bad news for you both," I said, figuring it was best to get the worst over quickly. "Your friend, Marian Wright, has been involved in a traffic accident. I'm afraid she's dead."

Both women lapsed into silence. After a few moments Bruno said, "How can she be dead? She's in Arizona." It didn't make a lot of sense, but it defused the immediate shock. Both women twisted around to look at him.

"It happened here in Washington. We were supposed to meet her at the Salish Lodge in Snoqualmie on Friday night. Ms. Birchfield and I were driving to the meeting. For some reason we haven't been able to figure out, your friend stepped into the highway in front of Ms. Birchfield's car. We don't even know why she was there on the road. Or why she called Kathy."

"What?" Juanita Raykovich half stood out of her chair. "*You* hit her?" Kathy turned from the window, nodding, tears blurring her violet eyes. Nobody said anything for half a minute. Finally, Raykovich found her voice. "But how could that happen?"

"Right now, it looks like a bad accident and a worse coincidence," I said. "The State Patrol's investigating. I doubt they're going to find out anything we don't already know, though. As far as the coincidence goes . . ." I shrugged, not knowing what to say.

"Even when they get done with their report, you won't know what she was doing out there," said Bruno, knocking tears off the end of his nose with the back of his thick hand.

Susie Scudder tugged at her short skirt. "How could you hit her?"

"It happened so fast," I said. "Kathy didn't really have a prayer."

Bruno pulled out a handkerchief the size of a baby blanket and honked loudly into it. "No," he corrected. "Mrs. Wright didn't have a prayer." Bruno seemed more thoroughly shaken than either of the two women. Or was it that tears simply looked more touching on the formidable bodyguard?

After we had opened all the baggage that burdens announcements such as the one I had handed them, the "poor Marians" and so forth, I said, "Anybody know what Marian was up to last week?"

Juanita Raykovich slumped in her chair, pushed a wad of tissue across her face, dabbed at her frog eyes, and said, "It had something to do with our party. Marian was helping us."

"Party?"

The four of them looked at each other for a couple of beats before Kathy walked around the desk and cleared her throat. "It was really your gig, but I gave it to Bruno. I'm sorry."

"What was *my* gig?" I asked.

"Remember the yellow dog party? Those four guys who wanted you to find their dream girls? Juanita has a friend who knows one of them and he told her about it. She and Susie and Marian got to talking one morning and—"

"We all live in the same condo," said Susie Scudder. "See, we kind of had this book group. A readers' group. We would all three of us read the same book and then discuss it every other Saturday morning at brunch."

Kathy said, "They each had a man from their past they wanted to find."

"Dream guys?"

"You might call them that," said Juanita, glancing at Susie. "Susie was trying to locate a man she met in Sun Valley several years ago. I was looking for a man from my undergrad days at the University of Washington. Marian was tracking down her ex-husband."

"Not for long," said Bruno. "She found Chuck right away. In Arizona. She was looking for somebody else after that. A couple of somebodies. I never knew their names. You see, Mrs. Wright was trying to keep the costs down for Juanita, so she might even have been looking for Juanita's guy. There's no telling who she was tracking in Snoqualmie. Mrs. Wright even drove clean to Arizona in that little car of hers to save money. About wore it out."

"Until a few days ago, she was hunting for Juanita's guy," Susie Scudder said. "But she found him and was moving on."

"She didn't tell any of you what she was moving on to?"

"No."

"So what were you planning for this party?" I asked. "Johnny Mathis records? Wine? A cruise on the bay?"

Juanita Raykovich waggled her crossed leg and said, "Something like that."

I looked at Kathy, who said, "I gave the job to Bruno. I'm sorry."

"You give him my dog too?"

In the corner of the room, high on a file cabinet, stood a stuffed yellow dog, a gift to me from the men involved in the yellow dog party, the dog I thought had been stolen when Kathy threw my belongings into the hall. When I brought it up Friday night, she hadn't bothered to mention she still had it.

"Marian wouldn't have done anything stupid like stepping in front of a car," said Susie. "She had a friend years ago got killed crossing a street. She was always careful. You know what I think? I'm not sure these men we've been trying to dig up are all such upstanding citizens. What if she accidentally stumbled onto something illegal? A drug deal or something? What if . . ." Susie Scudder began crying again, holding her face in her hands. "A week ago she told me she was worried. Why did she need to see Kathy at that time of night? There are questions I'd like answers to."

"Don't look at me," said Bruno, dropping a massive hand onto the doorknob. "Things like this are way out of my territory. I'm superstitious about people getting killed when I'm working a case. I'm outta here. But you want to know something? The way Mrs. Wright handled individuals, she probably made somebody mad. Real mad. Mrs. Wright wasn't always the most delicate soul." He opened the door and left.

All three women turned to me expectantly.

I tried on a smile. "What?"

"Will you find out what Marian was doing when she got killed?" Juanita asked. "We'll pay you."

I looked around the room at the three women. "I guess I could do that."

CHAPTER 6

Bundled up against the wind, Kathy and I strolled beneath banners rippling in the breeze, past pier restaurants and the aquarium, walking and talking and letting the cold air off Elliott Bay chill us.

Years ago, a car filled with besotted marines and their girlfriends had skipped the curb here, flipped over the low concrete railing, and sunk slowly in twenty-five feet of water. The next morning a crowd mobilized to watch the police divers haul eight drowned partygoers out of the drink, all stiffened into various contortions by rigor mortis. It was hard to walk past the spot without thinking about it.

"I feel like a rudderless ship," Kathy said. "I flossed three times this morning. I must have taken twelve showers over the weekend."

"Then comes the sleeplessness. Irritability. Inability to concentrate. Bouts of depression. Some of it won't seem related to the accident, but it all is."

"You talk like some sort of expert."

"I killed somebody last fall, remember?"

"That was different."

I gave her a look, but she was watching the bay. "Tell me how you think it was different."

She mulled it over for a moment and turned to me. "Forget I said that. I'm sorry. And I treated you so abominably after it happened. How can you stand to be around me?"

"If I hadn't helped bag cadavers in the war, I'm not sure I could."

"What war? You weren't in any war." She grabbed my arm playfully, then kept hold of it. After we'd walked another block, she said, "Thanks for agreeing to look into Wright's death for Raykovich."

"I need the money," I lied. I would have used almost any excuse to involve Kathy in my life once more. "Besides, Friday night bothers me too. Why do you think Bruno finked out like that?"

"He *said* he was superstitious."

Despite the threat of rain, we walked beyond Pier 70 and into Myrtle Edwards Park, a long, narrow strip of grass and walking trail along the waterfront. Although we were passed by a few runners in tights and a man and a woman on in-line skates, it was too early for the noon joggers and bodybuilders who trickled along the waterfront from the downtown gyms and offices. We walked the length of the park to the grain terminals and then turned around and got slapped by a cold southerly breeze. The whole thing was beginning to feel a lot like a cheap date, and I couldn't have been more elated.

"Thomas, thank you for kidnapping me and taking me on this walk."

"You like it so much, I'll kidnap you again. Maybe later in the week."

"You know, I didn't leave the house all weekend."

"It's what happens. You hide out. You eat TV dinners. You run out of clean socks. Your circle of friends dwindles."

"The only people I've talked to are my brother, my mother, and you."

A ferry churned through the whitecaps heading toward Bremerton across the Sound. The little green antique trolley toting tourists up and down the waterfront was barely visible in the distance, though the wind carried the clanging sound of its bell clearly. A trio of gulls balanced on the breeze out over the bay, flapping occasionally and waiting for us to discharge bread or garbage or spit chewing gum into the water so they could scoop it up. In the distance we could see the road that went nowhere, the overpass in the sky that had been designed to join a pier that had never been built. Up the hillside to our left a band of office workers hunched near the back door of their building like rats in a garbage dump—banished cigarette smokers.

"Is Bruno any good?" I asked.

"He's honest. He puts in a decent day's work. I don't think he actually had much to do except guide Marian. Juanita Raykovich was footing the bill, so Marian wanted to pay for her share in time."

"Juanita rich or what?"

"Works in international banking. Takes a lot of business trips overseas. What happened was, her brother got killed in a freak accident a couple of years ago and she recently settled a sizable suit."

"Freak accident?"

"Yes. I guess last week they found the man Juanita wants to invite to the party. He's living in Spokane. Married with six kids."

"He get sucked into a jet intake?"

"And the man Susie is looking for may be living in Tacoma. Bruno found out that much."

"The accelerator got stuck on his car while he was trying to park on the ferry?"

"Whatever are you talking about?"

"The freak accident. Juanita's brother? His dentist had a seizure in the middle of a root canal? You can't say freak accident and then leave me hanging."

Kathy laughed. "Do you really need to know?"

"I have to be on the lookout."

"He fell into one of those sidewalk gratings downtown. It just opened up and swallowed him."

"I never walk over those." Kathy looked at me carefully to see whether I was joking, but I kept my face as blank as a kid lying to the teacher.

"You never do walk over them, do you?"

"Never, and neither should you. So who was Marian looking for? Somebody said her ex-husband?"

"At first it was her ex-husband, but she found him in the blink of an eye, or Bruno did. He was deceased. Why don't you walk over them?"

"What? You think I'm stupid?"

"But the chances have to be a million to one."

"Look what happened to Raykovich's brother. So what killed Marian Wright's ex?"

"The way I understand it, he went to the hospital for a broken hip and never came out. Blood clot, I think."

"So Marian was helping the other two."

"Yes, but she was also still looking into some aspect of her ex's past. At least, that's what I think she was doing."

"He was dead. What could she have been looking for?"

"She wouldn't tell anybody."

"And who are the others looking for?"

"Juanita's looking for a man she went to college with."

"For what reason? He's married now, right?"

"Ah, the reasons aren't important." We kept walking. I could feel the wind through my pants, through my socks. Kathy had to be colder than I was, but she seemed to be relishing it.

"Kathy, I've been thinking about this. Marian Wright was involved in something she thought was dangerous. The individual I saw driving away Friday night was sitting toward the middle of his car, almost centered up with his inside mirror."

"What are you saying? He's a mailman with a rural route, so he sits on the wrong side?"

"I'm saying I've seen Bruno cruising around town sitting like that."

"Why would he do that, though?"

"Trying to balance the speakers. Get in the exact center of the car. And the driver I saw leaving the scene. He was roughly the same size and shape as Bruno Collins. He had a square head and short hair like Bruno."

"Bruno is a sweetheart."

"He probably has an alibi anyway. I'll talk to him. Was Marian a smoker?"

"Marian was the worst kind of nonsmoker there is, Thomas, a reformed former smoker. A zealot."

"The ashtray in Marian's car had fresh butts."

"If she'd had a smoker in the car earlier in the week, she would have cleaned it out. You had to know Marian. Those butts were recent."

"So somebody else was in the car that night or that day."

"Had to be."

"Tell me about Marian."

"I wish I knew more. Marian's first husband was in the merchant marine. Died in World War Two in a submarine attack in the North Sea. She was very young and they had been high school sweethearts. Five years later, she got her teaching degree and married the principal of her school. Then he died of some sort of rare blood disease after only a few months, something he picked up in the Pacific in 1944. The last husband I know very little about. They were married more than thirty-five years. Chuck ran a car painting business on Capitol Hill that was only marginally successful. He paid the bills but never made much in the way of profit. Marian taught school. They had one son, in his late twenties now, but except for a few visits during the divorce five years ago, we haven't heard from him.

"I tried to talk her out of the divorce. I suggested counseling, but she wouldn't hear of it. They had a huge house in Edmonds. Lots of friends. What I learned was that she had gone to a doctor to see about what she thought was a woman's problem and was told she had syphilis. Her husband got home from work that night, she confronted him, he confessed he'd had an encounter with a woman at work after a New Year's Eve party, and Marian tossed him out. He was gone that night.

"He volunteered for marriage counseling, psychotherapy, hypnosis, whatever Marian wanted. But all she wanted was a divorce."

"And then what? Five years later, she wants to look him up?"

"Maybe to slap his face. I don't know. Maybe to patch things up. She never said." Kathy's cheeks were pale in the wind, and her hair, most of which was stuffed down her collar, was being blown away from her coat in long strands that whipped around in the breeze. "The sad part was she still loved him. I could see it."

"So your client had syphilis as well as a divorce from a man she still loved?"

"I only learned of the syphilis from the other attorney. I'm sure if I had spoken to her about it, she would have been mortified. She was a remarkable woman and I liked her a lot. And I'm not just saying that because I killed her. Oh, that sounds dreadful."

"There are tons of dreadful things you can say after something like this. Don't worry about it."

I wanted to tell Kathy how easy it was to begin liking someone you had accidentally killed. I wanted to tell her about the genuine cornucopia of affection I felt for Philip Bacon after that night on the hilltop in West Seattle where I put eight bullets through a wall into his back, thinking he was another man who'd trapped me in a vacant house and was trying to kill me. I wanted to tell her how fondly I remembered the way he combed his hair, how grateful I was for the one or two nice things he had said to me during the six months I'd known him. I wanted to tell her how much I admired his gentleness, about my sudden fancy for his mismatched eyes, my instant regret over the jokes I had played on him.

"Thomas, I can't tell you how much I appreciate you investigating Marian's death for us."

"No guarantees. In all likelihood, it was a simple accident."

"By the way, you lost your voice at McCormick's the other night, didn't you? It was funny to see you tongue-tied."

"Tongue-tied?"

"When we met."

"Me?"

"I thought it was kind of cute."

"Tongue-tied? What on earth gave you that idea?"

CHAPTER 7

It was noon by the time I caught up with Bruno Collins.

On the walk to his place from Pioneer Square, I happened on to his car parked at an expired meter, a vintage Chevrolet, pale green, with vanity plates: DETECT1. It was hard enough to tail someone or do surveillance without announcing yourself, so the plates might as well have said STUPID1. I pumped a couple of quarters into the meter so he wouldn't collect a ticket.

I knew little enough about Bruno Collins—only what Kathy had told me that morning and some gossip I'd scrounged up from others in the business. Bruno made his living scaring people, skip tracing, collecting debts, repossessing cars, riding shotgun for visiting politicians and celebrities—in effect, looking, acting, and being a tough hombre.

About a year ago, or so the story went, Bruno, accompanied by his ex-wife and her boyfriend, visited his eleven-year-old son's middle school on parents' night. Bruno found himself in his son's shop class, surrounded by power equipment, welding torches, sanding machines, a myriad of dangerous cutting and crushing tools. Skittish around such machines himself, Bruno's overactive imagination conjured up a thousand ungodly accidents. He watched and listened to the shop teacher for signs of slackness or ineptitude. A robust, laughing specimen who did not impress Bruno in the least, the shop teacher did not realize his lame jokes were making Bruno nervous and somewhat queasy.

When the session was over, Bruno marched from between a drill press and a power jigsaw, pushed a finger into the unsuspecting shop teacher's sternum and whispered, "Just remember. My *kid* loses a finger. *You* lose a finger." It was hard to correlate the Bruno of fable with the smiling, sometimes crying, slightly dim-witted, slightly frightened man I had met.

When I found him, Bruno was in a tiny shoe-repair shop near Second and Cherry, hunched over a backgammon board rolling dice with the shoe-shine man, the two of them looking as serene as clams in a bucket. Bruno's jacket was folded neatly across a chair; his shirtsleeves were rolled into doughnuts on his massive forearms.

"Talk to you a minute?" I said.

When he looked up, his face wrinkled into a frown. "Mrs. Wright was one of the nicest women I ever knew. Treated me real decent."

"Look, Bruno, I'm trying to find out what Marian was doing the night she got killed."

"For the women? You're working for them?"

"Well, you bowed out."

"It just gave me a creepy feeling."

"You mind telling me what you know about Wright's recent activities?"

With a flourish Bruno emptied the cup of dice onto the backgammon board and then exclaimed loudly, "Double sixes!" I waited for him to move his men. He placed one of his opponent's blots on the bar.

"She never said this, but I think she wanted to get back together with her ex. I found him in less than five days. First I tried the Veterans Administration. Then I remembered he still owned a piece of property on Capitol Hill. I called the county assessor and got his address from that. It was a P.O. box right here in Washington, but he hadn't lived here in years. Just picking up his mail. I mailed a letter to the P.O. box telling him he was part of a class action suit and we thought we had a check for two thousand dollars with his name on it. Turned out he was dead, but he'd been remarried and his widow sent me her address in Arizona.

"Now Juanita, she was looking for this guy she knew from college. Mrs. Wright found him too. But the one I did the most work on was Susie Scudder. Doesn't that sound like udder? Scudder, udder?" He chuckled. "She was looking for a man she dated four or five years ago. Met him in Sun Valley. He got her pregnant and now she's got the kid. Cute little rascal. But get this. The kid's father told her he was Eddie Murphy. She thought she had Eddie Murphy's baby. So I go calling all over Hollywood talking shit about how I got a client had Eddie's baby, and it turns out Eddie Murphy's never been to Sun Valley, and now I'm worried about getting hauled into court for slander. Not only that, but she's got a photo somebody took at the lodge of them together, and this guy doesn't even look like Eddie." Bruno laughed, rolled the dice, and made his moves.

"The comedian Eddie Murphy?"

"Right." Bruno watched his opponent roll, then groaned as he hit two of Bruno's blots and moved them onto the bar. I noticed Bruno played a gambler's game, waiting for the good rolls to save him.

"Off the top of your head, Bruno, you don't know what Mrs. Wright was doing last week?"

"Mrs. Wright was a take-charge kind of gal. When I found her ex-husband's widow, she drove right on down. Spent a week helping to find Juanita's man. Last I heard, she got Susie's search narrowed down to the Tacoma area. But I ain't worked on this in a week and a half. I'm telling you, she was a natural detective. A regular Mrs. Marble." He chuckled.

"You have an Arizona address for the ex's widow?"

"I'll give you everything I got." Rolling to either side like a ship on a contrary sea, Collins walked to the rear of the shop. I followed him behind the workbench to a desk in a corner with a lamp over it, photos thumbtacked to the wall alongside phone messages on Post-its. There was an answering machine and a loose beeper that clipped to a belt. The tiny shop smelled of shoe polish, old leather, unsmoked tobacco, and machine oil. A feather duster stood upright on the ends of its feathers by the high window under a faded cardboard sign for a brand of car wax that hadn't been manufactured in thirty years. A pastel boy with rosy cheeks and orange hair slicked down with Brylcreem smirked at us from another wall.

While Bruno riffled through papers in a drawer, I looked over his photos. Except for a Polaroid of his three current clients arm in arm with him, and Polaroids of five or six celebrities I assumed he had been bodyguard to, the photos were of people I didn't recognize. Women I took to be girlfriends. A picture of Bruno fishing with two men. Bruno at the horse track with friends. Bruno standing in front of a Mercedes-Benz with a singer of national repute whose name escaped me. And then Bruno's son, a carbon copy of Bruno, seven, eight, ten pictures of him at different stages of growth. Also hanging on the wall, a small plaster handprint painted gold, the type kids make in kindergarten and bring home for Mother's Day.

Bruno wrote the Arizona address on a scrap of paper and handed it to me, then gave me a sheaf of papers, one at a time, sorting the pages by hand. When he finished, I had sixteen pieces of paper of varying sizes: lists of names, phone numbers, organizations, schools, individuals—none of it collated. When I asked, he gave me the photo of his three clients from the wall.

"You didn't hear no rumors about me, did you?" Bruno asked, grinning.

"What do you mean?"

"You were looking kind of funny. I thought maybe you heard about me and the Swopeses."

"Not really."

"The Swopes brothers? Tussling with them outside the mayor's office and then getting into it with the mayor's driver? All that. It never happened. I don't know anything about their hydroseeding business or their little sister. By the way, their little sister beat up her boyfriend and put him in the hospital. And I don't know a thing about their mother's car."

"I never heard any of that."

"Good," Bruno said. We had been walking to the front of

the shop and now were watching the lunchtime crowd on the sidewalk on Second Avenue. "Just look at them out there. Lemmings."

"People have to make a living."

"Nerds in herds." He smiled at the rhyme. "Nerds in herds."

Halfway to the door I said, "Oh, by the way, Bruno, where were you Friday night?"

"Friday?"

"Yeah. Friday night."

A customer with shoes in a paper sack had come in, squeezing past us in the doorway. "I was at a party at my ex-wife's sister's over on the lake. My nephews' birthday. Both of them have their birthday on the same day. They're twins."

"How long were you there?"

"Oh . . . hey." Bruno smiled and then laughed. His high-boned cheeks grew tight as walnuts and shiny as buttons. The mustache stretched and thinned out. He pointed a finger at my chest and snapped down his thumb, mimicking a gun. "You're checking out my alibi. Very good. Check out the alibis. I like that. I was at my ex-wife's sister's, oh, till about ten-thirty. I like that. Checking the alibis."

He was still laughing gently when he headed back to the backgammon board.

CHAPTER 8

Tuesday morning I hopped the 9:37 A.M. United to Phoenix. It might have seemed a rash gambit, but I didn't have a handle on Marian Wright and I was antsy.

Chuck Wright, Marian's ex-husband, had retired to the Scottsdale-Phoenix region, had remarried, and then two years ago had died. Marian visited the widow three weeks ago. What I wanted to find out was why.

Driving across four states only to discover he was dead was one kettle of fish, but the papers Bruno had given me clearly indicated Marian knew he was underground before gassing up and heading south. It was a long trip just to stare at a gravestone.

And what could she possibly have learned in the desert to propel her into those further weeks of digging? I knew she had been helping with Susie Scudder's search, and Juanita's, but according to both Scudder and Raykovich, she had also spent considerable time on a confidential project of her own.

Yesterday I had phoned Susie Scudder and Juanita Raykovich, chatting almost an hour with Juanita, who wanted to talk down the accident until she had flattened it like a rug.

I went to the King County Courthouse and discovered the maiden name of Bruno Collins's ex-wife, then backtracked and found her sister, also divorced. Her sister *did* have twins and *did* live on the lake and *had* thrown a birthday party Friday night for the twins, but on the phone she was only too happy to shoot down Bruno's alibi, asking pointedly what sort of trouble he was in now.

I also phoned the Salish Lodge, but nobody remembered Marian Wright or anything unusual taking place on Friday, except for the highway accident down the road. They had no record of a dinner reservation for anybody named Wright.

Tuesday, it was seventy-six degrees at the airport in Phoenix, and the dry heat emanating off the concrete and runways felt soothing. I carried my jacket in one hand, a single travel bag in the other, and hailed a cab in the sunshine. "Where to?" he asked.

"Casa Grande."

"Thirty minutes." Outside the airport, some of the cactus on the desert was as tall as a house, the sand baking in browns, ochres, reds. I half expected to see a posse sitting on dusty horses on a ridge but realized that was as fatuous as travelers hitting the Northwest who expected to see logging trucks in downtown Seattle.

My cabdriver was a talker. He went on about Scottsdale and Phoenix having two distinct phases: the quiet summer phase and the winter phase when all the "stinking snowbirds" come back, "fuckin' with the economy," clogging the roads, hogging the utilities, and mucking up all the services. The cabbie had a hooked nose and a degree in architecture, but so far, five years out of college, no job prospects other than ferrying people from the airport, a job for which he seemed particularly well-suited.

"In the winter a hundred and twenty-five coffins a day get shipped north from our airport," he said. "A hundred and twenty-five."

"Coffins?"

"After New Year's and around Christmas it picks up, but those are the averages. They get their pension, the house is paid off, the kids are out of the nest. They come down here where it's warm in the winter so their bones don't ache, and we ship them back in boxes."

We took Highway 10 south to Casa Grande, passing the Superstition Freeway, Guadalupe, Sun Lakes, and roads that went to Tempe, Mesa, Apache Junction.

"It's an RV park," I said.

"Of course it is. I don't know why they don't stay in Wisconsin and buy heat lamps."

When we got to Casa Grande we found a street full of RV parks. It seemed everybody in the enclave where Chuck Wright's widow lived owned a bicycle or a tricycle, a potted plant, and at least one dog. Most of the dogs looked as if they lived off table scraps and hard candy.

The cabbie let me out across from a couple in their late seventies sunning themselves in lawn chairs, the mister in a Speedo, tanned teats drooping onto his ribs, the missus in a two-piece, no teats at all, their skins slack and stretched and a leathery nut-brown. They were holding hands, a bottle of tanning lotion between them on the ground. She gave me directions while he feigned sleep.

The widow, going under the name of Elizabeth O'Connel, lived in a thirty-foot Pace Arrow. Heat radiated off its aluminum walls.

I knocked twice before she walked heavily across the floor and fumbled with the door. She'd had some cosmetic surgery that made it hard to tell whether she was in her fifties or sixties, the judging made even more difficult because she wore enough makeup to ruin a good jacket. The roots of her hair were white, but the rest had been dyed a shade of orange-pink. She cracked the door, and I felt a couple of sniffs of cool air from inside. Peering down at me over rectangular half-lens reading glasses, a glossy magazine in one hand, she said, "Yes?"

"Mrs. O'Connel? We spoke on the phone. My name is Thomas Black. Working for Marian Wright's lawyer."

"You the detective?"

"Private investigator."

"Lawyers disgust me."

"You know how to save one from drowning, don't you?"

"How?"

"Take your foot off his neck."

She smiled in spite of herself. "Raymond's going to think I'm a terrible chump, but come on in." She wore silver Lycra leggings and a short-sleeved aqua sweater. Her feet were bare, knobby, and her toenails were painted pink. She ate right, and she exercised, and she flirted with good surgeons.

It was air-conditioned inside and roomier than I would have guessed—tidy, no knickknacks or anything that might roll around while barreling down the freeway. A Honda Civic with a towing attachment to its nose was parked outside the gate. She sat me against the wall on a narrow sofa that I assumed converted into a guest bed, then knelt beside an air purifier on the floor and tinkered with the controls.

"Dust mites, don't you know. They're everywhere. They sit on your face and eat the dead skin. Get in the pillows and bedding, everywhere. If our eyes were microscopes, we'd go insane."

"I've always suspected as much."

After she was satisfied, she pulled up a bar stool directly in front of me, crossed her legs, and looked me over. Her teeth were long and very white, and her smile was a pleasant surprise. "Tell me what you're after, and I'll see if I can help."

"It is my understanding Marian Wright drove down here."

"Three weeks ago."

"Would you mind telling me what happened?"

"I got a little teed-off with her, let me tell you. I'm still teed-off thinking about it."

"What did she say?"

"Nothing that I would repeat. Even though Chuck is dead, Marian still hadn't gotten over all the imagined slights through the years. She was a brittle woman who disguised herself as tough and so felt like she had to act mean. It wasn't attractive. I'm glad I never got bitter over my divorces. Raymond's due here in an hour. I still talk on the phone to Herbert. Frederick is dead or I'd talk to him too."

"What was the purpose of her visit?"

"She showed up one morning out of the blue trying to get me to show her Chuck's personal papers. Photos. The tax records. His phone book."

"And did you go along with it?"

"Everything but the tax stuff. It burns me up to think about it. I wasn't thinking. Chuck used to say she needed a six-second delay on her mouth. I could see why."

"Was she here long?"

"One visit. Maybe an hour."

"And did she tell you why she wanted to look at his papers?"

"A bunch of reasons. None of them made much sense. If you want the truth, I began to suspect right away she was out of her gourd. Chuck's been dead for two years, but she referred to him like he was in the next room waiting to do her dirt one more time."

"I'll tell you why I'm here. Marian Wright was killed in a traffic accident last week." I waited for a reaction, but there was none except her wiggling her toes.

"I can't imagine why you or her attorney would want to know what she was doing visiting me."

"Her death occurred under circumstances we cannot entirely account for."

"I hate lawyers."

"Do you suppose I could see what she saw?"

Elizabeth O'Connel got up, went into another room, and came back with a handful of manila file folders which she slapped down on the counter. I pulled up a bar stool and she stood up against me.

"We're homeless, you know. Vagabonds. We live in what is basically a truck with a stove in it. Raymond and I drive up to Ohio in the late spring to see his children." After a bit, she pretended to read the papers over my shoulder. She was a friendly woman, but her breath smelled like sour apples, and her breasts were making my arm sweat.

I found handwritten letters from somebody named Dee, brief and chatty and about as neutered of emotion as the printed greetings on a Christmas card. The letters were on top, so I assumed if Marian Wright had been the last one through these papers, she had put them back last. I found pages that had been ripped out of a personal phone directory. There were photographs of fellow sojourners from RV camps. Elizabeth O'Connel pointed out various friends, telling me where they wintered and which states they visited in the summer.

There were no photos of Marian. I found four crossed-out phone listings with area code 206, western Washington numbers. Two numbers for Dee. No last name. One for B.L. And one for Marian. Coming here had been a long shot. Elizabeth had engaged in a lengthy and probably caustic conversation with Marian Wright, yet, in spite of my prodding, she refused to give me any details. I could tell from her tone and body language I wasn't going to get any more out of her.

I picked up the papers and carried them over to the sofa, spreading them beside me so she had no place to sit. "What did Marian say about this?"

"She wanted to know who those phone numbers belonged to. And who was this Dee person."

"And who was Dee?"

"Couldn't say. Chuck never mentioned him."

"You ever go back to Seattle with Chuck?"

"Just once. We saw his son, who was living near the university at that time. Other than that, we had dinner with two or three of the men who used to work in his garage, saw the sights, picked blueberries, and then drove down through Oregon and northern California. To be frank, I need a little blue sky above my head. I didn't see any in Washington, and it was July."

"You have an address for his son?"

She walked over to the telephone and pulled a small book out from a nook in the wall, opened the magnet latch, and read off a phone number and street address in Tulsa. "We haven't kept in touch. Charlie never did like me somehow."

"What did your husband die of?"

"Blood clots. It was so quick." She spewed out the facts as if she were canceling the evening newspaper delivery instead of putting the lid on a man's life. He'd gone to the hospital for a broken hip and died six days later.

It took me ten minutes to copy the names, numbers, and addresses I wanted. I put asterisks beside the people she couldn't tell me about, notations and explanations beside the ones she could. Seven people in the directory were former employees. One had been a golfing buddy. He was dead now, she said. Cancer.

It was beginning to look like Wright had been interested in Dee. I assumed from the handwriting and from the flowered stationery that Dee was a woman, even though O'Connel assumed the opposite. I reread the letters: brief notes about two children who, judging by the context, were in school; reflections about a Ford Taurus bought secondhand; overtures to selling the car for instant cash. The last letter from Dee had come six to eight months before Chuck died, almost three years ago. There had been an intervening Christmas, but no card. They had either lost contact or somebody had removed the card and any later letters.

Outside, the two sun worshipers were gone, probably inside having a nooner. A collection of elderly neighbors in pressed shirts and slacks stood in a driveway visiting. Since talking to the cabbie, I had not been able to get coffins off my mind—coffins polished and gleaming and lined with silk, hundreds of them stacked in warehouses, spit-shined boxes waiting to be routed north from the airport, entire planeloads stuffed with corpses, the bodies laid out, made up, shaved, powdered, costumed, some snazzier than they had ever been in life. I could not help looking at these people and wondering how long before they would be shipped north.

CHAPTER 9

"**K**athy, this is Thomas."

"Where on earth have you been?"

"You miss me?"

"Actually, I thought you might be able to take care of the poodles."

"I'm in Arizona. I guess I should have told you before I left."

"I feel awful every time I look at these dogs, and they're driving me nuts, tearing my place to shreds. You don't have a dog. You like dogs. You have room."

"You'd rather they tear *my* place to shreds?"

"You've got a yard."

"And I'm a sap."

"I didn't say that."

"But you were thinking it. Anyway, I got myself a dog."

"When did this happen?"

"About a week after I got out of the hospital. He saw the buzzards circling and followed me home from Safeway, thought he might get in on some free meat."

"When we drove by, there was some old man on your front porch with a dog. That must have been him."

"If the dog looked as if he'd crawled out of the wrong end

of a tree shredder, it was L.C. If the old man looked about the same, that was my father."

"I should have gone up and introduced myself. I think he was feeding your dog a candy bar."

"L.C. used to live on garbage, and Nigel knows he has a sweet tooth. It's some sort of contest. If my dog likes him better than he likes me, Nigel wins."

"I'm sure you're mistaken. Don't you think?"

"Who knows? Anyway, I called to tell you I'm down here in Arizona backtracking Marian Wright. Bruno wasn't a huge help, so I figured to start from the beginning."

"Who's paying for this?"

"Near as I can figure, I am."

There was a long silence. "If Juanita doesn't want to pick up the tab for the travel, I'll reimburse you."

"Not on your life. You didn't authorize this. I did it on my own hook."

"Don't get noble on me, Thomas. You're not paying money out of your own pocket. No way. Have you found out anything?"

"I got some names and phone numbers, the same ones I think Marian Wright came out of here with. And I spoke with Chuck Wright's second wife. The widow."

"Is that who Marian saw down there?"

"Yes. I'm not sure why, but for the most part she refused to tell me what she and Marian discussed."

"Marian told me she was obstinate."

"I have the feeling Chuck Wright liked his women that way. Also, I found a phone number for Marian's kid. Did you already have that?"

"No."

"He's living in Oklahoma. I called him and told him his mother was dead. He wants to come to Seattle to help settle the estate. He's planning to borrow the plane fare and stay with a friend. He thinks he's coming into some money."

"I guess I didn't tell you. He's not in the will. I suppose you don't want to call him back and tell him?"

"I'm heartless, Kathy, but not that heartless. That's the kind of job we have lawyers for."

"I hope he's a twit. Otherwise, telling him is going to be hard."

"By the way, I still have your car."

"Keep it."

"I can't keep it forever."

The connection was silent. After walking with Kathy on the street, it had become obvious she couldn't look at a Firebird much less drive one. Firebird narcosis. Firebird tremens. I had been driving it with the intention of handing it over to Kathy the next time I saw her, but each time I tried, she said no. Then too, it smelled like her, had her music in the tape rack, her bobby pins on the backseat, her sunglasses in the tray, and I couldn't get enough of it.

"Tell you what I'll do, Sister. I'll sell it for you. Help you find something else."

"That would be good. Thank you. You know, I have an uncle lives down there. Scottsdale."

"Me too. Doesn't everybody?"

"So, when're you coming back?"

"You do miss me."

"It's these dogs. I have to get them out of the house." We were quiet for a long while, four states of silence. "You know what's really awful about them? These dogs?"

"What?"

"I don't think they realize she's dead. They keep going to the door and whining and waiting. I can't stand much more."

"I'll find a home for them when I get back. There must be a nice experimental lab around."

"Don't you dare."

We chatted for a long while after that, not about the case, and not about our histories. About nonsense, about a neighbor of Kathy's who kept fourteen cats, about international headlines, the crisis in Europe, crime, my father. We were like a couple of twelve-year-olds who had only just discovered the telephone. I told her the story of the coffins flying north every day. I told her about the funny feeling I'd had in the RV park, imagining all those people in their coffins. What I didn't tell her was the picture I'd had of her and me in that RV park, living in a motor home, her hair pink, mine gone, a couple of candy-fed dogs with bellies like barrels racing between our rockers.

By the time we were through, we had been on the line an hour and a half. Talking nonstop.

CHAPTER 10

Because the plane landed an hour late at Sea-Tac on Wednesday, it was two in the afternoon by the time I tracked down B.L. in a crisscross directory: phone numbers on one side, addresses and names on the other. B.L. stood for Bain Littrell. A man or a woman?

My call produced only Littrell's answering machine, a woman's voice sounding as if she'd swallowed Valium before laying a message on the tape.

"Yes, operator, I do take collect calls. I'll be out for just a while. Do your talking after the beep, and God bless."

Standing at Beulah's island in the office, I read through a copy of the autopsy report from the medical examiner's office. Wright's death had come as a result of severe trauma. There had been traces of drugs in her system, prescription drugs, antibiotics, though in minuscule amounts. They had found no alcohol in her blood. Also, beneath the fingernails of one hand they had scraped out tiny fragments of red paint. I assumed it matched the crimson of Kathy's Firebird.

"Kathy seen this?"

"Not yet," said Beulah. "She's up at the jail visiting a client. Are you going to move back in? I was wondering if we should clean out your old room. We've been using it for storage."

"It's okay." I grinned. "I'll let you keep your coats in there. And your broken-down TVs."

"We're not keeping our . . ." She laughed.

I phoned a friend in the King County Medical Examiner's office. "Esther. This is Thomas Black."

"I was just going home, and I'll miss my bus if I don't hurry."

"Just take a minute. You sent Kathy Birchfield's office an autopsy report on Rosemary Marian Wright?"

"I remember."

"There's something noted here about marks on her wrists."

"We were talking about that. It was strange for a traffic accident. There was chafing on both wrists and a large bruise on one. Mind you, she was over seventy and, judging by what we saw, prone to bruising. It could have come in the accident, but the regular all-around pattern of chafing didn't look consistent with the irregular trauma you expect from a traffic accident."

"You're saying she might have had restraints on her wrists shortly before death?"

"I'm saying they found some chafing on both wrists and a contusion on one. Make of it what you will. If foul play were part of the scenario, we would have said, yes, restraints were probably used. But it was an accident. That's what the State Patrol concluded. I'm sorry. I have to go now or I'll miss my bus."

"Thanks, Esther."

It was possible to get paranoid by dwelling on every little angle. Signs of bruising on Marian Wright's wrists threw everything out of whack. I began to examine my memories of that night for gaps, for misconstrued details, for wish fulfillment, falsities. Memory is quirky—and not nearly as accurate as we pretend. Together Kathy and I had gone through a tremendous shock, and shock always knocks your sensory perceptions askew. In my zeal to be the shoulder for Kathy to lean on, perhaps I had been too confident of my own perceptions.

What if the collision had been an elaborately staged murder to make people think Wright's death was an accident? Improbable, yes. Impossible, not really.

It was possible, remembering the way she'd stepped into the

roadway, that Marian Wright had been pushed; the way she was holding her hands, as if to balance herself; the look of surprise in her eyes. Maybe I was imagining that look of surprise. No matter how much we wanted them to be something else, memories were usually a muddy conglomeration stitched together from event, logic, suggestion, and outright guessing. It frightened me to recall how many witnesses I had interviewed over the years who swore their memories were facts.

When I phoned the State Patrol, they told me they were ready to release Marian Wright's Datsun to the executor of her estate, namely Kathy as her attorney; so I had Beulah arrange for someone to pick up the car the next day and take it to my house, where I could examine it.

After one of the paralegals helped me find Marian Wright's file folder, I took it to Kathy's office and thumbed through it, noticing as I did so a photo on Kathy's desk of her standing arm-in-arm with Philip. I was pretty sure the photo had not been there when I'd been in her office Monday.

Marian Wright's assets were a teacher's pension that would never keep up with inflation, various certificates of deposit, and a slim bank account. Most of what she had was tied up in her condo.

The family Bible, the baby photos, the memorabilia—all were headed for the Goodwill. The dogs were to receive a small stipend for their upkeep, their eventual home to be decided by her attorney, Kathy. Wright's sister, who was cooped up in a Montana nursing home, would reap the bulk of the loose change. As for her son, Charles Simpson Wright, Jr.—he wasn't mentioned, not even best wishes for the holidays. I wondered what filial crimes lay beneath this mother's snub. When I'd spoken to him, he gave no hint of bad blood in the family, but then, a stranger calls and tells him his mother is dead, he wouldn't blurt out, "That's okay, I didn't much care for the old bag."

Wright's doctor's name was in the papers, and I phoned the office, gave the receptionist some mumbo jumbo about a sudden death and pressing legal matters, and got him to call back in ten minutes.

"Dr. Blood? My name is Thomas Black. I'm an investigator working for Katherine Birchfield, Rosemary Marian Wright's attorney."

"So that *was* her. I saw it in the paper and didn't know if it was the same woman. I'm sorry."

"What I'm calling about is the status of Mrs. Wright's health at the time of her death."

"Yes, I see. Uh, I'm not positive whether I should get into that over the phone. Perhaps if you have the attorney—what did you say her name was?—bring along a copy of the death certificate and her power of attorney . . ."

"You going to be in all week?"

"I golf Thursdays."

Parking Kathy's Firebird in a lot on Fifth Avenue near the main branch of the public library, I went inside past a troupe of bearded citizenry on the patio, shopping carts beside them, heaps of spare clothing, sleeping bags, plastic sacks of whatnot. Four weeks ago a man had died overnight of hypothermia in a doorway, and the city in its guilt had opened the lobbies of several public buildings to the homeless, allowing them to spread their sleeping gear on the marble floors after ten at night as long as they cleared out by six the next morning.

In the religion section I found a Bible concordance and looked up the phrase that had been pasted to Marian's dashboard: *Thou hast broken the teeth of the ungodly*. It was in Psalms, and as many of the Psalms were, it was a lament for the righteous in trouble. The full text read: *Arise, O Lord; save me, O my God: for thou hast smitten all mine enemies upon the cheek bone; thou hast broken the teeth of the ungodly.*

The phrasing painted a picture, but not the one you might expect an elderly woman to cherish. I wondered whose teeth she wanted broken.

For half an hour I sat in the Firebird in the parking lot on Fifth and made calls on my cellular phone. I dialed all the numbers out of Chuck Wright's personal directory, reaching a total of eleven people. Six others did not answer. One number was disconnected. Some hadn't heard anything from Chuck Wright for five years, yet each of the people I spoke to had been contacted by Marian in the past three weeks. A man named Biggs had been a member of the same Lions Club as Chuck Wright.

Biggs told me Marian had phoned and asked if he knew anybody named Bain. Or Dee. Or nicknamed D. Marian hadn't bothered to tell Biggs her ex-husband was deceased, and he was shocked when I told him they were now both dead.

Back at the office I hung around waiting for Kathy to show up, holding my breath with an eye on my stopwatch, and when I tired of that, measuring my biceps with a piece of string. When Beulah caught me using the string to calibrate the circumference of my skull, she got to laughing so hard she had to fetch a cup of cold water to keep from going into hysterics. A guy like me has to appreciate an easy laugher like Beulah.

I phoned Bain Littrell once more. Sounding breathless, she told me she'd just come in the door. After I told her who I was and what I wanted, she said, "I'm sure I don't know anything about any accident." Her voice was livelier than on the answering machine, but not by much. She agreed to speak to me if I drove out to her place.

Traffic was heavy as I drove alongside Jefferson Park Golf Course on Beacon Avenue South, which sported a spacious, grassy median that ran for miles under a canopy of high voltage wires. A low cloud sank on this end of the city like a tent sagging in the rain.

Littrell lived just off Beacon on Juneau Street, where all the houses were small and tidy, the trees bare, the lawns dormant. Her narrow driveway consisted of two strips of concrete laid through the grass. The drapes were drawn. The house looked to be probably two bedrooms and no more than a thousand square feet. It had been painted recently, and the gutters and storm windows were new.

The Acura Legend parked in the driveway, windshield salted with a fine mist, didn't seem to match the modesty of the house. I waited a few minutes before a brunette woman in a light blue dress opened the front door and storm door, holding them until I brushed past her.

Once in the house, she said, "Bain Littrell," and shook my

hand confidently. I gave her one of my cards, the one without the burp gun on it.

She was a pretty woman, but not so pretty as to make your knees buckle. In her late thirties, maybe a few years older than me, she had a softness to her features that portended a sloppy, saggy middle age. She had short, dark hair and the sort of tasteful and discreet makeup job little girls tend to get all wrong when they copy it. She was tall and walked well and had a studied composure about her, as if being careful to avoid any expression that didn't complement her. Because of this, her face was almost as lifeless as her voice. On top of all that, she had the mien of a woman who would advertise for companionship in a church magazine.

"As I mentioned on the phone, I'm trying to track down some information on a woman you might have spoken to in the past few weeks. Marian Wright."

She considered the idea long enough to suck her front teeth with her tongue—an uncharacteristic move, I thought, for someone with such studied facial expressions—then shook her head. I wondered if the question had made her nervous. "No, I don't know that I recall the name."

I showed her the photo I'd taken from Bruno's collection, holding two fingers over the other clients so only Marian was visible. "Look familiar?"

"I don't believe so. No. This involved an accident, you say?"

"Yes, but if you've never seen her, I suppose there's no point in burdening you with the details."

"There is always the possibility I spoke to her on the phone and forgot. What is it you think she might have wanted?"

"Marian? Oh . . . hard to say." She was lying to me, so I saw no point in filling her in.

I looked absently around the pristine living room. A crumpled sack of groceries only partly put away sat on the end of the kitchen table. She'd been home for at least the thirty minutes it had taken me to drive here, but had not put the groceries away. What had she been doing?

"I guess that's it then?" she said, rocking back on one heel.

"One more question, if you don't mind? You know a man

named Chuck Wright? Ran a car painting place up on Capitol Hill. The Queen's Arms Paint. It's still there, although somebody else owns it now. You mighta had a car painted there once?"

"I really don't think so."

"How about somebody named Dee? You know anybody who goes by the name of Dee?" She continued to shake her head. "Elizabeth O'Connel? No? Well, then, thanks for your time."

"Don't worry about it." She gave me another blank look, blinked, then walked me to the front door and, despite the drizzle, stepped out onto the uncovered stoop with me. Littrell wore a sort of stylized sainthood I'd seen some women slide into for various reasons: they'd had an ugly divorce, they'd embraced religion, they were ill, they'd been assaulted, or maybe they had a man in prison, which I believed, because of her phone message, was the case with her. A man in the slammer was the most obvious and, I had found, commonplace reason for women to take collect calls on their answering machines.

An elderly man across the street who'd been eyeballing Bain lost interest when his wife toddled out of their house clasping both hands around the belly of a small dog that had clearly done something wrong.

By the time I got to my bungalow in the University District, I found Nigel in the kitchen fixing dinner. He must have used the door key I had given him so he could feed the dog when I was in Arizona. I parked in the driveway at the side of the house.

My place had a mother-in-law apartment in the basement, and Nigel had not been shy about hinting it would be the perfect hideaway, advising me there might not be too many years left for us to get to know each other, since he had suffered one heart attack already. When I told him there were already two people living there, he suggested in rather highfalutin language that I toss them out on a technicality. He was fond of insinuating that somehow it was my fault he had disappeared and hadn't been back for any of my birthdays or my broken bones or my good grades. The fact was, after disappearing into the void for twenty-five years, he had known where I lived but had not contacted me, while we had had no clues at all about him.

Sporting my green apron over his yellowed dress shirt and tie, Nigel had all four burners glowing. In the living room his shabby blazer was slung neatly over a chair. L.C. was hunkered on the kitchen floor next to two dachshunds awaiting airborne snacks.

"Now don't get yourself in an uproar," Nigel said. "The boys and I have got everything under control. You want to work out, read the paper, whatever, just go on ahead and do your business. This is going to take another hour. Had no idea your old man was a chef, did you?"

"Nope." I thumbed through the accumulated newspapers until I located the two-paragraph accident notice. It mentioned Kathy's name as the driver. I hoped she didn't see it, and if she didn't, that one of her friends didn't point it out to her. I then found the ad I had placed in the classifieds under WITNESSES SOUGHT.

There were several messages on my machine, one from Nigel, who heard his own voice and gave me a live version of the message over the sound of himself on tape, so that I couldn't understand either one, two messages from prospective clients, and one from Kathy saying she wanted to meet me for dinner tomorrow night at Mitchelli's. No messages yet from any prospective witnesses. I didn't bother to ask Nigel to repeat his message a third time. It was something about dinner.

Taking my father at his word, I rigged up my wind trainer in the spare bedroom, opened the windows wide enough to feel the fresh air and listen to the rain dripping from the eaves, tugged on a pair of cycling shorts, and climbed onto my new Eddy Merckx. After pedaling for forty-five minutes, a glance around the kitchen told me I would be up late. He had fried sausage slices for the pasta and had dropped at least one piece of eggplant coated in grease on the floor. The side order was deep-fried calamari, and several pieces of that had been kicked under the cupboards, so the floor was like an ice rink. I stretched, showered, and had dinner with the father I never knew and hadn't seen in nearly thirty years.

"You got ladies cruising your house here, Tommy. Up and down the street waiting for you to come out. I saw one last night. Pretty ladies. When're you going to get spliced?"

"Anytime you say. You pick her out. I'll marry her next week."

"Is that sarcasm? Do I ask you for sarcasm?"

I was four when they divorced, and after the age of seven, he stepped out of our lives the way a drunken rope handler falls out of a blimp, noiselessly, without warning and pretty much forever, except for one birthday present two years later, a picture book on the American Indian, a book I kept near my bed until the pages came loose and drifted out one by one. I could still remember long passages from that book. I knew there had been no letters. No phone calls. No visits. But when I was twenty-five, Mother told me there had been no support payments either. At first I had been willing to make excuses for him, but the more I saw of the world, the more I realized the importance of family, and the more I learned of the fragility of childhood, the less empathy I had for him.

When we finally reunited, I had been wary and, seeing that, he gave me a song and dance about how much he loved me, how much he'd thought about me over the years, how much I meant to him. All of it was hard to swallow.

Before my sister looked him up, the most recent word we'd had on Nigel was that he was somewhere in Utah prospecting for uranium. Utah had seemed like a pretty good place for him.

CHAPTER 11

Thursday morning, Susie Scudder sat on a high window seat in Marian Wright's condominium kicking her bare feet, which did not reach the floor, and watching Tobey while he tried to negotiate a deal with me. The boy wanted to swap a plastic rocket that had seen better days for the leather bomber jacket Kathy had given me two Christmases ago. The jacket would have engulfed him, and I let him try it on so he could see for himself, but all it did was whet his hankering for it. His mother had one lined with rabbit fur, but he wanted to be a pilot and he needed *this* one. He needed the aviator glasses in my pocket too.

I was sitting cross-legged on the floor, and Tobey was at eye level, wiggling and gnashing his teeth as if he had to pee. He had curly hair, a chocolate complexion, and gray-green eyes that fixed on you and did not weaken. In the end I traded him a penlight for the rocket, then lost the rocket for an extra stick of bubble gum he'd found in his mother's purse. He was happy with the deals and ran around whooping and crashing into furniture and swinging his arms wildly. His mother tried to calm him down, but all he did was climb into her wooden clogs and work them like stilts.

The three-story condominium was on Sixteenth Avenue at the south end of Capitol Hill. It was newly built, eight units, two on each floor and two in the basement, maybe ten years old, and sat on a narrow lot with narrow apartments on narrow lots to either side. Marian and Juanita owned side-by-side units on the top floor, with a view of the downtown Seattle skyline in the distance and, closer, the campus of Seattle University.

"The sunsets must be magnificent from here," I said.

"Even from my place downstairs," said Susie, patting the bench seat for Tobey to sit beside her. He looked at her and then raced across the bare wooden floor and skidded on the knees of his jeans.

"Want more gum?" he said.

"I do, but I don't have anything to trade."

"I can take . . ." He gave me a sly look. "Money."

"Tobey," said Susie. "You come over here and sit down this minute. Stop bothering Mr. Black."

It was a large, open apartment with pine floors, colored throw rugs, matching wooden furniture, and very little amiss. The patio had been rebuilt into an atrium with three birdcages and a host of hothouse plants inside. On the wall over a credenza hung a series of photos, several that were obviously Marian's family when she was a child. One had been taken apart recently, the frame loose. I took it off the wall and removed the frame.

Folded lengthwise along the bottom edge, the photograph had been inserted into the frame so that you could not see the torn stockings on the women or the one barefoot kid who I thought might have been Marian herself around the age of twelve or thirteen. Names penned on the back with a fountain pen confirmed my theory. Everyone in the photo looked austere, as if they'd been staring at the sun just before the photo was snapped. I wondered who'd disassembled it and how long ago.

One snapshot must have been Marian Wright's son, Charles Simpson Wright, Jr., although there were no pictures of him after about the age of eight, which struck a chord with me. I had been eight the last time I saw Nigel, on a whirlwind trip through Tacoma, a one-night stop to win his wife and children back, a roll of the dice that went bad, and then a long, dark retreat into obscurity with his Geiger counter.

"How long did you know Marian?"

"Let's see, we moved in after Tobey was born. It must be almost four years."

"You see a lot of her?"

"Marian didn't approve of me being a single mother, but she got me the job at the bank. You should have seen the recommendation she wrote. Baby-sat for me on a moment's notice. Never took a dime."

Tobey was on the bench seat, leaning sleepily against his mother when Juanita Raykovich burst through the door, heels working the hardwood floor like castanets. Raykovich was gussied up in a dark raincoat over a lighter business suit.

"So," she said. "What can we do for you, Mr. Black?"

I got up off the floor and squeezed Tobey's foot. Suddenly shy, he clasped his mother with one arm and pinched one of her small breasts with the other. "For starters, tell me what you were really doing looking for these men."

Juanita and Susie exchanged glances, tried to speak at the same time, then Juanita took over. "Do you really need to know that?"

"I need to know what Marian knew."

"It was my idea." Juanita went to a window alongside the atrium, stood with her legs apart and stared outside. Her auburn hair fanned across her back at the level of her shoulder blades until it spanned the width of her. Headlights from the early morning traffic on Broadway glimmered through the atrium glass. "We heard about your yellow dog party and decided to throw our own."

"For your dream guys?"

The two women looked at each other and giggled. "You don't get it. You really think if three women get together to find men from their past it's to do them favors?"

"What did you have in mind?"

"Look, a man wants a woman from his past, it's because he's thinking romance—or, more accurately, sex. A woman wants a man from her past, it's revenge."

Susie Scudder laughed and said, "Don't look so shocked."

"You going to hire hit men, or what?"

"Nothing that exotic," Juanita said. "I can't see how the details are pertinent. Besides, Susie and I have decided to go ahead with our plans, and we don't need them broadcast all about."

"Look," Susie said, "I really have to get to work and get Tobey over to his day care. You got any more questions for me?"

"Yeah. Who were you looking for?"

"I thought Bruno was going to fill you in."

"I got his version. I'd like yours."

She spoke quickly. "Five years ago on a ski trip I met this actor. I was young and not all that sophisticated and away from home literally for the first time with some girlfriends, and he gave me what I later figured out must have been his standard line. I was simpleminded enough to fall for it, okay? It was what everybody used to do, you know, before all the diseases. When he comes to this party, I'm going to serve papers on him. Force him to get a blood test. Make him do right by Tobey. That's all."

"You lose track of him?"

"I never had track of him. I think he was married." She glanced down at Tobey, who didn't seem to be paying attention. The penlight was screwed into her thigh. "It was the only time I ever did anything like that. Everybody else was doing it. I thought I was being cosmopolitan." Susie gathered up her purse, a knapsack containing Tobey's paraphernalia, and went to the door.

"Now he owes just a little back support," said Juanita.

"Tobey's the best thing ever happened to me," said Susie, opening the door. "But I can't do it alone."

Juanita saw them out, then strode hippily over to the atrium windows and looked at the cityscape. Beyond the skyscrapers the sky was pink, dark clouds to the north. She watched the headlights on Broadway and the snow on the Olympic mountain range across the Sound as the morning sunlight began to bombard the slopes.

I turned to Juanita. "And your dream guy?"

"I wish you wouldn't call him that. They were nightmares. All three of them were pigs."

"You met in college."

"My first year of college, my first semester. I was big and awkward and didn't know a thing about grooming or makeup. I'd come from Moses Lake, and everything about Seattle dazzled me, including the men at school. Burt took advantage of me in a way that took me years to recover from. Now I'm going to give him something that might stick in *his* craw for a while."

"You don't want to tell me what he did?"

"Not even if it was relevant."

"And Marian was after her ex?"

"He gave her syphilis."

"He was against the divorce, claimed he still loved her."

"Men are always against the divorce. And they always still love you. They give you running sores and then think they're doing you a favor wanting to stay."

"She told you exactly why she was going after him, didn't she?"

"What makes you say that?"

"Susie doesn't know. Bruno doesn't know. Kathy either. People have to confide in somebody."

"Marian was incredibly embarrassed over it."

"Go on."

"Chuck gave her the HIV virus."

"Did she have AIDS yet?"

"Yes. Small symptoms. Marian was monogamous during the marriage, celibate after the divorce. Chuck gave it to her. There was nothing else it could have been."

"What was she after?"

"I don't know what she was thinking. I only know she alternated between being so depressed she couldn't get out of bed and being so angry she sometimes carried a butcher knife around in her purse."

"Depressed enough to kill herself?"

"*That* I don't know."

"When did she find out she was HIV positive?"

"Maybe six weeks ago. She didn't want Susie or anybody to know. We never spoke about it without her reminding me I had promised not to tell anyone. Marian had always taken an extremely moralistic view of AIDS. She said once she thought it was a plague sent by God to afflict sinners. She kept trying to figure out what her crime was. I think her way of coping was to go after Chuck."

"Was she quite ill?"

"Not yet."

"So why visit Chuck's widow? What was the object?"

"When they got their divorce, Chuck admitted he'd had sex with a younger woman, but he never told Marian who. She blamed her almost as much as she blamed Chuck. She wanted to find and punish her."

"With a butcher knife?"

"Of course not."

I brought out my notes. "She ever mention anybody named Dee?"

"Not to me."

"Or Bain Littrell?"

"No."

"So what's the deal with her son?"

"Is he involved?"

"I don't think so. Just curious."

"I don't know what happened exactly with her son, but she was a wonderful person."

With Juanita on my heels, I went through Marian's effects. Her closet contained some hats her mother had collected. A lot of fake jewelry. A great deal of clothing that was no longer fashionable. In a corner in a shoe box under three pairs of shoes I found a .32 caliber revolver that looked as if it had never been fired. There were no bullets. The closet smelled the way my grandmother's closet used to smell, of mothballs.

At her small credenza I located a tidy clip of bills, her checkbook, and some writing materials. Over the past year she had doled out substantial amounts of money to different charities, several hundred dollars at a whack, and this at a time in her life when she was driving to Arizona to save on the airfare, collecting tinfoil in used sheets, and writing notes to herself on the back of junk mail.

One surprise was a loan note written out to Susie Scudder, five thousand dollars to be paid back in monthly installments. Susie seemed to have missed the last few payments.

I found no record of activities during the last few weeks. Nothing concerning her ex-husband. Not a clue to tell us who she had met with Friday.

Marian Wright had an extensive collection of books, mostly literary authors. The bedroom had an Apple computer in the corner with a plastic cover over it, a box of diskettes beside the computer.

I sat at the desk. Juanita was leaning over me, so when I turned to her, my face was buried in a waterfall of hair. "So what are you going to do now?" Juanita asked.

"Look over her telephone bills. And I want to go over that computer in the other room. Sweep the disks for records she might have been keeping. Then I need to take a look at her car when it comes back today."

"That's it?"

"It's as far as I've thought ahead."

"You should be following Burt."

"Who's Burt?"

"The dolt Marian found for me, the dolt who messed with me in college. Burt Roberson. He's got six kids and lives in Spokane. I want you to go over there today and follow him. Put a tap on his phone. The whole bit."

"I'll get to him."

"Today would be the best."

"There are other things I need to do first."

"Today."

"Listen, Juanita. You want to supervise every little angle yourself, hire some high school kid." She glared at me, eyes bulging even more than normal.

"I pay the bills, I call the shots. Isn't that fair?"

"It's fair if you've got somebody laying carpet. But I'm good at what I do, and that's not how I work."

"Roberson is a son of a bitch. One way or another, he's probably responsible for Marian's death."

"You have reason to believe he was in town?"

"Marian died. And she had tracked him down. That's reason."

"From what I can see, she tracked down a lot of people." It had been a mistake to let her hang around and kibitz while I looked through the condo. She had glimpsed the checking records over my shoulder and had learned of Marian's loan to Susie, a loan I was fairly certain she had been ignorant of.

Juanita took a small sheet of trembling notebook paper out of her purse and handed it to me. The paper said, *Hemstad Electronics, Spokane, Washington. Burt Roberson, Vice President.* It had an address and three phone numbers, plus a fax number. She said, "You prove to me he wasn't here, and I'll give it up."

I sat in Marian's kitchen, picked up her phone and dialed the first number. A woman answered, kids shouting in the background over a loud TV playing cartoons. "Ma'am, this is Hoody at the Four Seasons in Seattle. We have what looks to be a very expensive pair of glasses somebody left here last week, Friday I believe, and we think they might belong to your husband."

"My husband was in the hospital Friday morning. He fell on the ice the night before and broke his tailbone."

"But he does come to Seattle on business?"

"And he has stayed at the Four Seasons. But not Friday."

"Now, lemme see here. Your husband is B. Robertson, is that correct?"

"Roberson. No T." She spelled it.

"My apology, ma'am. I'm just trying to get these very expensive glasses back to their owner. In situations like this the hotel feels an obligation to guests. Please excuse the imposition."

I hung up, glanced at Juanita Raykovich, then pushed a kitchen chair toward her. She remained standing, shaking her hair out—in the event that I hadn't already seen how much of it she had—her face tight, eyes white all the way around. "He was in Spokane Friday. Cracked his tailbone on the ice Thursday."

"Says who? His wife? He knows he's in trouble. He put her up to it."

"You don't believe that?"

We let it sit between us for a few seconds. Finally, she said, "You're stubborn, aren't you?"

"I know how to do my job is all."

"No, you're stubborn. I don't like stubbornness in a man. Or an employee. Maybe I should have hired somebody else."

"Nobody's asking you to like me. Just to let me do my job."

Juanita turned and walked out of the condo. Eighteen years was long enough for most glaciers to melt, yet she still carried around every original cold ounce of hate.

CHAPTER 12

In front of Mitchelli Trattoria a trio of panhandling winos created a ruckus with two bicycle cops while I breezed past and grabbed a booth in the far corner. Kathy came in behind me.

"Been here long?" she asked, stepping past a waiter with steaming plates in his arms.

"All my life."

"How did I miss out on that?"

She still had a hard time with her smile, this one so dim some would have considered it a frown. The only other time I had seen her this moody was right after I killed Philip. After the waiter had taken our orders, I said, "Talk to Raykovich today?"

"No. Why? Did she fire you?"

"Not yet."

"She had trouble with Bruno too. I heard she gets a little bossy."

"How did Bruno handle it?"

"Did exactly what he was told."

"That's not going to work here."

"Why not?"

"Because I'm not Bruno."

It drew a genuine smile from her, the first of the evening. "You haven't changed."

"You'd be surprised. But look. I found out Marian Wright had AIDS."

"I know."

"You know? Why didn't you tell me?" Kathy reached down and handed a battered leather briefcase across the table.

"I just found out. Somebody from the Salish Lodge called this morning and said this had been banging around for a few days."

Propping the briefcase open in my lap, I encountered a jumble of notes, loose scraps of paper, credit card receipts, and lists of names with cryptic messages next to them. The briefcase was Marian's, but the odds were minimal that the hodgepodge inside was her doing. Everything else about her had been orderly and precise.

One pocket was pregnant with letters, sealed, stamped, addressed, but not mailed. One had been slit open. "Go ahead. Read it," Kathy said.

Addressed to a woman named Pamela Mainprice in Edmonds, a community north of Seattle, it appeared to be a form letter printed on a computer:

Dear Ms. Mainprice:

It is my sad duty to be informing you that through the activities of one of your recent partners you may be and most likely have been utterly infected with a virus called HIV. Because I found out I was infected I have been conducting a study and have constructed a tree of death of which you are but one of so many branches.

If you care to pursue the issue or if you sincerely wish to take a look at my tree of death I would be more than willing to confer. The sapling was planted more than five years ago, so you may already be aware of your condition although there is no guarantee. Several people involved are either deceased or ill. If this is the case with you or any of your loved ones, accept my condolences.

At the bottom of the letter was Marian Wright's phone number alongside a scrawled signature.

"You imagine receiving a letter like that?" Kathy asked.

There were seventeen of them. Most of the addresses were in the Northwest. One was in Montana. Another in Florida. "I wonder how many she's already mailed."

"My guess is none. Where do you think she got AIDS? Isn't that an awful question? Everybody wants to know where somebody got it. Like it's the most important aspect instead of the least important."

"Marian didn't think so."

"But this AIDS business does bring up other possibilities, Thomas. You asked me if Marian might have been contemplating suicide. She was dying anyway, but maybe she wanted to make it look like an accident to make sure her life insurance paid off."

"I don't know why. Her money's going to her sister in a nursing home. The rest to charity. This morning I went through her apartment and found her phone bill. Three weeks ago, driving through California on her way back from Phoenix, she spoke to a woman named Bain Littrell in Seattle. Then about a week later she called her from Tacoma, twice, spent forty minutes on the phone the second time."

"And?"

"Littrell claims she never heard of Marian."

"Why would she lie?"

"I don't know. I've been trying to find this person named Dee who seems related to Littrell somehow, but I've been hitting dead ends all day. The post office, everywhere."

We were midway through a meal of fettuccine Alfredo, when she said, "Thomas, I just need to say a couple of things. And then I want to ask one question. After that, I'll put it behind me forever."

"What are you talking about?" I filled my mouth with ice water knowing full well what she was talking about.

"First of all, I'm ashamed for the way I behaved."

My teeth were immersed in ice chips so that my words came out in a gargle. "Don't worry about it."

"I realize what happened with you and Philip was not your

fault. But I have this one question I want to ask you and I want you to give me a straight answer."

"I'll try."

"When Philip died? That night you two were up there at that vacant house together? Did he say anything? You know, afterward?"

"You mean after I shot him?"

"Yes."

"About you?"

"Yes."

I wiped my mouth with a napkin and strained to read her eyes. My desire was to anticipate what she needed to hear, but then, after I did, I couldn't bring myself to mutter the words, partly because I couldn't lie, not about this, not even if it was a lie Kathy needed, but mostly because it wasn't my job to make Philip any more of a martyr than he already was. He had lied to me that night, as he had lied to me other nights. He had died so quickly he hadn't time to expel the air from his lungs, much less roll over and whisper quiet nothings about the woman we both adored.

"You were on his mind, Kathy. Very much so. But he didn't say a word."

"Nothing?"

"He had no time." I drank the entire glass of water, gulping the ice lumps and feeling the coldness sink deeper and deeper inside me.

We didn't say much for a while, and then she began crying. It is inevitable that when you sit at a busy restaurant with a woman and she's crying, everybody assumes it is your fault.

It was one of those hair-raising breakdowns that are hard to watch, the kind where she gets a funny look in her eyes as if she is going to tell you something she has no words for, and then the tears begin dribbling down her face almost of their own volition. Then her shoulders begin to heave. It took a long time before any sound came with it, but when it did, it was as if she were wearing earplugs and could not hear how loud she was.

She kept trying to tell me she was sorry, but she couldn't make the words distinguishable, and the more she tried, the more times she failed, the louder her sobbing grew, until the patrons at the tables around us were listening, until the waiters and waitresses had all stopped in their tracks. Until I thought I was going to get arrested. I could see the headlines: MAN MAKES WOMAN CRY IN DOWNTOWN EATERY.

It was hard to guess what they believed I had done, but I was on the wrong end of murderous looks from everyone but the baby in the corner booth. Draping my arm around Kathy and carrying her briefcase, her purse, Marian's briefcase, and Kathy's coat didn't help. Still crying, she stumbled between the tables, walking like a swimming-sideways goldfish during its last hours.

Twelve minutes later when we got to her apartment on Queen Anne Hill, Kathy was still apologizing, still crying. Nothing I did or said had any effect.

By eight-thirty she had apologized so many times I was embarrassed for her. Trying to distract herself, she asked about Nigel. My explanation quieted her, so I kept talking.

"I hadn't seen him in almost thirty years, and he kept kissing me. In my other family the men don't kiss each other, so I didn't know how to act. And then he started kneading my shoulders and wondering aloud how much weight I could pick up. Like I was a starving horse he had found in a field. We had dinner at Ray's Boathouse, and by the end of the meal he was almost a godfather to our waiter. I think he wanted to impress us with how much of a regular guy he could be. On the way out, he got the waiter's address and promised to write. I thought he was nuts. There was an enormous basket of matchbooks, and he scooped up so many my sister thought he was going to get arrested."

"You don't like him even a little, do you?"

"The part that makes it tough is he's always telling me he loves me. And then there's usually a long pause while he gives me time to say it back. But I hardly know him. So I end up being the son who's too cold to tell his own father he loves him. He tells my sister I'm cold. And she tells me."

"And, of course, he knows she will. Tell you."

"Naturally."

Kathy's shoes were off and her feet were tucked under her, and she had snuggled into the crook of my shoulder, her hair solidly under my chin. She had stopped crying. "When he says he loves you? What do you really want to say?"

"I don't know. Something about disappearing for twenty-five years."

"But you don't."

"How can I? He lives in some old lady's basement in New Jersey."

"How does your sister handle it?"

"She says I'm cold."

"What's he been doing all this time?"

"Got kicked out of the Air Force, where he used to fly P-51 Mustangs. He prospected for uranium in Utah. Lived in Arizona. And maybe Texas. Then went back to Philadelphia and moved in with his mother. I think there was a failed marriage or two in there, but he won't cop to it. He lived with his mother until she had to go to a nursing home. After that, he moved in with the elderly woman next door, stayed there seventeen years until one night he had a psychotic episode that scared her enough she gave him the boot. He says he sold airplane parts all those years, but until he put in some time as a watchman at a warehouse complex, he didn't have enough quarters to qualify for Social Security, so I don't think he sold shit."

"You *are* bitter."

"I didn't think I was until I started talking about it."

By the time I had fed the poodles and driven home, it was almost nine.

Nigel was on my front porch feeding Vitabones to L.C., sucking on a cigar, and munching from a bag of fried pork rinds. Of late, he had been in the habit of walking the three miles from my sister's place and waiting for me to show up. It was cold on the porch, and Nigel looked as if he had been there a good while. I parked my truck in the long driveway behind Marian Wright's Datsun B-210, which was behind Kathy's Firebird, then walked alongside the house past the cars to open the back door and let Nigel in.

The back porch light was out. None of the neighbors along the alley had their lights on either, and the end of the driveway and the backyard were dark. I felt my way along the house to the wooden steps that led up to my rear porch. The slight odor of tobacco smoke hung in the air. I took two steps up the staircase before I sensed somebody was in the yard with me.

Something banged the wooden railing beside my right arm. I heard the loud, tinny ring of metal on wood and a hard object nicked the back of my elbow.

I hopped up four steps before another blow caught me across the back of one thigh and stung like a cannon shot, although the wooden railing seemed to absorb most of the impact. Otherwise, the blow might have broken my leg.

Instead of continuing up the stairs and getting cornered on the dark porch, I vaulted the wooden railing into my backyard, sprinted several lengths across the soggy grass, pivoted, and squared off with my assailant. Or assailants. My leg throbbed. Had he hit my elbow that hard, he would have crushed it.

The only light was a vague haze in the driveway generated by the street lamp in front of the house.

Knowing speech would act as a homing device, I kept quiet.

Briefly silhouetted against the haze, he stepped away from the house and moved toward me. He was a large man, tall and bulky, and walked with stubby little steps like a rooting hog. He had a squared-off head and short hair. He obviously could not see me—I could barely see him—and he was going wrong. The problem was, he was going only a little wrong. The other problem was the object he carried appeared to be a baseball bat.

Moving beyond the vague glimmer from the street lamp, he was soon backed by my garage, where he became virtually invisible.

CHAPTER 13

We stood in the darkness for what seemed like hours but was only as long as the average man could hold his breath.

The yard had frozen and thawed a dozen times during the winter, so what we had beneath us was a layer of mud and grass that pulled at our shoes every time we moved, making a sound like an old man sucking his dentures.

I gathered he was trying to adjust to the lack of light, since I was doing the same. One never has real darkness in the city, and my night blindness was largely the result of having gotten out from behind a pair of bright headlights minutes earlier.

An aluminum baseball bat makes a certain low-pitched whoop when pulled through the air quickly. I heard the noise three times as he came closer.

When he got too close, I leaned back and fumbled around for one of the bricks lining my rose bed, but felt only wet grass. He continued swinging over my head while I crab-walked backward. He must have heard my clothing rustle or one of my joints pop, because he turned and faced me squarely for the first time.

I dove into the wet grass and tumbled and rolled.

Behind me, the bat struck the ground with dull thuds. On my knees at the far end of the roses, I finally found half a brick, clawed it out of the ground, and hurled it. A clean miss, for it tumbled dully across the sod on the far side of the yard. I found another and pitched it through the air. It struck something soft and dropped to the earth. Bingo.

"Fucking Christ," he grunted in a hoarse whisper.

Now that I had his range and his attention, I hurled two more. He cursed and thundered across the turf in my general direction.

On hands and knees I scrabbled toward the garage. He should have been running behind me, but he had underestimated my original position and tumbled over me as I bisected the yard.

The collision forced the wind from my lungs and, for a moment, I thought his knee had broken my shoulder. My right arm refused to work. Groping along on my belly, I crawled away before he could get to me, for it was easy enough to bean this bozo with a brick in the dark, but I certainly wasn't capable of wrestling anybody this large.

As I crawled, he got up and began pummeling the ground behind me. I rolled and got to my feet and backpedaled, then danced sideways and stopped. He had been using the noise of my clothing on the ground for a target, and when I stopped, his radar screen went blank. As I tried to keep from breathing too loudly, the tip of the moving bat brushed my lips. It might as well have been the wingtip of a jet in flight. I stepped away and put my fingers to my mouth. My lips were numb but intact. Another half inch and my teeth would have been scattered about the yard like popcorn.

Cradling my head, I continued to backstep, yet somehow he found my range and followed, pulling the bat through the air in front of me.

"Nigel!" I shouted. "Get the police! Nigel! There's someone in the backyard. Call the police!"

The bat whacked me across the ribs, a glancing blow, but the next one would do more damage. Covering my head and face with my arms, I stepped into him. It happened in the space of a single second.

My timing was lucky enough that I bumped into his face as the bat and part of his arm wrapped around my left side. His breath smelled of stale beer. For a moment or two he couldn't figure out what was happening, couldn't comprehend that I was close enough to dance with.

In the second it took me to move into him, I slapped my left arm down and trapped the bat against my body while simultaneously ramming the heel of my right hand toward a spot in the darkness that should have been the base of his nose.

Like a poleaxed ox, he dropped at my feet. The bat was in my hands now, and I stroked it across his legs twice, doing my best to crack bone. Before I could take a third swing, a pistol went off in my face.

The pop deafened me. It also lit the yard up for a fraction of a second and converted me into a genuine, albeit temporary, blind man.

Seeing nothing but the lightning-white flash, I swung the bat hard one more time and thought I heard the gun whir off into the dark.

I stepped back and took stock. As I pondered the situation and wondered whether he still had the gun, I heard him working the latch at my back fence. I got a glimpse of his beefy backside as he made his escape. Then the lights came on next door.

My retired neighbor, Horace, stepped out onto his porch in a long underwear top and striped railroad coveralls. "That you, Thomas? I thought I heard a shot."

"You did."

"You start firing guns off in this neighborhood, I'm gonna call the police."

"Call the police."

"I will. I'm warning you. I'll call the police."

"Call them."

"You think I won't?"

"I want you to call them."

"I'll call the damn police on you. You can't fire guns out here."

"I didn't fire it. Somebody fired at me."

"You think I won't? You ex-hippies. Who do you think you are? I'll call the goddamn police." He slammed the door.

"Call them," I yelled. When I got to the front of the house, Nigel was lounging in an old chair he had asked me to leave on the porch for him, smoking a stogie and nuzzling his two dachshunds and L.C.

"What happened to you?" he asked. "Been playing in the mud?"

"You didn't hear me yell?"

"Been sitting right here enjoying the night air." He puffed on the cigar self-importantly.

"You didn't hear the damn gunshot?"

"I raised you, I woulda taught you not to use that sort of language."

"You didn't hear a gunshot?"

"In the air corps I heard plenty." As I unlocked the front door, I noticed Nigel had brought along a shabby suitcase. He flicked the glowing cigar butt onto my walkway.

"Somebody's going to have to pick that up," I said.

"Nonsense. It's compost. You know what your trouble is? You're too easy. That's why people walk all over you."

"You didn't hear the gunshot?"

"Son, if there'd been a gunshot, I guess I would have heard it, now, wouldn't I?"

I picked up the phone, dialed 911, and talked to the operator while Nigel lectured in the background. My sister, he said, had gone emotional on him, had some sort of breakdown and booted him out, thus he needed a place to sleep, just for the night, him and his dogs. If I turned him out, they could tramp the sidewalks until morning, him and the boys, the way they'd done in Paterson, New Jersey. He could arrange to be back this way by eight if I could find it in my heart to dole out a little coffee and half a piece of dry toast for breakfast. When I hung up the phone, I said, "Sleep in there. But those two have to stay outside."

"Tommy, the boys've never stayed outside."

"L.C. stays outside. So do they."

"L.C.'s got a good thick coat. Look at Briggs and Stratton. Look at 'em. They'd catch pneumonia."

"God shouldn't have made dogs without hair."

"Now don't you go taking the Lord's name in vain, Tommy. Not while I'm around. I'll bet you don't eat beef either. You probably got no strength. You get mugged often, do you?"

"Yeah, sure. About twice a week."

When the police came, they found a .38 caliber revolver in my backyard, bagged it, and put it in their trunk along with the aluminum baseball bat. The canine unit arrived, and the handler went off at a good clip with his dog, returning twenty minutes later. My assailant, the handler suggested, had probably gotten into a car not far away and was on the other side of town by now.

Still a little shaky from the fight, I cooked for two that night—a salad, salmon, and steamed rice—while Nigel settled into the living room, rearranging furniture, dusting the mantel, and turning on the television. When I went through the phone messages, there was one from my sister, who said, "I think Nigel's headed your way, Thomas. Don't let him in. Whatever you do, you cannot let him in. You were right." The other message was from Beulah in Kathy's office. "Thomas. The car should be at your house by the time you get home. I got Bruno to go out to the tow yard and pick it up. Ciao!" Bruno Collins! Good grief. One of my suspects had been given a free hand with the evidence.

After dinner, I went out to the driveway with a flashlight and scoured the Datsun. The gas tank was over half full so I doubted she'd been out of gas Friday night. The cigarette stubs were still in the tray. I inspected the interior, the mechanical condition of the car, the tire wear, and learned nothing except she bought retreads, carried maps of six states, and had a tape player but no tapes.

As long as I was already outside, I went to the garage and prepared a spot for the dogs. Nigel spent almost an hour trying to "settle the boys in."

With my father outside, I sorted through Marian's briefcase. Besides the unmailed letters and the receipts, the only thing I found to pique my interest was a notebook she had sketched in. One page had a hand-drawn chart. At the base, the word MAR-IAN, a horizontal line drawn to the word CHUCK. Another horizontal line was drawn from CHUCK to ELIZABETH. Above CHUCK was DEE, connected by a vertical line. Dee. The mysterious and, so far, untraceable Dee. Yet Marian must have located her, because Dee's name was connected to five men's names horizontally, and then vertically to BAIN. Was this her tree of death? The drawing implied that Marian thought or knew Bain and Dee were linked.

Spreading out the papers from the briefcase, I searched for a phone number or address for Dee, but all I found were credit card slips for gas and lunches.

I was stuck with Bain. Bain Littrell.

In the shower, I found bruises on my rib cage and the center of my back. One knee was sore and beginning to swell. My lip had been puffy all through dinner. Nigel had stared at it disapprovingly. I stood under the hot spray thinking about the man in the backyard. The lightbulb over the back porch had been unscrewed only far enough to go dark. I had tried to give it to the SPD in case he'd burned a print onto it, hoping they might match it in the new county fingerprint computer, but they assured me they were too busy to process it.

As far as possible suspects, there had been a battering husband whose wife had hired me to get her and their two children away from him, but that had been last summer before I'd gone to the hospital. The husband had been a big guy, recently released from jail. Then there was Bruno Collins. He had been here today and might have hung around. Bruno had lied about his alibi, and I still hadn't had the time to find out why.

When I went to bed, Nigel was hunched over a small drawing board working the stump of a cold cigar in his mouth, a compass, T-square, and a mechanical pencil in hand. He rumbled about the house until the wee hours.

By seven I was so stiff I could hardly get out of bed. After my morning ablutions and a glass of water, I went into the spare bedroom and climbed on the wind trainer for a little over an hour. It was raining outside, the overflow from my gutters beating a tattoo that kept company to National Public Radio. The body heat generated from the workout loosened me up a bit.

I had showered and was halfway through breakfast before L.C. stumbled, like a drunk after a binge, into the kitchen from the direction of the living room. "What the hell are you doing in here?"

The dog stopped in his tracks, dropped his head, and lowered his ears. In the living room, Nigel was asleep in his clothes on top of the bedding, even though I had made up the sofa with sheets and blankets. The dachshunds slept under his arms.

"Nigel, you see anybody hanging around the house last night before I got home?" It took three repeats before he opened his eyes, and before he did, he felt around for his dogs the way a miser felt around for his sack of gold.

"Now what are you doing, Tommy?" He yawned and stretched out a foot.

"Just a question. You see anybody last night?"

"Well, yeah, sure, there was a fellow in the driveway."

"*My* driveway?"

He yawned. "Yeah. You're not looking so hot, kind of like a corpse somebody warmed up in a microwave."

"What'd he look like?"

"Well, he was big. Looked like a ball player. You got closer than I did. I didn't even pay attention."

"Why didn't you tell me this last night?"

"You didn't ask."

"Was he white or black?"

"Now that is hard to say. It was dark."

"You can't describe him at all?"

"I just did. He was big."

"Didn't it seem a little strange that there was a man in my driveway?"

"How do I know what you keep in your driveway?"

"Thanks, Nigel. By the way, I left a note on the table." He was asleep before I closed the door. Lazier and more worthless even than my father, the dachshunds hadn't bothered to open their eyes.

CHAPTER 14

It was snowing lightly by the time I got to Bain Littrell's house on South Juneau Street, the flakes large and wet and interspersed with fast-falling raindrops, the air crisp and moist, so that my breath walked out in front of me.

No one answered Littrell's door.

Across the street I found the old man who'd been staring at her lasciviously two days earlier. It was a street full of pre-WWII boxes, his a carbon copy of Littrell's. I told him I was a private investigator seeking information on his neighbor. You would have thought I'd asked him to help judge a Miss Nude Universe contest.

"Mother," he shouted. "We have a detective in the living room. Trying to pick up manure on that Littrell woman across the street."

"Not manure," I said, closing the front door behind me and heeling my shoes onto a sheet of butcher paper laid out for that purpose. "Just information."

"She done something wrong?"

"It's about somebody she knew who was in an accident."

The man's name was Stober. He introduced his wife as Mother but she wasn't my mother so I didn't call her anything. He wore pressed slacks and a shirt buttoned to the neck. His wife wore a spotless dress and a pressed apron. The heat in the house was high enough for an incubator, but they both wore sweaters. Hearing the commotion, their little rat dog came into the room and began sniffing me. They told him to quit, but anybody could see he wasn't going to give up a good thing.

Stober and his wife sat next to each other on the sofa and held hands. I sat on a second sofa across from them and praised their house.

"Been here ever since I got the job in the shipyard," said Stober. "Over forty years. We were renting an apartment in the University District before that. Mother and I met at the post office. But we never had no neighbor like the Littrell woman before."

"That's not so," Mother said. "Remember Pat Oswald, Daddy? He drove the Corvair?"

"Some days she don't even budge from the house. Other days she's in and out. No rhyme or reason. We used to ask her to watch after Sardine because he gets lonesome when we're gone, but she always said she was waiting for a call and might have to go out." The dog had climbed onto the sofa and was nosing my crotch.

"How long has she been across the street?"

"Let's see . . . five years in May. We had her here once when we had a block party at Christmas. She stood in the corner over there by the hi-fi and didn't say a word."

"She first moved in, we thought she was a Gypsy. Remember?"

"She would hammer over there. I thought she was making patio furniture to sell off the back of a truck." Stober laughed while his wife gave him a loving, moon-eyed look, probably the same look she had given him back at the post office.

"But here's what she does. Mother found out one morning. She visits elderly relatives. She done it once with an aunt, and when the aunt passed away, why, she left most everything to her. That's what she's living on. Now she visits relatives. If they got money. Talks to them old folks when they're lonely and gets herself put into the will. She's owned a new car every doggone year she's been here too. Wish I had a bunch of rich relatives about to kick the bucket."

When I got outside, the sky was filled with falling snow-flakes. Tires whistled on the snowy pavement at the stop sign at Beacon. When Littrell's Acura Legend showed up, the hood was steaming and warm, snow wedged down on the windshield where her wipers had packed it. I phoned the plate number to a friend in the P.D., and he shortly confirmed it belonged to Bain Clarice Littrell. The address was current, and she was not making payments to a bank. He dug up her driver's license too. She was five-foot-eight. Brown eyes. Brown hair. A hundred thirty-five pounds. Thirty-eight years old.

Half an hour later Littrell came out, climbed into her car and headed toward the freeway. She wore jogging shoes, blue Lycra tights, and a red sweatshirt. It was snowing pretty good now, and I had to admire her spirit of adventure. In Seattle, people didn't normally drive in the snow if they could help it.

She went north on I-5, got off at the Ravenna exit, drove to Green Lake, and launched out on the walking path that looped the lake.

In the parking lot I slumped down behind the steering wheel, paged through a cycling catalogue, and got colder and colder. My ribs still hurt from the thumping I'd taken the night before, and I was stiff from being in the truck. I wondered if one of these elderly relatives she visited might not be the Dee I was looking for.

She walked the entire circumference of the lake and then drove back to her place, stopping once at a supermarket. When it got late and I figured she was bedded down for the night, I went home. On the way, I used my cellular phone to call Bridget, an operative I used from time to time. I'd sent her out to Snoqualmie to the same stretch of road as the accident. It was the same night of the week and the same time, and a lot of the same cars would be passing. "How are you doing?"

"In an hour and a half I got almost eighty plate numbers. I missed a couple. The weather's so bad, though, a lot of people probably stayed in."

It was a good list to have, although I might not call anyone on it. Most witnesses to an accident went home thinking they weren't needed.

It was late when I got home. The windows of the Firebird and the Datsun were opaque with snow.

I was lucky the house hadn't caught fire. Nigel had baked nachos on a cookie sheet and left the oven on. Melted cheese had dripped onto the oven door and hardened into a black crust. Cheese drippings swooped across the floor like starter swatches on a Jackson Pollock painting. On the table the cookie sheet sat without a hot pad under it. A jar of mayonnaise stood warm and uncapped and spotty with broken chips stabbed into the jelled mess.

A note on the kitchen table said: *Have found suitable accommodations nearby. Left you a little snack if you are so inclined. Your dog, L.C., seems to be content with me and the boys, so I took the liberty of adopting him. Knew you wouldn't mind, since you don't seem to have the time or inclination to give him the companionship he requires. Your loving father, Nigel.*

Maybe it was just the long day, but somehow, stealing my dog seemed like the worst insult I'd ever suffered. I'd had a dog who'd been murdered, but this seemed infinitely worse.

I went downstairs and knocked at the basement door. When Hank Torgerson, my renter, answered, his bulky body blotted out the small doorway. He had slumped shoulders and long blond hair and was similar in size to the man who'd attacked me last night. In fact, for a moment last night I'd thought it was Hank. "Chester still up?"

"Conked out a while back. What's happenin'? The baby-sitter told me there was somebody up in your house flushing the toilet from about two on."

"My father. He must have gotten up at two. Listen, Hank. There was a guy here in the yard last night trying to do me some damage. The police were here and the neighbors have been alerted, but just the same, he might be back. About your size. Carried a baseball bat and a gun."

"Keerist! Are you kidding me?"

"He came at me like he knew what he was doing."

"Friend of yours?"

"It was dark. It might have been. The cops haven't found him, and I have a feeling they won't. I want you to keep a close eye on Chester."

"Thanks for the warning."

"You see *anything*. You hear *anything*. I want you to tell me."

"Sure, Thomas. Sure."

"I'm sorry about this. I wanted this place to feel safe for both of you."

"Hey. Life in the big city."

Five weeks ago I'd spotted Hank a block from the Greyhound depot sitting on a stack of luggage, trying to make sense of life, a man worn down by the abrasion of petty failure. His kid was chatting with strangers and swinging around a parking meter like it was a maypole. I couldn't get over the contrast between the two: innocence guarded by despair. They had been out of their apartment in Oakland two months, living in their car until it caught fire, and Chester tended to think of their predicament as high adventure.

When I spoke to them, I found out Hank had recently turned down an opportunity to work for a contractor tearing down old houses in the Regrade because he didn't have anyone to look after Chester during the days. Carting their luggage around with them, they had been sleeping in shelters and unlocked cars. At least two of those nights the weather had been below freezing.

I took them home, ran a couple of background checks on Hank, and rented my basement apartment to them.

I had to float Hank the rent on the first month, but he paid me back quickly enough. A pregnant teenager two doors down began baby-sitting. Hank was saving toward a car, and it looked as if he might be in line to get a full-time position with the contractor. I felt a tad smug about it, even though the discounted rent was hurting my bank balance and despite the fact that the last time I'd done something like this, the recipients of my largesse had walked off with my television set.

CHAPTER 15

Early Saturday morning, Trina, another part-time operative, showed up wearing a bright red coat, the collar obviously taken from the hide of an electrocuted fox. Beneath the coat she had on a cinnamon-colored bodysuit with a ring attached to the zipper that would have served better as a door knocker. I found a less conspicuous coat for her in my closet.

"Nobody's going to take any notice of me," Trina said, pulling the zipper to her chin. Zipped, the cat suit was tighter than ever.

"If it was just you and me, it would be different."

She pulled the zipper back down a few clicks and said, "Don't stare."

I laughed, because I was being very conscientious about not staring and she knew it. Tall and athletic, Trina worked on a road crew for the state and often lugged a sack of cement around on her shoulders all day. Maybe because she wore a helmet and boots at work, the last thing she wanted in her private life was to be overlooked.

What made Trina's services indispensable in certain surveillance operations was that her hearing impairment had forced her to become adept at reading lips.

I said, "We need to be inconspicuous. I'm following a woman who's seen me before."

When we went out to the Firebird, Horace was alongside my driveway hosing down his sidewalk. After it froze up he'd come back out and salt it. In his late seventies, Horace wore railroad coveralls and most of the time had the frantic, slightly frustrated look of a man chasing a mole around the yard with a pitchfork.

"You and your old man are about as dissimilar as two human beings can get, that's all I got to say."

"You've seen Nigel?"

"You got none of his genes. You ever listen to him? Your old man's some kind of genius. He could have easy taught college."

When Trina came out the back door behind me, Horace gave her a suspicious frown. A moment later, my dog, L.C., drifted out from beyond Horace's basement walkway, head lowered, eyes avoiding me.

"L.C., what the hell are you doing over there? Get back in your own yard before Horace washes you down. Come on, boy."

Looking dazed and somewhat confused, L.C. glanced lackadaisically back in the direction from which he'd come. Horace should have been apoplectic, but he only grinned. I had it figured out by the time my father, wearing only slacks and the shabby sport coat, stepped out onto Horace's wet patio from the basement door and scratched his shock of wiry hair with one finger. His bare toes curled on the cold pavement. "Mornin' to ya, Tommy."

Horace said, "Your old man's gonna stay with us. We're fixin' up a nook for him in the laundry room. 'Course, myself, I'd be ashamed my old man had to rent out a place next door."

Nigel ran his tongue around his teeth, scratched L.C. behind the ears, and avoided my eyes as studiously as the dog did. After a few moments he said, "I don't know how long I'll have to bunk here, Tommy. I hate to do all that packing and traveling back to Jersey and lose my train of thought. You know, kiddo, we get the rights problems and the marketing straightened out, a doohickey like the one I'm working on could be worth millions."

"Another invention?"

"Millions."

"You wanted to stay out here, you should have treated my sister better."

"You haven't spoken to her, have you?" he asked quickly.

"Haven't had time."

"She's suffered a misunderstanding, but I'll straighten her out. And won't be in your hair long. Half a year, max."

"Half a year?"

"I knew you'd be intrigued, kiddo. As soon as I get the kinks worked out, I'll show you a rough draft. Don't worry about me. I'll just bed down here behind Horace's washer and dryer. Cheap rent. Good food. Fine friends. What else could a man want?"

Horace grinned so hard his teeth showed. "He's a real philosopher, ain't he?"

We took the Firebird. Trina wore the canvas hiking jacket I had given her, but carried her fur-lined coat in her arms the way a child carried a blanket. It was a long shot, staking out Littrell's house on a Saturday morning, but around eleven it paid off.

Littrell came out, got into her car, warmed it up for seven minutes, drove to Seward Park Avenue South near Brighton Street, stopped at the curb, and tapped her horn. It was only a five-minute drive.

She had stopped in front of a large, two-story house with four old American cars in the driveway. After some moments, a man in a suit came out, a long, dark raincoat flapping in the breeze.

He was a big man in sunglasses, with close-cropped hair, what was left of it, burly shoulders, and a rolling gait. He stubbed a cigarette out on the parking strip with his toe.

"You get a look at 'em?" I asked Trina after we had driven past.

"Just for a second. He said, 'You were lucky to get me. I

was planning to visit my daughter and the kids in Shelton for the . . .' I didn't get the rest."

We followed them into downtown Seattle. She let him out across from the Stouffer-Madison Hotel, then drove west on Sixth. Trina said, " 'Yeah, I'll be there. Piece of cake.' "

By the time we saw Littrell again, she was feeding a meter on Sixth near Lenora. We swung into an alley, parked Kathy's Firebird illegally, and followed on foot. It was windy, and the sky was a cold, gray ceiling.

We followed her into the Westin Hotel, where she met with two Japanese men in business suits, laughing, all of them. When I'd spoken to her before, she'd given no hint she could become this animated.

She wore a dressy coat over a plaid jacket and a paisley skirt, pumps, as if ready for a day at the office, except this was Saturday. They adjourned to the bar and eventually took an elevator upstairs. They talked about drinks, computers, and the Sonics, all of which Trina reported to me dutifully.

An hour and ten minutes later Littrell rode the elevator down to the lobby and strode purposely out into the weather. Neither gentleman accompanied her.

Keeping a block behind, we followed. She took Fifth Avenue to the Stouffer-Madison and found a parking spot in the garage under the building. It felt cold enough for snow, yet it was raining, not hard. I let Trina out after making certain she had the redial on her cell phone set to my number. She left just a whiff of her drugstore perfume in the car.

Keeping tabs by phone, she told me Littrell was meeting a little, bald-headed man in the lobby. The large man she'd picked up earlier was looking on. She went upstairs with the small man and came back down fifteen minutes later looking none the worse for wear. I was beginning to get the idea that these weren't elderly relatives.

I picked up Trina and we followed the Acura back to Seward Park South, where Littrell let the man out and headed back toward town.

She drove to Capitol Hill to a florist on Madison where she

purchased a bouquet of yellow and white flowers, then went another four blocks to Sixteenth. It took her five minutes to find a parking spot. After she locked up, I got out and told Trina to keep the Firebird in a holding pattern. I went to Littrell's Acura Legend and propped a sixteen-penny nail under the passenger-side rear tire.

Littrell walked up Sixteenth to a three-story house, white with blue trim, climbed the concrete steps into the front yard and went around to the back. There were similar dwellings on either side, across the street an apartment building. I followed.

There was a wheelchair ramp to the back door from a small private parking area off an alley. A large green Dumpster was overflowing with rotting floral arrangements. I opened the lid with one finger and saw some IV line tubing and about two hundred color photographs, all of which appeared to be personal in nature: people, relatives, pets, somebody's Corvette. I had a pretty good idea what this place was. Strangely, it was less than ten blocks from Marian Wright's condo.

After a few minutes of waiting beside a brick garage across the alley, a man collecting aluminum cans came along and we struck up a conversation. An ex–bank clerk, he did odd jobs in a nearby apartment building in exchange for a small room. He was explaining how his girlfriend, who had recently gained over a hundred pounds, had jilted him to marry his brother, and was asking my advice because the brother had cheated on her and he wanted to rat on him. Before we could put order into his universe, Littrell came out the back door and went around the front of the house.

I dialed Trina and told her to stand by. "But what do you think?" the aluminum collector asked. "You think she would come back to me if she knew she was being two-timed?"

"I don't know. I try to mind my own business," I lied.

At the top of the wheelchair ramp I rapped at the back door of the blue and white house. After a minute a pale woman in jeans and a white T-shirt answered, her short brown hair sticking out where the arms of her wire-rimmed glasses pushed through. She had a small, round face with a wedge of fat under her chin. "Yes?"

"I'm sorry. I followed Bain up here, and then I kind of got turned around. Is she still here?"

"Bain?"

"Yeah."

"That must be the woman who just left."

"I feel like I should have been here more often, you know."

"Maybe you could come back. Deanna's probably going to need to sleep the rest of the afternoon."

"If I could just look in on her. If I come home tonight without at least seeing her, I'm going to get murdered."

She led me inside. Two stories with a basement, the house had apparently been a residence at one time, later a rooming house, and most assuredly a small apartment building too, for there were painted-over numbers above each room. Now it smelled of cafeteria cooking, medications, bleach, sickness, and sweat. An office door just inside the back entrance bore a sign: BATES REGIONAL FACILITY.

Many of the rooms were open, and I saw several men on their backs in bed and one in boxer shorts working his way slowly to a small desk in his room. All of the occupants were deathly thin and had either no hair or short hair growing in clumps, like concentration camp survivors.

On the second floor in a small bedroom, she lay in a high hospital bed. The nameplate on the door identified her as Deanna Ayers. Her eyes were closed, but I sensed she wasn't sleeping. Her face was bony and bruised-looking, and the lump she made under the sheets didn't look nearly large enough for anyone thinking about living through the night.

Ready to tip over, a small vase next to her bed held fresh yellow and white daffodils. She had a TV, mostly empty hangers in the closet, and a wall filled with children's drawings. One of them was done in yellow and red crayon, and across the bottom in teetering, misshapen letters was printed MOMMY, I MISS YOU.

On the way out I stopped at the office door. "Tell her I was here. I'll be back."

"Sure."

"You guys don't call her Dee?"

"No, but I know her family does."

"How long has she been here?"

"Five weeks."

"And how is it looking?"

"Well . . . you saw."

CHAPTER 16

We located Littrell five minutes later on Twelfth Avenue near Marion Street in front of Seattle University. The tow driver was jacking up her car to remove the tire with my nail in it. We trailed her until after nightfall. She visited the Alexis Hotel and then, at the corner of Madison and Terry, the Sorrento, a small luxury hotel that resembled a foreign embassy.

As I swung into the circular drive in front of the Sorrento, Trina hopped out in time to lip-read the room number when the desk clerk gave it to Littrell. An hour and a half later Littrell emerged and walked down the hill toward her car.

"We aren't going to follow her?" Trina asked after I'd gotten out of the car.

"I'm beginning to get the basic idea."

Once in the Sorrento, I put a toothpick in my mouth, then another. In the elevator I tipped my hat back and unbuttoned my coat.

It took him a while to answer his door.

Packaged in an overlarge silk robe, he was about five-six, in his early forties, slight of build, with a bouquet of dark hair at the neck of his robe and another spray of it on his pallid legs. His skull was a shiny dome, and his features were knotted with caution.

I showed him a plastic badge, painted silver with red letter-ing: VICE SQUAD. Kathy had given it to me as a gag gift two Christmases ago.

"Hotel Owners Association operative," I said. "You gonna let me in, or you just gonna stand there with your fly open?"

"You, uh, you said you, uh, were—"

"I'm just here to give you some neighborly advice, but if you need this to be official, with the warrants and the hand-cuffs and the wife getting a phone call in the middle of the night and the article in the paper, we can do that."

The door swung wide. When he had closed it behind me, he said, "What do you, uh—"

"Your ID. Pronto." I flipped open a notebook and put a pen on the page while he raced across the room and came back stiff-arming a wallet at me. "License only."

His name was St. Clair. He seemed a man who rarely got any sun. He lived in Redmond, a twenty-minute drive from the Sorrento. I jotted some notes and returned the license.

"I don't know," he said. He had a slight overbite. "I mean, what did I do wrong? Was there anything—"

"You had a prostitute up here?"

"I entertained a guest."

"You realize the world is not the place it was ten years ago. There are epidemics."

Before I could stop him, he padded across the room and re-trieved an expended condom from the wastebasket, dangling the mess between two fingers. I made a face. He stared at it, then at me, dropped it into the wastebasket and stepped into the bathroom, where he washed his hands.

When he came out he said, "The Hotel Owners Association, you say?"

"We investigate morals offenses in our hotels. Right now I'm compiling a master list. Your guest's name?"

"Tawny. You're not going to put me on a master list, are you?"

"Not you. Tawny. How long you been seeing her?"

"About five years. Off and on. Sure. Put her on the list. I

tried to take her out on a real date a couple of times, but she laughed in my face. What do you want to know?"

When I was through with St. Clair, Trina and I drove to my place, where I calculated her hours and wrote her a check. I went inside and telephoned Kathy but got no answer. It was almost seven and dark out. On the back porch I picked up L.C.'s water bowl, chipped the ice out, scrubbed it with a brush, and then hammered the ice out of the bowl Nigel's dachshunds had used.

Feeling moody, I put on my Hottest Girl Groups of the Sixties CD, loud, and a few minutes later thought to phone Scottsdale. Elizabeth O'Connel answered after one ring. The music came close to drowning out our conversation, but I didn't turn it down.

"I recently learned Marian Wright was HIV positive," I said. "You knew that, didn't you?"

There was a long pause. "Yes. Yes, I did."

"Is there any particular reason you didn't want to tell me?"

"You mean, other than the fact that I'm HIV too?"

Although I should have been, I was not expecting the revelation. She'd undoubtedly acquired it from the same source Marian had. "I'm sorry."

"It's something you live with. Chuck and I both knew about it . . . at least we knew *he* had it. I guess I should have investigated more, because after he died, his doctor was adamant I be tested."

"Do you think you could tell me what Marian Wright actually talked to you about now?"

"You're still chasing around after that old hen?"

"Yes, I am."

"You know, they say when you own a boat, the happiest two days are the day you buy it and the day you sell it. Marian was like a boat to Chuck." It wasn't the story I'd heard, but it was what she needed to think. "She wanted to know where Chuck got the HIV. Chuck had told me he got it from some woman in Seattle. But now you and she have me doubting Chuck. Maybe it wasn't a woman. Maybe he was playing around with little boys. I don't know. It's infectious, this distrust. I hate it. And I hate you for bringing it to me. And that old hen, both. Did you know she threatened to send Raymond a registered letter saying I was infected?"

"Who's Raymond?"

"He *was* my third husband. He moved back in after Chuck passed on."

"And he doesn't know?"

"No."

"Elizabeth, you can't be having relations with a man who doesn't know you're HIV-infected?"

"I don't know that what I'm having or not having is any of your business, Mr. Black, no more than it was any of her business."

"She ever send the letter?"

"She did not."

"Chuck ever tell you the name of the woman who supposedly gave him HIV?"

"I never asked."

"So who is going to tell Raymond you've got it?"

"When I find the time, I will." Her voice had grown more tremulous with each word. "Is that good enough for you, Mr. Black?"

"I guess it'll have to be." I was beginning to see what Marian had been up against. When I finished this case, I would have to reflect long and hard about spilling the beans on Elizabeth O'Connel, and maybe others. Pundits would be calling me an old hen.

A few minutes after we hung up, the front doorbell rang. Susie Scudder stood on the welcome mat, Tobey scampering across the porch behind her, harmlessly karate-kicking the chair I'd left out for Nigel. Susie wore jeans, Dr. Marten boots, and an imitation of an Air Force parka. Her blond hair was pulled into a knot at the top of her head and was shiny with tension. Her look was pleasant, hopeful, and businesslike.

"Well, this is a surprise. Come in. Both of you. Terrific. What can I do for you?"

"We don't want to be a bother. I had to leave early the other morning, and I was wondering if you needed to talk to me anymore."

"Mom, can we go to McDonald's?" Tobey asked. I took their coats, and as I did so, the doorbell rang again.

I glanced out the window and said, "Tobey. Watch this." He ran to the tall, narrow window alongside the door and pressed his face eagerly to the glass. "What do you see, Tobey?"

The four-year-old spoke slowly. "A kid."

I opened the door on the barred, rectangular peephole and heard a froggy voice say, "Hey, Buuuuud."

"Who's there?"

"Me."

"I don't see me."

"No, not you. Me. I'm down here."

"Where's down here?"

"It's me, Chester. Right down here."

"Who?"

"You have to open the door, Buuuuud. I'm down here. Chester!"

I looked over at Tobey. "Should I open it?" Genuinely puzzled, the four-year-old glanced at his mother, then me, and shrugged. I opened the door.

Shoes untied and on the wrong feet, the buttons on his shirt in the wrong holes, Chester stood with his hands on his hips giving me an exasperated look through his Coke-bottle glasses, the same look he gave me every time he came upstairs. He said, "Heeeey, Buuuuud," and walked in as if the house were his and we were servants. He was maybe two years older than Tobey, not much taller, and his constant scruffy state was a stark contrast to Tobey's immaculate clothing and hair.

"Your dad downstairs?" I asked.

"He's at work."

"On a Saturday night, huh? I hope he's getting overtime."

"Double-time, Bud."

"Good for him. Where's Liseea?"

"On the couch. Sleeping." He looked around for something to appropriate, grabbed Tobey, and headed for my television.

Susie and I sat at the dining room table. Chester began running a black-and-white video Kathy had left months ago: *Arsenic and Old Lace*, starring Cary Grant and Priscilla Lane. Chester had already seen it a couple of times.

"Have you found anything?" she asked.

"Some. I'm probably moving a little slower than Marian did, but that's because she stirred up a lot of sediment and the waters are murky."

"Before we started this, she used to go down to the city council meetings and raise holy hell. I saw her chew out a cop once after he pulled her over for speeding. She beat the ticket in court, but that wasn't good enough. She wrote letters to the cop's supervisor and the mayor trying to get him in Dutch."

"Did she tell you she was HIV-infected?"

"What?"

After I'd explained, she hugged herself and glanced at her son in the living room. "I should have known something was going on. She was so intense those last few weeks. Marian, Marian, Marian."

"How much of what she was doing the last week had to do with you? Do you know?"

"Not really. Somehow she got a list of customers from the weekend I was at the ski lodge five years ago. They faxed it to her. It turned out Tobey's father never registered under the name he used with me, so she had to call a bunch of people to find him."

"That was the Eddie Murphy name?"

"Right. He told me he was Eddie Murphy. He didn't really look that much like Eddie. A little bit, but . . . it was so impossibly romantic, and we seemed to click the way I'd never clicked with anybody in my life, and then he told me he couldn't have children. It seemed like a no-lose proposition. It was bad enough to have the baby, but when my folks saw Tobey was half black, they just about ate the carpet." Susie had always been standoffish and formal with me, and this was the most human look I'd had from her.

"Marian located him?"

"Wednesday a week ago in Tacoma. She said she was going down to check him out, but I'm not sure that she ever did. His real name is Abdul Sarwar. But he checked into the resort under the name of Ransom Marbles." I had seen both names in Marian Wright's papers, along with addresses and phone numbers.

"Abdul? Is he a Black Muslim?"

"I guess so."

"He know he has a son?"

"Marian swore she wasn't going to tell him. But here's what I've been thinking. It's the reason I needed to talk to you. If somebody was frightening Marian, it was probably Abdul. Listen, he had scars on his back he said were bullet wounds. He was a black belt in some martial art; I forget which. If Marian saw him, she ruffled feathers, and his were the wrong feathers to ruffle."

"*If* she saw him."

"I don't know if she did."

The doorbell rang, and I excused myself. On the porch I found Liseea, Chester's baby-sitter, looking sleepy-eyed, seventeen, tall, and lethargic. She was eight months pregnant. "He's parked in front of a video," I said. "You might as well come in too."

After introductions, Liseea sank onto the sofa next to Chester, fluffing his hair with her fingers. Chester, without taking his eyes off the movie, socked her leg lightly.

Before Susie and I could resume our discussion, the doorbell rang again. When I opened it, Kathy was on the stoop in her black coat and clasping a small purse, her mother's car pulling away from the curb behind her. "I thought I'd surprise you, but I see you already have company. Let me come in, and I'll call a cab."

"Don't be silly. I phoned you a few minutes ago, but you weren't home. Why don't you stay for dinner? We'll invite the whole gang."

It was hard to believe how small and shy she looked, this woman who for years had made a daily habit of straying up from her basement apartment to ambush me at meals, during naps, and more than once, in the tub. Not that I had ever objected, except for the times she'd brought mini-tours through.

Susie chopped vegetables and built a green salad while I sliced olives and sausages to drop into a pot of spaghetti sauce we had simmering on a back burner. When Hank arrived in grimy work clothes, I introduced him around and he went downstairs to wash up. When we wouldn't let him help in the kitchen, he tried to interest a drowsy Liseea in conversation while Chester filled him in on the plot of *Arsenic and Old Lace*.

"You've still got my movie," Kathy said.

"I watch it quite often. It reminds me of you."

"You've seen it more than once?"

"Fifteen times, maybe twenty."

She smiled. "Sure."

By the time the gang had wolfed down dinner and we had done the dishes, the windows in the kitchen had steamed over. Polishing one of them with a dish towel, I spotted a glowing ember in the backyard next door. It was still there a few minutes later, so I went to the back porch and hailed Nigel.

"Why don't you come on over?"

"Don't want to bust in on you and your friends. I'm fine." He was standing in the rain.

"Don't be ridiculous. Come on over."

After he'd toweled off and the introductions had been made, Nigel memorizing first, last, and middle names with no little amount of showmanship, Kathy asked if he'd eaten. "Oh, I threw something together with a can opener and a hot plate."

He downed two heaping plates of spaghetti. He had carried a wet dachshund into the house in his arms like a baby, and the dog captured the attention of the boys. After eating, he talked to Hank about construction, to Liseea about motherhood, to Susie about his flying career and his two brothers who'd been killed flying in past wars, and to Kathy about the politics of nuclear energy, all the while pointedly ignoring me as if I'd been blackballed. By the time we'd dished up Goo Goo Cluster ice cream, eaten it, and rinsed out the bowls, he had used his resonant voice, inquisitiveness, and obvious love for animals to charm everyone in the house, including me.

After a while Chester and Tobey ran through the house and asked if they could feed the dogs on the back porch. Nigel made a move to get up from the sofa where he was expostulating on what was wrong with the Pentagon, but I waved him off.

I went to the kitchen. What to fix? One dachshund and my ex-dog, Last Chance. A hot dog and a turncoat. I prepared two bowls, the first brimming with Alpo, the second a mixture of Alpo and peanut butter. It didn't take long for L.C. to look up from his chow and start smacking his chops loudly. He knew he was eating something he shouldn't, yet he was an unrepentant scavenger and couldn't quit. The more he gobbled, the louder the smacking noises. Before long the boys were in hysterics. It was the sort of prank boys loved.

When the evening broke up, Hank, Nigel, and Chester went down the inner stairs to the basement, ostensibly to talk construction and test Hank's stores of beers, in reality so Nigel could check out the basement like a hermit crab seeking a new shell. Minutes later he came back up, his voice choked. "What happened to the dog?"

"Huh?"

"What did you feed the dog?"

"What dog?"

"Your dog."

"I don't have a dog, Nigel. You have three dogs and I don't have any."

"You know what I'm talking about. He's down there drinking water like there's no tomorrow. What did you feed him? A chunk off a salt lick?"

"Not anything I wouldn't eat myself."

Nigel gave me a look so withering it actually made me feel a pang of guilt. Kathy's ex-fiancé had been the one who told me about feeding peanut butter to dogs. I never would have thought of it on my own, but that didn't make me feel any less of an idiot.

I drove Kathy back to her apartment on Queen Anne Hill.

We got out, walked around to the steps leading up to her unit and stood in the lee of a shingled wall, sheltered from the wind and a cold drizzle. Across from us the lights of the city and the Space Needle were blurred by the mist. I said, "I'm glad you came over."

"Your dad is a character. Does he always work a crowd like that?"

"He was in particularly good form tonight. Are you going to want your car back?"

"I've been taking the bus to work. Walking to the store. I'm all right for a while."

"And after that?"

"I'll figure out something."

"Has anybody ever told you those eyes of yours are like quicksand? They suck a man in by the boots."

"It just so happens the grocer told me this afternoon."

I leaned down and kissed her. Her lips were hot and her cheeks cold and damp. Although she didn't pull away, she kept it brief. "I know you're going through a bad time," I said.

"Yeah, the worst year of my life."

"With Nigel hanging around talking about my childhood, I'm starting to get some perspective on my own life. I'm over thirty, and I've always been alone. I didn't realize how alone until you left."

"I missed you too."

"Did you?"

"Didn't you think I would?"

"I don't know what I thought. Are you coming back?"

She shrugged and looked at the ground. "I don't know."

"I can wait, you know."

"Maybe you can, but I don't see an end to it. I really don't."

"I can wait a year. Whatever."

"A year? I don't know. It might be longer than a year."

"I could handle a couple of years. Five, maybe even ten."

"You'd find somebody else."

"There is nobody else."

She kissed me on the cheek and dashed up the stairs to her

apartment, her hips moving under her coat, a toss of her long hair and a flash of her ankle as she rounded the corner. I heard the sound of keys jangling in the lock, a dead woman's poodles yipping behind a door.

CHAPTER 17

Sunday night I took a room at the Edgewater Inn on Alaskan Way on the waterfront. The Beatles had stayed there the first time they came through Seattle, and my sister had purchased a square of carpet from their room, which as far as I knew, she still owned.

When I shouted that the door was open, the woman made her way into the room and peeked into the bathroom, where I stood in front of the sink, my face cloaked in shaving lather, a golf hat on my head. It was seven o'clock, and she was nothing if not prompt. She wore high heels and a designer raincoat. Her dress was tight across her hips. I knew she didn't recognize me. She said, "Are you Krebs?"

"Come on in. Make yourself comfortable."

If I hadn't already known, I would have guessed she had been in a lot of hotel rooms, both from the way she moved around this one and from her total lack of curiosity. She stripped off her raincoat and draped it across a chair, then, swinging it by a long strap, centered her bag on the coat. "So. You must know St. Clair pretty well?"

"Not really."

"What do I call you?"

"Maynard will work."

"Well, gee, Maynard, he gave you an awful impressive rec-ommendation for somebody who doesn't know you very well."

"Actually, it's not G. Maynard. It's Maynard G."

She smiled. It was warm and professional and generic, the same one she might have handed out to the mailperson or the dishwasher repairman or any of her customers. "Maynard. I like that. It's a sensual name. How would you like to pay for this, Maynard?"

"How about cash?"

"That will work. Did anybody ever tell you you have nice arms? You work out, do you?"

I doffed the hat, cranked both faucet handles until the sink was churning, splashed my face, toweled off the remaining suds, and stepped into the bedroom. She had been unzipping her dress. I said, "Might as well keep that on."

Seeing people out of context frequently jars a person, a fact I was counting on. It took her ten seconds to stop gawping. "You!"

"Odd circumstances to be meeting under, don't you sup-pose, Ms. Littrell?"

"You're not Maynard Krebs."

"Maynard G.? No. Although, for a couple of years when I was a kid, I wanted to be. You never watched *Dobie Gillis*?"

She zipped her dress back up and sat on one of the chairs in the room, crossed her legs, and faked another smile. Her voice had gone dead and flat again, as if she were only alive when she pretended to be for a client. "What is this? A hustle? I hate private investigators. I'm warning you. I can hurt you."

"I thought we'd chat."

"Why here?"

"For one thing, here you can't lie about what you do. And I knew you were going to lie about what you do."

"I charge people for chitchat. Better put a hundred and fifty on the table before my friend shows up or he'll thrash you to a raggedy pulp."

"And you'll love every minute of it, won't you?"

A flash of color rose in her cheeks. Oddly, she seemed easily embarrassed. "I think I will."

The door to the room opened—Littrell had most likely unlocked it on her way in—and the man who'd accompanied her
to the Stouffer-Madison yesterday swaggered into the room,
walking like a plump rich kid on his way to the john after eating too much dinner. He made the doorway look small, not because of his height, for he was of average height, but because of
his width. He had a home haircut, tiny feet, and button ears,
but as near as I could tell, those were his only small features.
He wore an unbuttoned raincoat over a suit, the same clothes
he'd worn yesterday. I could see that an epaulet and one pocket
on the raincoat had been torn and hastily resewn.

"How's the nose?" I asked. Both his eyes had black circles
under them. His nostrils were packed with a reddish crud and
with rolled-up strips of gauze.

When I shifted my weight, he pointed a short, thick finger
at me and said, "You don't give no trouble." His voice was
worn-out, high and soft, not a forced whisper but as soft as a
whisper, as if he'd recently had throat surgery. It was peculiar
enough that I was sure he turned heads whenever he opened
his mouth. The only conceivable way to mask such a voice was
to whisper. The man in my backyard had whispered.

Without turning away from me, he directed his gray eyes toward Littrell. "What's going on?"

Littrell said, "Just do it. Get rid of him."

"He pay up?"

"Don't worry about the money. Just do it."

He swiveled his tiny eyes from Littrell to me and back to
Littrell. It was clear he did not understand the situation. He
looked like a stupid man, but I didn't let it impress me. Littrell
carefully reached for her raincoat and eased into it, as if any
abrupt movement on her part might spark trouble.

"You look to me like you could use a lesson in humility,"
she said.

"I've always been humble," I said quickly. "In fact, humility
is something I take great pride in."

The man pulled two small objects out of a pocket in his
raincoat and folded them into his fists. Taped rolls of quarters,
I thought. Arms held high like John L. Sullivan, he stepped

toward me. He had the cold and somewhat scary eyes of a man in the act of killing a chicken; a man who'd killed so many chickens he could daydream about other things while doing it.

I leaped onto the bed, got it bouncing, and put my fists up, grinning and bouncing. He took a swing at me, but I was bounding around on the bed, so he caught only part of my thigh. It felt like I'd been hit a glancing blow by a locomotive piston. In fact, it was all I could do to keep my legs under me. "Before we start," I said, smiling, "why don't we let the lady step out onto the balcony? We wouldn't want her to get caught in the cross fire."

"Ain't gonna be no cross fire."

"Just the same." I stopped bouncing and dropped my arms until he lowered his fists and turned his head to Littrell. It was hard to dislike such a gentleman. She pulled open the sliding glass door and stepped onto the balcony, closed it, and stood facing the dark water. I thought she moved with a certain amount of grace, and I wondered if there wasn't a word for somebody who was graceful while having you beat up.

"Look," I said, "I know how it works. Some pasty-faced twit who maybe does twenty-five sit-ups three times a week wants to tie Bain down and you stand in the doorway and he rips his shorts. You might even have to twist a little, lily-white arm every once in a blue moon. But life is too short for the whuppin' we're both about to take."

"Just you."

My ribs had been keeping me awake at night, and not a day had passed that I hadn't thought about how close I'd come to losing my teeth to that baseball bat. "I'm going to take a whuppin', sure. But it's going to cost you. And then, there's the off chance I'll get lucky and drop you."

He was more skittish than he was willing to let on, probably because of last Thursday night. If he was the man who'd attacked me, he hadn't fared much better than I. His eyes didn't betray him, but his skin was glowing pink and he had started to sweat. "I'm getting paid to do you. I do you."

"She's out there in the wind. She can't hear what we're saying."

"What are you trying to tell me?"

"You and me, man. We can work this out."

"Without scrapping?"

"Yeah. Right. Now you got it. Without scrapping."

"You yella?"

"What she expects is for you to take care of her, right? I mean, that's your actual job."

"I whup clients."

"What are you, fifty? It's time to start working with your head instead of going home with bloody knuckles."

He thought about it briefly. "What've you got in mind?"

"You let me talk to her. I walk out of here. You walk out of here. She walks out of here. We're all hunky-dory. What's wrong with that?"

"Talk? I thought you wanted to bang her."

"You kidding? I wouldn't go to bed with her on a dare."

"Why not? You a fag?"

"I'm in love with somebody else."

He dropped his hands to his sides. He knew about love. He wasn't going to admit it, but he knew about love, and I could see that we had a connection now. I could see it plainly in his dull gray eyes. He looked at Littrell on the patio. His strange elf voice dropped. "She expects me to punish you. I don't see any way out of it." He stepped forward and swung twice, missing both times. He stopped moving and put his hands down. "She's out there expecting a show. I gotta give her a show."

"Listen, buddy. I'm not going to hurt her. I never was. What I wanted was to ask her a few questions and to meet you."

"Me?"

"People tend to hold grudges. Somebody's holding a grudge, it's nice to know what he looks like."

"What are you talking about?"

"Somebody tried to break my legs the other night. I didn't get a good look at him."

"You think it was me?"

"Yes."

"So this was a setup?" He looked around the room warily.

"More or less."

"I don't hold no grudges. With me it's all business. Everything's business. During the week I drive a potato chip truck. The truck is where my heart is. Matter of fact, I been thinkin' of giving all this up."

"So, what do you say we bring her back in and I ask her some questions and we all go home? What's wrong with that?"

"But what are we going to tell her? We can't let her think I backed off. I don't want her thinkin' I'm yella."

"What if we tell her I begged, and you say you felt sorry for me."

"Won't wash."

"Why not?"

"She knows beggin' don't work on me. I got a rep. People beg, I break their fingers."

"Tell her I have a heart condition and if you hit me I might go down for the big count. You don't want to get the rope over a heart condition. How's that?"

He knuckled his chin and stood with his hands at his sides, looking me over. "Okay. I'll get her back in here. But you make it good. She can get real mad."

"And you step outside so I can question her."

"Outside?"

"Just there on the patio. Nice night. The waterfront. Some of this stuff I'm going to ask her about is private." I bounced off the bed onto the carpet and held my hand out. We shook.

"Just for the record," he said, "it wasn't me the other night."

"Glad to hear it."

"I set out to break somebody's legs, they get broken."

"I know that." He turned, opened the sliding glass door to the patio, and called Littrell in, then stepped out past her. She looked at me like I had come off the bottom of her shoe.

"It's okay," he said. "He'll explain."

"You'll explain what?" Littrell asked, stepping into the room with her arms folded across her breasts. As he closed the sliding glass door behind himself, the room filled with the cool smells of salt water, diesel oil, and just an insinuation of Littrell's perfume. When we were alone, she said, "I don't get it. What happened?"

"We decided to be mature about this."

Littrell looked from the man on the patio to me and then back. "That doesn't sound like Houser. Let me get him back in here."

"I wouldn't do that. People have life experiences. They grow. He's in a growth phase right now. Don't take it away from him."

"Did you offer him money?"

"I don't have any money on me." He was leaning on the rail smoking a cigarette.

"So what's really going on?"

"What's going on is I ask some questions and you answer them."

She gave the man on the patio another disbelieving and slightly disgusted look, then sat in the same chair she'd laid her coat across earlier. She crossed her legs and installed her bag on her lap. "I don't know that I should be doing this."

"Why don't you start with the gasbag out there?"

"His name is Fears. Houser Fears."

"Who is he?"

"An ex-con I employ when I have a new client."

"Spend time in the joint with your husband, did he?"

"I live alone."

"Did you know he fired a shot at me Thursday night? He could have killed me."

"I don't know anything about that."

"Sure. Blow it off. I don't blame you."

"This old woman you're working for—"

"I'm not working for her, okay? She died in an accident, and I'm looking into her last few weeks."

"She came to me and asked a lot of questions. She was not a likable person. You've spoken to her. You know what I'm talking about."

"She was dead when I got into it."

"She was very unpleasant. And beyond the unpleasantness,

she began contacting my clients. She threatened two of them. Two I know about."

"How did she find your clients?"

"Hired a private investigator, I would assume." Littrell's look was scathing.

"The woman is dead. Nobody cares who your clients are."

"If I have AIDS, they might."

"Do you?"

"No."

"Did she say you did?"

"That's exactly what she said. She said she thought my clients should be informed. Listen, Black. I know the rules and I play by them. Everybody uses protection, and I'm tested every six months."

"It's so safe, why get tested?"

"Why not? I don't believe an old woman like her could have found out who my clients were on her own. You found out for her, didn't you? You're another one of those sanctimonious—"

"It wasn't me."

"She threatened me and even began pestering a friend of mine. I didn't like it."

"Which friend?"

"You wouldn't know her."

"If she lives on Sixteenth in a hospice, I might."

"If you know about the hospice, you know what's going on with Dee. Wright found out she had AIDS, made some false assumptions, and thought Dee and I worked together."

"You didn't?"

"Dee was never in the life." The room was silent for a moment. "Don't look at me like that. I hate people who get all moralistic when they talk about the life. *You* work your tail off to earn a master's degree in economics and then hire out to a clothing company for nine dollars an hour and see how long you last. I went three and a half years trying to make ends meet!" Fears had been right about the temper.

"So you sent Fears after me."

"I sent nobody." She stared at the carpet. Her voice grew subdued and flatter than ever. "Wright told me her husband got

the HIV virus from Dee. She wanted to sue Dee. When she realized Dee didn't have anything, she decided to track down the
person Dee got the virus from and sue him—or her. She
thought I was involved."

"Were you?"

"No. She had this vision of a whole legion of irresponsible
degenerate men and women running around screwing unin-
fected people and passing the disease around. She was on a
crusade."

"Dee corresponded with Marian's ex-husband in Arizona.
What was that all about?"

"Years ago they had a fling . . . Dee always thought fondly
of him."

"What do you know about it?"

Bain crossed her legs the other direction and sat more
primly than ever. "For a while Dee worked in a copy place next
door to the garage Chuck Wright used to own on Pine Street.
One New Year's Eve the garage threw a party. Deanna was going through a lot of problems in her marriage right then—she
always was—and Chuck had been paying a bunch of attention
to her, which was just what she needed. They ended up in the
loft of the garage while everybody else was getting smashed
downstairs. They met again a week later, and then Dee decided
it was wrong and cut it off."

"And?"

"And right about then Dee's marriage to William blew up.
Dee and Chuck kept writing even after Chuck remarried. He
told me once on the phone he still loved Dee. But then, he told
me he loved both his wives too."

"Why were *you* talking to him?"

"I was the contact. Dee never stayed in one place long
enough for him to keep tabs. She was always looking for a job
to pay the bills. One night I even gave her a slot on my schedule. It didn't work out. I guess it was a good thing, because two
months later she learned she had AIDS."

Littrell focused on the tip of her foot. She was a good one
with eye contact when she wanted to be—eye contact being one
of the tools of the trade—and had given me soul-piercing looks

when she thought I was a client, but now she didn't know whether I was going to let her go or twist her arm. Outside, Fears flicked his sparking cigarette into the water and took another one out of his pocket. I knew the odds were that he had been in my backyard and she had put him up to it.

"Do you know where Dee got the virus?"

"Her husband. William went to Trinidad with some buddies, and they all came back with either the clap or AIDS."

"You told that to Marian Wright?"

"Yes."

"Where did you and Deanna Ayers meet?"

"Vanderhoef Sports on Rainier Avenue. I worked in the office for a couple of years after college, and she was in the order department."

Before driving home, I spotted a homeless man and a woman who was obviously mentally ill sucking bent cigarettes in the doorway of a vacant building under the Alaskan Way Viaduct. I offered them the room key to the Edgewater, then drove them to the hotel while they sat in stony silence. Later I realized they must have thought it was some sort of scam.

CHAPTER 18

It was snowing again on Monday morning, the type of wet Northwest snow that rarely sticks, and if it does, is gone in a few hours. My lawn looked like a battalion of tiny green bayonets poking through the white. In the street, snowflakes alighted and liquefied before you could focus on them.

The way they faded reminded me of the way a memory fades when you try too hard to remember it, the way I had been trying too hard all winter to conjure up Kathy's face, knowing the harder I worked at it, the farther the memories would be pushed away, until at last they vanished completely. All winter the image of her smile had been vanishing, and before I knew it, all I had left were a few photographs limp with handling.

Kathy had never been up to speed on cars, so I wasn't surprised when the Firebird didn't have cables in the trunk. I bought a set at an auto supply store six blocks away and tossed them into the backseat, then drove to a medical office on Broadway where I hand-delivered two letters from Kathy Birchfield as well as a Xerox of Wright's death certificate.

Dr. Blood was in his forties and wore horn-rimmed glasses and a goatee that made him resemble a beatnik poet more than a doctor. Holding my letters in his delicate hands, he read them twice each. He confirmed Marian Wright was HIV-infected and that he'd had to hospitalize her for a period of three days during which she neither spoke, nor ate, nor, as near as anyone could tell, slept, except under sedation. It had been an exceptional reaction, made even more exceptional on the third day of her stay at Swedish Hospital when one evening, without a word to a soul, she got out of bed and skulked out of the hospital. "She always was hardheaded," said Blood.

According to Blood, Marian Wright had, years ago, contracted syphilis. Along with a mild arthritis, she had been battling eating problems her entire life and had never carried as much fat as a healthy woman should. But her most pressing ailment had been the lack of sleep. On a good night she might doze three or four hours.

"She worried. That was her problem. Worrying was a hobby with her. You find people like that. We usually assume it's psychological, but I sometimes wonder if it isn't an imbalance in the brain's chemistry."

"What did she worry about?"

"She'd come to me once a month with a little bump or a feeling that there was something wrong with her and I'd run some tests and tell her everything was all right, but she used to do the same thing with her dogs, her car. Nothing was ever quite right, but none of the experts could find anything wrong."

"Until you found her HIV?"

"It kind of made up for all those imaginary complaints, didn't it?"

Blood studied the medical examiner's report and told me the drugs in Marian's bloodstream at the time of death would not have caused dizziness or mental problems, at least not anything that would convince her to throw herself in front of a moving car.

The hospice wasn't far from Blood's Broadway office. A young man in a T-shirt and jeans answered the back door and told me Deanna was having a bath and wouldn't be available for half an hour. He ushered me up the stairs to a small kitchen and sitting room at the west end of the building.

After a while a boy and two girls in their teens came in, the boy weeping, the girls touching and comforting him. I sat on a

dirty couch and scanned a *Time* magazine that was eight weeks
out of date. The boy had tested negative to the HIV virus but
sobbed that he wanted to have AIDS because his girlfriend
down the hallway did. The girls were trying to talk sense to
him, but from the sound of their arguments, he had been in
this morose frame of mind for weeks. They repeated the scene
four or five times like drunks too inebriated to get it right or to
remember that they'd only just played the scene, rehearsing
tirelessly the way only teenagers experimenting with emotions
can.

The floor show was beginning to pall when a chunky
woman in a white T-shirt and tan shorts came in and looked at
me. "Can I do something for you?"

"I'm waiting for Deanna Ayers."

"She's in there watching *The Price Is Right*. Somebody say
you couldn't go in?"

"They said she was having a bath."

"Oh, gosh. That was ages ago. Go on in."

She was propped up in a hospital bed staring at a television
somebody had perched precariously on a bureau top. She wore
men's pajama bottoms with camels on them and a man's ribbed
sleeveless T-shirt. Her arms looked like they'd been formed
from plastic coat hangers, and her chest was flat as a boy's.
When I knocked on the door frame, it took her a pitifully long
while to roll her head over to see who was there.

She weighed no more than ninety pounds, her face emaci-
ated, eyes sunken. The back of her near hand was riddled with
sores from months of IV needles. Her mussed hair grew in
clumps. Her glassy brown eyes mirrored pain and apathy and
only a little curiosity. "Deanna Ayers?"

"Do I know you?"

"My name is Thomas Black. I'm a private investigator. May
I come in?" With one bony hand she slowly signified that I was
to turn down the volume on the game show she had been
watching. Feeling as though I were pulling a thumb out of a
child's mouth, I silenced the television. "I'm trying to backtrack
Marian Wright's travels during the past couple of weeks."

"Oh, I couldn't talk out of school about Marian. She's been very kind to me."

"I guess you didn't hear what happened. She was killed Friday a week ago. In a highway accident. And you wouldn't be talking out of school. I'm working out of her attorney's office."

"Marian's gone? That's so strange. I was just thinking about her."

I told her how it had happened. She didn't show a whole lot of emotion, but then, she didn't look like she had a lot to spare. "Do you think you might tell me what you two talked about?"

"At first, all she wanted to know was why I gave AIDS to her ex-husband. I didn't even know he had it. It was something Chuck and I never talked about. He knew I was ill, but I never gave him any details and he never asked."

"Was there anything else?"

"Where I got it. Did I ever do drugs. Who I had sex with. We discussed my sex life, pathetic as it was, for hours, literally. We talked about it so much it got to be like we were talking over my old tennis matches in high school. I remembered all sorts of things I hadn't thought of in years." We were silent for a moment while she swallowed. Her eyes rolled to a water glass beside the bed. I tried to hand it to her, but she clearly wanted me to help her drink. Leaning close to the bed, I tipped it to her chapped lips and waited. It was like waiting for a heavy stutterer to get a word out.

"I know this must be exhausting for you," I said after she'd sipped. "Tell me when you're too tired. I can come back."

"No, you stay. There's not a whole lot of people who want to spend time with me. I had friends, but when it takes a couple of years to croak, people get burnt out and move on to other projects. One friend told me she had too much yard work. Maybe the others are visiting sick people who have the refinement to die at a quicker pace. What else do you want to know?"

"Everything you told Marian Wright."

"Sure, but let me say something first. If I ever gave it to her husband, I did not do it knowingly. Chuck and I had sex two times, and he wasn't inside me for more than three minutes—

total. I just don't think he got it from here. Besides, women don't pass the HIV virus off as easily as men. Chuck tried to help me out at a bad time in my life. He was a real nice guy. And I felt bad that what we did ruined his marriage."

She stopped talking and closed her eyes for a few moments. When she opened them, she said, "Marian wanted to know all the people I had sex with in my life. She made a kind of a graph which she kept showing me so I could check if it was right."

"Did she talk to these people?"

"That was the whole idea. Tracing the HIV the way the post office might trace a lost letter. She would come back here and tell me what they were doing now. In a way, it was kind of interesting. A gallows version of *This Is Your Life*."

I pulled a small notebook from my inside jacket pocket. "Would you mind naming the people for me?"

"There was my husband, Bill, of course. He gave it to me, although he's not sick and claims he doesn't have it. It doesn't seem fair, that some people get it and carry it around for years and never even know it, and other people, three months later they have AIDS."

"No. It's not fair."

"I'm sorry I said that. I promised myself a long time ago I'd stop talking about it being fair or not fair. It wears me out. So there was Bill. Then there was Chuck. That's two. I think we came up with five names. That's not too much of a tramp in this day and age, is it? Sleeping with five men? For a twenty-seven-year-old woman?"

"Probably not." Twenty-seven? Good Lord. I might have been willing to concede she was as young as late forties, but twenty-seven?

"I had girlfriends who slept with five different guys a month. Now they're married and living in Federal Way with their hubby and kids. And *I'm* here." Despite what she said, there was no self-pity in her voice. To her it was all irony. I wondered if I would be so sanguine in the face of my own death.

"I don't think you did all that much wrong."

"From my point of view it was four too many passes on the

roulette wheel. But I try to look at the positive aspects. This morning I feel pretty strong. That's positive."

"Your husband and Chuck. Who else?"

"A man named Ransom. That was in college. He was something. You know? One of those guys I didn't really figure out until years later. First he made me feel guilty by insinuating I didn't want to be friends with a black man. Then, after a while, if I didn't want to kiss him, he claimed it was because he was black, and if I didn't want to sleep with him it was because he was black. I never did catch on. Not until later. Did you already tell me why you need to know all this?"

"It's intrusive, and I apologize. Wright was doing some investigating the day she died. We're trying to find out what was going on."

"She was nice to me. After the first. I guess she felt sorry for me."

"She identified with you. We've got three. Who was number four?"

"Some man I didn't even know at the time. We met in his hotel room. He told me he was originally from Schenectady, New York. There was a time when I wouldn't have told a soul this, but it doesn't matter anymore. I did it for money. My girlfriend makes her living that way, and she thought I might try. I hardly remember it now, although I know at the time it was all I thought about for weeks. I do remember I made him wear a condom, but he took it off halfway through. That was two years ago, just months before I found out I was HIV-infected."

"So he might have given it to you?"

"Bill gave it to me."

"How can you be sure? Didn't you say he claims not to have it?"

"Bill and two of his friends got it in Trinidad. His friends are sick. I'm sick. And Bill's fine. Doesn't even have a pimple. But I know I got it from him." She let her head sink back into the pillows and closed her eyes. I waited.

One wall was dotted with photographs similar to the ones I'd seen in the Dempster Dumpster the first time I visited. Featured in the photos were two little girls who didn't look anything like the woman in the bed, but then the woman in the photos who I knew had to be Deanna Ayers didn't look anything like the woman in the bed. The woman in the photographs had big brown eyes and long, stringy, blond hair; looked about seventeen.

It was almost five minutes before she opened her eyes. When she did, she greeted me with a weak smile. I said, "You doin' okay? Want me to call someone?"

"No, I do this all day. It feels kind of peaceful, really. Mostly it's the meds. You got more questions?"

"Apparently Wright wasn't as positive as you are that you didn't get it from one of your other contacts. Did Wright talk to you more than once about any of these people?"

"All of them."

"Remember any of what she said?"

"She thought they were jerks. My ex-boss, I guess, threw her out of his house on Mercer Island."

"He must be number five. We'd only gotten to four when you drifted off."

"Randolph. I worked at this sporting goods company on Rainier Avenue."

"Vanderhoef's Sports?"

"How did you know?"

"I met another person who worked there."

"He was my boss. Randolph Vanderhoef. I think we did it once."

"When?"

"About four years ago. It's a long story."

"And no protection?"

"I never would have remembered. I guess not."

I assumed she'd been drinking when she'd had sex with Vanderhoef, but there was something in her eyes that made me back off on the question. I would ask about it later. "What about the others? Protection?"

"None of them really. Not Ransom. He was sterile. And he said he didn't have any disease. You know, now that you have me thinking about this, Marian got real mad talking to Ransom. Wouldn't tell me why. I forgot about that. But she was mad at all of them. After I told her how Bill, my ex, treated me, she offered to file a lawsuit in my behalf."

"So being angry at Ransom wasn't anything new?"

"Except she was *really* mad."

Following Marian Wright's reasoning, since she believed Dee had given the HIV virus to Chuck Wright, who had in turn, given it to Marian, anybody Dee slept with after Chuck would not be relevant. I asked her what order she had slept with these men. The sequence should have been: Ransom, the college boy; Bill, the ex; Vanderhoef, the ex-boss. Then Chuck, and then the trick from New York, who probably wouldn't have been pertinent, and even if he had been, Marian had no way of locating him. I couldn't recall a more grotesque interviewing session: standing in the room of a half-dead woman, cross-examining her about her past sex life.

On my way out of the building at the back door, I ran into a man in his late twenties with two children in bright dresses and bulky ski coats. They had already passed me when I turned and said, "William Ayers?"

He squinted at me from the shadows of the unlighted hallway. "Do I know you?" The two girls stopped in front of him and stared at me while he placed his hands on their heads as if they were melons.

"I was visiting your wife. Ex-wife. I'm trying to track the movements of a woman named Marian Wright. Did you ever talk to her?"

"Why don't you two go up and see Mommy," he said, turning the girls' heads around so they were looking at him instead of me. "And remember, don't get on her bed. She's very fragile."

"Like a glass princess?" the younger girl asked.

"Just like a glass princess, Jenny."

"Can we visit Chad too?"

He was quiet for a moment. "Chad isn't here anymore." As the girls ran into the building, he looked at me harshly and said, "What did you say your name was?"

"Black. Thomas Black." He took me outside. He wore a forest-green jacket that complemented his brown eyes, and had long, swept-back brown hair. He was a small man and slender, and for some reason didn't fit the image I'd had of the husband of the woman upstairs. There had been no photos of him on the wall, a fact I hadn't noted until now.

"What are you to this Wright woman?"

"I'm investigating her death."

"She died? How'd that happen?"

"Hit by a car."

"Yeah? I would have thought she probably stroked out talking somebody to death. What do you want from me?"

"Did she speak to you?"

"Accused me of giving Dee the virus. She's not the first person to accuse me, but she's the first one to nut out on me. She actually came to the mill where I work and sprayed a sign on my truck with shaving cream. 'HIV positive. Steer clear,' it said."

"What'd you tell her when you spoke?"

"I told her to lay off. But she wouldn't quit. She figured I gave it to Dee and Dee gave it to her husband. She thought I owed her money, I guess. Finally, I went to my doctor and had him write a letter saying I was clean as of the last time he tested me, which was about eight months ago. I'll show it to you."

"I don't think that's necessary."

Hot under the collar now, he strode down the wooden wheelchair ramp to a red Nissan truck with deer lights on a roll bar, unlocked it, stretched across the seat until only the cuffs of his tan pants and cowboy boots showed, and fumbled in the glove compartment. He came back and thrust an envelope into my hands. It contained a letter from a doctor in Bothell who asserted William Dean Ayers tested negative for the HIV virus on May tenth of last year. While I read it, he said, "This is a hell of a country, when you have to carry paperwork proving you don't have the plague."

"It probably isn't going to get any better," I said.

"That's right. You better get your own paperwork."

He ripped the letter out of my hand and strode up the wooden ramp. I called after him, "Did that satisfy Marian Wright?"

He turned back, still angry. "What do you mean?"

"Did she stop bugging you?"

He shrugged. "Yeah. I guess."

"Then why does your ex-wife upstairs still think you gave it to her?"

"You can't listen to her. She's on medication. We all know where she got it. Slutting around."

It was a spiteful sentiment, and he didn't wear it well. Besides, I believed her version of her sex life, and it did not paint her as a slut. At this juncture, Dee had absolutely no reason to lie, but William Ayers—now here was a man I wouldn't trust to check the air in my tires.

CHAPTER 19

On the drive to Tacoma I used the cellular phone to call the doctor in Bothell who'd written the letter exculpating William Ayers of having AIDS. Dr. Fleischman assured me the letter was genuine and added that Ayers had given instructions to pass out the information to anybody who called. When I asked if there had been others, he told me of an older woman who had given no name. I didn't need a name.

There was a chance the man this doctor had tested was not the man I knew as William Ayers, but I discounted it. Paranoia was for when I'd been knocked around more. There was plenty of time for paranoia.

Tacoma was fifty miles south of Seattle, a trip most people who had a choice took only during nonpeak driving hours, yet lately the area had become so congested it almost didn't matter what time you drove; it was always jammed.

According to Wright's notes, Ransom worked for an insurance company on the third floor of a building a block off Pacific Avenue in downtown Tacoma. I parked the Firebird at a meter that still had time on it and walked. The sky was gray and cold, and thunder rumbled out over Commencement Bay, sounding like a rock avalanche. Up the hill in the residential areas, dogs were barking, moms were calling their kids in, and putterers were turning off their home computers lest any of them tempt a freak lightning strike.

It was a ten-story building, and Wright's notes saying it was on the third floor were wrong. It was on the fourth. When I got off the elevator, I walked to the receptionist's desk and gazed out over a hundred partitions, a worker squirreled away in each cubicle.

The receptionist was a motherly, buxom black woman with bright red lipstick and straightened hair that curved back in at her neck. She regarded me with smiling eyes. "Can I help you?"

"I'd like to speak to Abdul Sarwar."

Using her large, muscular arms, she pushed herself up and off from the desk, then chaperoned me through the partitions. I followed along in a sweet boulevard of perfume until we reached a desk that was vacant. She turned to leave and said, "He'll be back. Lunch isn't for a while."

I sat in his chair. I knew plenty of people who had jobs like this, but it looked like my version of hell. Outside, thunder rumbled, but the windows were too far away to see lightning. Beyond the papers and the blue-covered reference books lined up neatly against the partition were photographs of three small children and a woman with cocoa-colored skin and gaps between her teeth. When a man walked into the cubicle behind me, I stood.

"Mr. Sarwar?"

"Yes." He had a soothing voice; a low and relaxed tone, and skin so dark it was almost a true black.

"I speak to you for a few minutes?"

"In what regard?"

"A woman named Marian Wright." He looked mildly alarmed.

"They don't like us handling personal business on company time, but I suppose I can cut you a minute out of my schedule. I'll have to work into lunch." From the look on his face, I had little doubt that he *would* work into lunch. It was hard to relate this diligent company man to a scoundrel who would use racial guilt to flummox a young college coed into the sack, a man who, I had been told less than two hours earlier, had sworn he was sterile when he was obviously not.

"Nieces and nephews?" I asked, gesturing at the photos.

"Just exactly what are you here for?"

When I told him who I was and what I was doing, he peered at me through a pair of rimless round-lensed glasses. After he had done that in his own quiet, contemplative manner, we shook hands. He was five-foot-nine or -ten and wore pressed slacks, a tidy narrow belt, and a shirt with military creases so sharp and straight I immediately wanted one just like it. He sat, spun his chair around expertly, and rolled to the far corner. "Now, why would a private investigator want to talk to a lowly claims examiner?"

"Is that what you do here?"

"It might not seem too exciting to someone who probably gets into car chases every week, but I like it. Five years in March."

"Never been in a car chase. What was your name before you changed it to Abdul Sarwar?"

"Before I changed it?" He tightened his small brown eyes behind the rimless spectacles. "Thomas Black." I laughed, but he didn't even crack a smile.

"A woman named Marian Wright came and spoke to you, didn't she?"

"You didn't bring her with you?"

"She was killed in an accident. I'd be grateful if you told me what you talked about."

"I'm sorry she was killed, but the lady was a stone fruitcake. I took her down to the coffee shop and we spoke for a while, and then one of the security guards for the building tossed her butt out of here. She tried to duke it out with him. An old lady. Probably somebody's grandma."

"Why'd she get kicked out?"

"For yelling and making a scene."

"What did she want?"

"Mr. Black. You know what she wanted, or you wouldn't be here."

"What I know is hearsay. What I would like is your version."

"Let's lay out the hearsay first."

"Okay. She probably told you she knew you had had sex with a young woman of her acquaintance. This would have happened back in college."

Sarwar rolled his eyes and laid both his hands flat on the arms of his chair. "I did a lot of things before I found Allah."

"Was that one of them?"

"Oh, I had sex all right. And probably in college and probably with a young woman. Mr. Black, I have shaken off my previous life. I don't understand why it keeps getting dragged up."

"I'm working for friends of Mrs. Wright's, in conjunction with her attorney. I'm just trying to trace her movements the last week of her life."

He thought about it while adjusting his glasses with the fingertips of both hands. He had long, elegant fingers and manicured nails. "She claimed I slept with some girl named Dee or Gee or something like that. It was a long time ago, maybe eight or ten years, over at BCC. I attended Bellevue Community College, but I don't remember her. I told her that."

"What did Wright say?"

"Well, it ran the gamut. First she called me a liar. Then she threatened to come upstairs here and tell my boss what a horrible person I am. Then she told me I had AIDS. That's when I got up to leave. She started grabbing at my shirt and yelling all kinds of crazy things."

"And that's when Security kicked her out?"

"That's when."

"You see her again?"

"She called. Same day. Maybe twenty-five minutes after they kicked her out. She sounded more reasonable, so I spoke to her again. It was one of my dumber decisions."

"And how did that conversation go?"

"She believed me, I guess, that I didn't remember sleeping with this *person*, but she wanted to find out other stuff."

"Like what?"

"My birth name. She already knew it, so I don't know why she asked."

"Ransom Marbles?"

"Actually, it was Sonny Marbles. I came up with Ransom around the time I hit my teens. Got tired of people calling me Sonny. I won't deny I used to work white chicks. Nothing dumber than a white liberal chick never been around a brother before. Almost any angle you worked paid off. Mostly I used the guilt rap. I probably used it on Deanna."

"Deanna?"

He looked at the floor and shook his head. "Well, maybe I do recall her. After I talked to the old lady, I started reminiscing."

"But you didn't want to tell me?" He didn't answer. "When Wright phoned, what else did she say?"

"You mean, after she threatened my job and telling my wife I had AIDS? After threatening to tell my kids? After all that?"

"Yeah."

"I don't know what else she was planning, because I did what you would have done."

"What's that?"

"I racked the phone on her."

"There was another topic she must have brought up. Maybe earlier, downstairs?"

"Why are you so sure there was anything else?"

"I'm beginning to learn how Wright thought."

"Yeah, I guess there's no harm in telling you. She wanted a list of every woman I ever slept with. She got a notebook out and wanted to start writing. I told her I wasn't giving her any list like that. My wife saw a list like that, I'd never see sweet potato pie the rest of my life."

"You see her again?"

"Not really."

"When was her visit?"

Abdul compressed his lips against themselves as if he were going to blow through a straw. "Little over a week ago. Listen, she invited me to some party, hinted around that I might be a father. You know, that I might have a kid I don't know about. This Deanna have my kid?"

"I couldn't say."

"It wasn't a boy, was it?"

"Couldn't say."

"Sure, well, listen, I got work, man."

"Before I go. You ever been to Sun Valley?"

"Sun Valley?"

"Pretended you were Eddie Murphy? Slept with another woman you probably don't remember?"

"Was that old witch tracking every girl I ever knew?"

"You were in Sun Valley five years ago pretending to be Eddie Murphy, weren't you?"

The coincidence would have been hard to swallow in a B movie, but I'd come across worse. I'd once tracked down a lost sister for a man who, years earlier, had lived not only in her building, but in her old apartment. As adolescents they'd taken clarinet lessons from the same teacher despite living seventy miles apart. Whether or not this particular coincidence meant anything was another question.

"Eddie Murphy? I haven't thought about that in years. Right before I converted, man. What could I do? You find a chick dumb enough to believe you're Eddie Murphy, you have to fuck her." He laughed to himself.

"Is that how it works?"

"It's how I used to think. Now? I don't even look at white women anymore." He gave me a brief glimmer of a smile, then wheeled his chair around to work. When I left, it was thundering outside.

CHAPTER 20

As I followed Marian Wright's trail, I half expected somewhere along the line to come upon a man or a woman who *was*
HIV positive and who *was* glibly passing the disease around the
countryside in the manner of the notorious airline attendant
chronicled by Randy Shilts in *And the Band Played On*. But so
far I had no evidence pointing to such an ignoramus. The the-
atrics in this situation had been Marian Wright's stridency, her
accusations, her willingness to chase down every contact Dee
ever had, as well as the contacts' contacts, her willingness to
hurl threats willy-nilly.

An hour and ten minutes after visiting Abdul Sarwar, I was
back in Deanna Ayers's bedroom in the hospice. Her children
and ex-husband were gone, and she was watching television
again. I rapped lightly on the partially open door. "I hope you
don't mind another visit?"

"Are you kidding?" she whispered. She seemed to have lost
strength in the hours I'd been gone. I told her I didn't believe
she'd gotten the virus from her ex-husband. She wrestled with
that for a moment and said, "No, I probably didn't."

"Marian must have told you the same thing."

"She may have. I get confused."

"Can we assume you did not get it from a transfusion?"

"I'd never had a transfusion."

"Or from IV drug use?"

"Definitely not."

"Can we also assume you inadvertently passed it along to Chuck Wright, as Marian Wright assumed you did, as opposed to getting it from him?"

"Chuck told me I was the only woman he ever cheated with, and I believed him."

"Because if we make those assumptions, then your contact was probably Ransom Marbles, who now goes by the name of Abdul Sarwar. Either that or your old boss."

"Randolph?"

"Right. Randolph Vanderhoef. Those two. Unless you've left somebody out."

"Nobody. There were five. You know him?" She seemed to have forgotten large chunks of our earlier conversation.

"Vanderhoef? I know where you worked. Vanderhoef's Sports. You told me."

"It was the creepiest thing. We were working late one night, and I generally rode the bus home, and it was going to be midnight by the time I got home so he gave me a ride, but on the way he said we had to stop at one of his rentals. It was vacant except for some old furniture. He offered me some wine, and I began to get a bad feeling about why we were there. I said no to the wine, and he started laughing at me, like I was some ninny who thought every man in the big city was out to ravish her. I got embarrassed and drank it.

"Next thing I knew it was morning and I was on the sofa with a blanket over me. I mean, it was literally the next thing I knew. It took me days to figure out the wine had been spiked. It had to have been. I had a headache for ten hours, and I only had one glass. *That* I remember."

"Did he have sex with you?"

"I don't know for sure. I know my clothes were rumpled and my bra was off, but I couldn't tell if I did it myself or if it was from sleeping on that old couch or what. I know I threw up in my sleep."

"Did you go to the police?"

She looked at me, barely breathing. "That's a man's question."

"Yes, I suppose it is."

"By the time I figured out what happened, a couple of days had passed. I knew at that point no blood test was going to turn up anything. I thought about telling Bill, but I was afraid Bill would kill Mr. Vanderhoef and end up in jail. Nothing else ever happened, so I just thought maybe everything would be okay. I wanted to pretend it never happened, and I did, basically, until Marian showed up."

"What did this Randolph character say when you woke up on the couch?"

"He was gone. I called a cab and phoned in sick the rest of the week. I told Bill I'd felt worn-out at work and had fallen asleep in a pile of ski pants. If I hadn't been so sick, he never would have believed me."

"What did Vanderhoef say when you finally confronted him?"

"Another man's question."

"You never confronted him?"

"Maybe I just got woozy on the wine. And he had a way of making you feel like you were stupid."

"Dee, if your husband is clean, and Abdul Sarwar is clean, which I haven't ascertained yet, you probably got infected that night by Vanderhoef. Although the john you slept with is still a possibility."

"Marian figured it the same way." Dee had been watching an afternoon movie on television. A scene solicited her attention for a few moments. When she turned back to me, she said, "What do you mean she identified with me? You said that earlier when you were here. Marian Wright identified with me. What did you mean?"

"Marian was HIV-infected."

Dee was quiet for a moment. "That explains a few things. You know, she never said a word."

"I didn't think she would."

I stopped off at the International House of Pancakes on Madison and scarfed down a lunch, picking up a section of the morning *Post-Intelligencer* to keep me occupied while I ate, except I couldn't concentrate on it.

CHAPTER 21

Vanderhoef's Sports was on Rainier Avenue a stone's throw from the new I-90 overpass. Many of the shops and businesses along Rainier Avenue were in obvious financial hot water or had already gone under: storefronts in want of paint, boarded-up buildings, dilapidated business signs with missing letters, rusty padlocks on canted doors. Because the first influx of Italian immigrants had settled here, the area had long been nicknamed Garlic Gulch and there were still quite a few Italian families in the surrounding neighborhoods, although the majority to the east were black, to the west, Asian.

The weather had cleared. Driving Rainier Avenue north to south, I aimed the Firebird directly at the base of Mount Rainier—in such a manner that it appeared I might drive to it in minutes. Rainier was still considered an active volcano, and since Mount St. Helens had blown its lid in 1980, numerous nitwits had been entertaining nightmares about Rainier erupting. I had them regularly.

Vanderhoef's Sports was in a formidable brick building, nearly a block long, half a block deep, and three stories high, windows grungy with road grime.

At the north corner of the building I discovered a narrow, unpainted stairwell, wooden steps deeply worn by years of foot traffic. The stairs led to a large production area with an open wooden floor made of unfinished planks. The high room stretched almost two hundred feet in one direction, forty in the other.

At a series of long tables, eight or ten Asians were sorting, folding, and packaging various athletic jackets and garments. Off in a corner, two men machine-stitched logos onto baseball caps. Bundles of clothing peeked from huge cardboard boxes. Portable racks sagged with garments on hangers. The place reeked of new clothing, dust, and old wood.

In a far corner stood a covey of glass-walled offices. In the first office I found a woman working a calculator as she clutched a can of Coca-Cola in her free hand. Despite the NO SMOKING sign in red lettering over her head, she had a burning cigarette dangling from her lips. With all the dust and flammable clothing and cardboard cartons, it was like watching someone smoke in an oil refinery.

"Can I help you?" she barked. She wore her hair in a pixie cut and had a small head, smooth, pale skin, and large brown doe eyes.

"I'm looking for Randolph Vanderhoef."

"Hallway to the right, two doors down. Oh, shit." She got up and walked me there, carrying the Coke and the cig.

In a suite of refurbished offices in the center of the building's east side I found Vanderhoef on the telephone.

It was a plush office, as were the other offices I'd passed, though the others were empty and dark. It had a sumptuous carpet, mahogany walls, an enormous glass-topped desk, fax machine, computer, and television. A large antique seal maker sat on a corner of his desk. One wall had a poster, a blown-up photograph of a well-muscled woman rock climber, behind her a thousand-foot drop. The other wall in his office had hand- and footholds built into it, presumably for climbing practice, a chin-up bar, ropes, a pair of packs, pitons, carabiners, and other climbing paraphernalia.

Vanderhoef hung up and smiled a smile that would have brought out the stars at noon. "You must be Russ! You *must* be Russ."

In his late forties, his hair was rust-colored, his brush of a mustache brown. He was built like a kid. His head was huge. His legs were not so short as to put him in line for the circus, but short enough. Yet, he was thick, his arms, legs, even his ears. He was my height, but then, I had legs. He had a potbelly and a little waggle of fat hanging on his jowls, but his handshake could have cracked river rocks.

He fixed me with sparkling blue eyes, one of which had been blackened recently. I noticed also that he crossed the room with a limp. "My name is Thomas Black," I said. "I'm a private investigator."

He stepped back a pace and grinned a snarly grin. "Oh, yeah? I thought you were somebody else. Don't worry about it. I got nothing against private peepers."

"I'd like to check a couple of matters with you if you don't mind."

He retreated to the edge of his glass-topped desk and leaned against it, folding his arms across his chest. He wore rumpled slacks, wing tips, and a dress shirt with an ink stain on the cuff. He was the right size to have been the thug in my yard the other night.

Glancing at the ropes and pitons in the corner, I said, "Do a lot of climbing?"

"My share. I do my share."

"Around here?"

"In the Cascades, some. Eastern Washington. You haven't lived until you've done Yosemite. I've been to Europe. South America. I teach too. Sleeping in a hammock twelve thousand feet in the air."

I laughed. "The only way I sleep twelve thousand feet in the air is on a jet."

"When I first got into it, there were only a few of us. And we knew all the other climbers. Nowadays, you drive up into the mountains to your favorite practice rock and you half expect a kid to come out and hand you a parking stub. You go hand over hand to the top of a four-hour pinnacle and there's gum wrappers stuck in the crevices. Life has turned obscene on us. But you didn't come to talk climbing."

"No. I'm told you had a woman named Deanna Ayers working here a couple of years back."

"Sure. I remember her. Yep."

"What can you tell me about her?"

"Seemed like a real nervous type. Neurotic as a squirrel in a rotating dryer."

"Is that why she left? Nerves?"

"Never said why she left. Just one day gave her notice and took off. I thought maybe she had trouble in the family. Her old man used to whack on her once in a while. She'd come in all knotted up. Fact, I still owe her wages. You know where she is, I'd like to see she gets them."

"Who hired her?"

"I did myself. Why? Who are you working for?"

"An attorney representing the estate of a woman who might have talked to you. The woman's name was Marian Wright."

"Old woman?"

"Yeah."

"Out."

"Look, I know she might have been irritating, but she was in a bad way and she—"

"It's time to leave. Now. Out."

"I'm not working for her. I'm working for her estate." I moved toward the door. "What about Littrell? Remember her? Used to work here?"

"Littrell?"

"Bain Littrell."

"She involved with the old lady too?"

"She ever work here?"

"In the office. Sure. About the same time as the little blonde. Littrell's trouble was, she was a dyke."

"Was she?"

"When you're around them a little, you can tell. Now get out."

"The old woman's dead."

"I don't give a shit if she's outside the door singing with a barbershop quartet. You got anything to do with her, I want you out."

In the corridor a man in a loose-fitting suit passed me, heading for Vanderhoef's office, having been escorted by the lady with the small head. She was standing outside the corridor door when I got there. She still had the Coke and the cigarette.

"Done so soon?" she asked, her head bobbing in an odd little jig, like the head on a jack-in-the-box.

"We didn't get on too well. You see an older Caucasian woman come in here and talk to him in the last two or three weeks?"

"You're not a cop?" We were walking together now.

"I was a cop. I'm working for an attorney just now."

"What? Vanderhoef do something wrong?"

"Not that I can tell. He owns all this?"

"Inherited it. Just after the war—the big war he used to say, WW Two—Vanderhoef's father started the company and got it going. But then he got into some sort of financial jam—women with babies is what I heard—and this guy named Albert Leffingwell stepped in with a bundle of cash and they became partners. Leffingwell and Vanderhoef. I think Leffingwell got his money back East running a bunch of service stations. They went from a balancing act to grossing over ten million a year.

"Leffingwell had only one kid. A daughter. Vanderhoef had only one kid, Randy. They got married. There are rumors about their marriage, but you hate to spread rumors. Well, I'll tell you anyway. It's supposed to be on the rocks."

"Say, listen. Did the old lady talk to you at all when she was here?"

She looked beyond my shoulder at the closed door I had come through. "It's almost two, and I haven't had lunch. You buy, I'll talk."

"Sounds like a deal."

CHAPTER 22

We took Kathy's Firebird a couple of blocks north on Rainier Avenue to Stan's Hamburger stand, where my guest ordered enough food for the Donner party. Congenial to the point of intimacy, she offered each menu item to me before attacking it. "Bite?" she said. "Want a bite?"

She wore jeans and a paisley long-sleeved blouse with a blue down vest over it; hiking boots with neon laces and little round clasps with smiley faces on them. For some reason her sleekness reminded me of a seal. It wasn't until I'd wolfed down a deluxe burger and slumped semicomatose against the driver's door that I remembered I'd had lunch at the IHOP.

Her name was Mary Ellen Richardson, a maidenly handle for such an earthy woman. "How did Vanderhoef get the black eye?"

She spoke through a mouthful of greasy food. "Fell off the climbing wall at the U."

"The limp too?"

"He's always had a limp. I don't know what that's from. He doesn't talk about it. So, this old woman was crazy, right? What was her name?"

"Wright."

"She told me, but I'm terrible with people's names."

"What makes you say she was crazy?"

"Everything. Randy threw her out, and then afterward she called me five or six times. I could tell. Cuckoo. Cuckoo."

"Maybe a little bit. What did she want from you?"

"Wanted to know who Randy was balling. I couldn't figure what her angle was. At first, I thought she might be Faith Vanderhoef's mother. But somebody told me Faith's mother was dead."

"Vanderhoef do a lot of fooling around?"

Mary Ellen pushed an onion ring into her mouth until the O deformed like a Hula Hoop with a boy sitting on it. She wore a ring on every finger of her left hand and one on the thumb of her right. "I guess you could say he does a lot of fooling around."

It occurred to me that Mary Ellen was playing me like a beetle on a string, that she might be planning to take our conversation back to Vanderhoef.

"What did you tell the old woman?"

"I gave her a few names. Why not? The funny thing was, she didn't only want to know who he had balled. She wanted addresses. Phone numbers. What was she doing, publishing a directory?"

"You mind giving me the list you gave her?"

"Listen, if I'm going to tell you everybody Randy ever screwed, I'll need more time than just lunch. If I even *knew* everybody. He's what they call—excuse my French—a cocksman." Tilting her head, she watched to see how the vulgarity affected me.

"I'm trying to find out what she was told. That's all."

Mary Ellen swiped at her face with one of the paper napkins in her lap, crumpled it, and let it roll onto the floor of Kathy's Firebird as if I were blind. "Right out front, I want to say, there's no way. He's not gay, and he doesn't use drugs. He doesn't have AIDS."

"Where does AIDS come into it?"

"Well, you know. She accused him of it."

"Of being HIV positive?"

"Yeah."

"Let's suppose," I said, "that she was tracing the transmission of the disease from a person who definitely had it but who'd had a limited number of contacts. Let's suppose she ruled out all other contacts except Vanderhoef."

"If that's what she did, she made a mistake. He fucks like a fruit fly. He had it, so would a bunch of other people."

"Like who?"

"Well, he would have passed it along to Jennifer and Janice."

"Who are they?"

"Jennifer works downstairs in shipping. She's a whiner, if you like whiners. Little bitty thing. She used to have my job, but she whined her way out of it. And Janice works in the Tukwila plant. She used to work downstairs at the job Jennifer has now. I know Randy had an affair with Jennifer because she told me about it while it was going on. That was maybe two years ago. And he told me himself he slept with Janice."

"Does he talk about his affairs like that?"

"Sometimes."

"Did you tell this to Wright?"

"I must have. She wanted to know who Janice and Jennifer slept with after Vanderhoef. Yup. I guess I did."

"Who *was* after?"

"You think I know all about my boss's sex life?"

I smiled. "You seem to."

"Not because I'm nosy, but I'm in kind of a unique position. I do the payroll and time sheets, so I get to hear the gossip. So let me tell you. Jennifer is now married to Craig, who worked here at one time. He's downtown working for the Port now. But before she married Craig, Jennifer had a hot and heavy romance with Bill, who used to be one of our drivers. And Bill must have slept with six or seven different live-in girlfriends over the past two years. He never uses a rubber. He told Jennifer it was like swimming in a raincoat. So if Vanderhoef had it and he gave it to Jennifer, who by now must have given it to Craig, her new husband, she also gave it to Bill, who must have given it to six or seven, and still counting, girlfriends. See why I don't believe this? All those people couldn't have it. Pretty soon half the city would have it."

"Maybe half the city does. What about this other woman? Janice?"

"Janice gets PMS every month like clockwork and expects everybody to feel sorry for her. She tried to keep it quiet between her and Randy because she was engaged to this uppity downtown lawyer. But then she married him, and they were divorced six months later. The lawyer's since got a new wife—I think she's maybe all of nineteen and already PG. So, they would have it. The baby too, probably. And now Janice is going with Ralph, who is one of our sales reps, but when they were first going together, Ralph was still seeing his ex-wife. So now, if you can believe all this, Ralph and his ex-wife and probably whoever she's with now have it. No. I don't believe it."

When I drove her back to Vanderhoef's Sports, I said, "Can I have your phone number?"

"I'm living with a guy right now, but call after ten on Saturdays."

"What I—"

"He goes golfing on Saturdays. Or you can get me here." She smiled, reached across, pulled me off balance by the shoulder of my coat, and bussed my cheek. I didn't bother to tell her the phone number was in case I had more questions. Nor did I bother to wipe the tiny smear of grease and lipstick off my cheek, at least not until she was out of sight.

I called home and retrieved the messages on my machine. The first was from Juanita, who wanted me to escort her to the party tomorrow night at Salty's in West Seattle. An odd request, I thought, given our history. Was this the party they'd been planning all along? The one they'd been arranging for weeks?

The second message was from the regional manager of a chain of department stores where I had been hired to delve into a systematic pilfering of the electronic goods. I had been running two hidden video cameras and working undercover for a couple of weeks when my father asked me to have dinner at McCormick's, but since that night I'd been calling in sick to the department store. It hadn't been fair to them, but they made it even by canning me.

I felt like stretching my legs, so, hoping to catch Bruno off guard, I walked to Second Avenue near Cherry Street to the shoe repair shop where he kept an office in the back. But he was not in. When I got back to Kathy's Firebird on Western, I dialed Bruno's cellular number. "Hey, buddy."

"Who's this?"

"Thomas Black."

"Oh, yeah? How you doin'?"

"Just great. Listen, thanks for bringing the car over to my place."

"Didn't have nuthin' else to do."

"How'd you get home?"

"A friend followed me in her BMW."

"You didn't see anybody hanging around my house, did you?"

"We got to your place about four. It was just getting dark. No. I didn't see nobody."

"Sure?"

"I didn't see nobody."

"How long did you hang around?"

"A minute or two." One of the reasons I'd wanted to see Bruno in person was to see if he had a broken nose or if somebody had smacked him with a brick recently. "I guess you want to know where the tapes are, yeah? I figured she's a dead lady, right? She's not going to be listening to no tapes. Chances are, whoever got the car woulda just thrown them away."

"You removed tapes from Marian Wright's car?"

"Man, I love New Age music. Besides, there were only ten of them."

"Bruno, how could you do that?" My voice rose in pitch.

"I didn't think anybody would notice." His voice rose too.

"What else did you take?" My voice rose higher.

"Nothing." His voice was a screech.

I took a deep breath. "And where were you Friday night two weeks ago?"

"Friday night two weeks ago?"

"You told me you were at a family birthday party. For your nephews. The family says you never showed."

"You telephoned my ex-sister-in-law?"

"Checking alibis, was all."

"Listen, Black. You know these lines are open. People can hear. You're going to the party tomorrow night, right? I'll talk to you there."

"You told me you stole tapes from a dead woman's car, but you won't tell me what you were doing two Fridays ago?"

"I forgot about the open line. Look, just for the record. I never took nothing. And this other thing. It involves certain people of the feminine persuasion. Enough said?"

"See you tomorrow night."

"Get some rest. From what Juanita tells me, it's going to be a humdinger."

I drove several miles back to Rainier Avenue, found a spot a block away from Vanderhoef's where I could watch the employees' parking lot, and sat, thinking mostly about the job but partly about getting fired.

At six Vanderhoef came out and climbed into a Mercedes. On Mercer Island he stopped at a convenience store and bought a magazine and a pint of cream. West Mercer Way snaked around the island, becoming East Mercer Way at the southern tip. It was the kind of road old people in Oldsmobiles drove on Sunday afternoons, enjoying the view of Lake Washington and the Seattle shoreline across the water, as well as the kind of road teenaged boys took their fathers' Porsches on late at night, driving too fast, wide-eyed girls in the seats next to them.

I couldn't stop thinking about Vanderhoef's black eye. So Vanderhoef had been limping all his life. So what? But why would he slam me around with a baseball bat? At the time it happened, he couldn't have known who I was. The one person with a possible justification was Bruno Collins, but the only reason that sprang to mind, besides pure cussedness, was that he didn't want anybody to learn how badly he'd botched the job those three women had hired him for. Either that or he'd been involved in Wright's death and was trying to discourage me from digging into it. Then there was Houser Fears and his black eyes.

Vanderhoef turned off West Mercer Way toward the water and headed down the hill into a maze of lanes and avenues. I waited a few minutes, then coasted down the hill and located his car in front of a huge, multistoried house directly over the route the hydroplane races took every August on Lake Washington.

I drove back up to West Mercer Way and parked straddling the property line of two residences, where each neighbor might easily think my vehicle was visiting elsewhere.

Forty-five minutes later I was listening to *All Things Considered* on the radio when the Mercedes emerged from the side street and headed north, Vanderhoef driving. A narrow-faced blonde sat in the passenger seat. She was in her thirties, maybe ten years younger than Vanderhoef. I followed them to dinner and a store and then home. It was an unproductive evening. I should have quit sooner but for some reason didn't.

After two lunches and no dinner, I was starving. At home my machine was full of messages. Alice, a woman who worked for one of the local insurance companies and who often looked up driving histories for me, had called and given me a rundown on Thornton Budden, the man who'd been driving the hay truck the night of the accident.

Two years ago in Arkansas he had been involved in a fatality involving a tractor trailer rig he was driving. After the accident, he got into a physical altercation with one of the bystanders and was jailed, though no charges were pressed. Five years ago his truck had been involved in a chain reaction collision in Southern California in the fog. Fourteen cars had been destroyed in the pileup, though nobody died, and blame was never assigned. Eight years ago his license had been revoked for a one-year period, again in California.

Discovering he'd been in an accident with a private investigator, Budden wouldn't have been enthralled at the prospect of having his record researched and maybe having his license pulled for good. A man with Budden's history might find out where I lived and try to put me out of the picture, even though the State Patrol was going to have the same information. I didn't think he was quite large enough to match the silhouette I'd seen in my backyard, but wearing a bulky coat and carrying a bat . . . adding a little bit of hysteria on my part, it could have been him.

There were five calls on the ad in the paper, but it was too late to answer them. One was from a man known to every lawyer in the Northwest: Albert Leedom, a crackpot who answered all the witness ads.

As I was falling asleep my answering machine picked up a call. A woman with a feathery voice asked if I would investigate a car wreck she claimed to have had five years ago involving the governor of the state, an accident she said had been covered up by the State Patrol with the help of the FBI. Everything about her said Nutcase, including the fact that she urged me to call her as soon as possible but forgot to leave either a name or a number.

CHAPTER 23

Tuesday evening, the evening of the party, a car dropped Kathy Birchfield off in my driveway. She quickly stepped across the wet lawn and climbed my front steps.

When I opened the door, a backdrop of purple and pink scalloped clouds tarnished the western sky behind her and made Kathy's dark hair and black coat stand out. The weather had cleared, and at night the roads now glistened with black ice. Thousands of Washingtonians had emerged from their winter depressions like dizzy kittens coming out from under a blanket.

"You just come to help your favorite guy get dressed?"

She stepped into the living room. "Actually, my date is picking me up here."

"Here?"

"I didn't particularly want him to know where I lived. He's the guy Juanita wants to tell off. She figures doing it over a P.A. system in front of a hundred and fifty people will make her feel better. I tried to talk her out of it. By the way, what did you pick out to wear?"

"Don't trust my judgment?"

"A man who thinks the most underrated rock 'n' roll singer of all time is Rick Nelson?"

"I never said that."

"You did."

"I said 'Travelin' Man' was arguably the best rock 'n' roll tune ever recorded."

"That's just as bad. Maybe worse."

"I was kidding."

"So what *was* the best rock 'n' roll tune of all time?"

"The best rock 'n' roll tune ever? You think I keep obscure facts like that in my head?"

"I know you do."

I waited long enough for an imaginary drum roll. " 'Johnny Angel.' "

She laughed so hard she had to sit down on the davenport, tears dribbling down her cheeks until she caught them with the knuckles of her thumbs and the backs of her hands.

When she had recovered enough to speak, she said, "Shelley Fabares couldn't sing. Even *she* knew it. Come on. You have to be at Salty's in forty-five minutes. Get in there, boy, and get dressed." She pushed me roughly toward the bedroom.

"By the way," she said, as somebody knocked at the front door, "anything going on with the investigation?"

I sighed. "A little. Tell you later."

"I'll get the door. After the party?"

"Sure."

"Here?"

"Or wherever. We can come back here in my truck."

"Good. I love your truck."

I went into the bedroom and dressed. When I came out, I met a man in my living room, a short, grinning blond with a round face and a paunch that looked tight as a drum. He wore a suit that was snug twenty pounds ago, and carried a corsage as if it were a bird on his finger. He kept jutting his chin out in an effort to make his neck comfortable in the small collar. The grin was what got me, like a pickpocket in a school for the blind.

Kathy cleared her throat and said, "Excuse me. Thomas, this is Burt Roberson. Burt, Thomas."

We shook hands. He had a repertoire of nervous mannerisms, including one where he repeatedly rode up on his tiptoes. He was taller than Kathy, but only marginally. Of Scandinavian stock, he had pale skin and paler eyes and lips that took on a shine when he pulled them into a smile. He bobbed his arms off to his sides like a self-conscious weight lifter, though I doubted he'd ever lifted weights. Using his front teeth, he gnawed a tiny wad of gum.

"He your brother?" Roberson asked, as if I weren't in the room.

"He feels like a brother sometimes, but no, we're just friends. Burt, would you mind getting the car ready? I'll be out in a minute."

"Noooooo problem, little lady." He scooted to the door, saluted me, winked at her, then came back and presented her with the corsage, and was gone.

Kathy came over to me, stood on tiptoe, and kissed me lightly on the lips. "You look just terrific."

"Same *to* ya, little lady."

A car horn honked outside, and I watched out the window as she skipped down the front stairs to where Roberson waited in a cream-colored Cadillac.

CHAPTER 24

Salty's was in West Seattle on a promontory of land directly across the bay from downtown. From the restaurant's banquet room downstairs, windows and decks looked out across the glassy bay toward the Lilliputian lights of Seattle's skyscrapers.

It was twenty after seven when I arrived. The banquet room was shoulder-to-shoulder with women in fancy dresses and men in suits or sport coats.

Like a large, black beach ball that had been held under water and released, Bruno Collins popped out of the mob near the front door wearing a dark suit and white sneakers and carrying a drink. There was no visible damage on his face, and I couldn't help noticing he was not moving as if somebody had plinked him with a brick a week back. But then, fat acted as a cushion, didn't it? I stepped close and tugged on his sleeve.

"Oh, there you are," he said, bunching his face up into a smile, cheeks like black walnuts. His eyes were bloodshot, and he'd missed more than one spot shaving.

"Hey, Bruno. How you doin'?"

"Pretty fair. Pretty fair."

"Bruno. You were going to tell me where you were two Fridays ago."

"Oh, yeah, sure." He looked around conspiratorially. "I have this friend, Carol. This is sacrosacred, right? You're not going to tell nobody?"

"Who is Carol?"

"My best friend's wife."

"And?"

"Friday night I was gettin' pussy."

"Bruno!"

"Don't look at me like that. Carol and I knew each other before she hooked up with Tony. Then she met Tony and I didn't see her for a while. Next time I saw them, they were together."

"And you never told Tony about your former association with his wife?"

"How do you tell a guy you fucked his wife? It's not something you can work into a casual conversation, you know. Like how about them Sonics? By the way, I jumped your bride a few times."

People I recognized from Kathy's office began to wander past. Beulah and a couple of her girlfriends. Then some lawyers I knew. A judge. Susie Scudder. A woman who was a local news anchor and her husband. And then, off in one corner talking animatedly to a waiter, Nigel. What the hell was he doing here?

"Bruno, how can you sleep with your best friend's wife?"

"Hey, I'm not proud of it," he said, proffering a grin that stretched his mustache like a piece of old rubber. "She came to me one day and said she was going to have an affair. I said, don't do that. And she said, why not? And I said, because Tony'll get mad. And she said, Tony's already mad. And I said, why's he mad? And she said, because he thinks I'm having an affair."

"So you figured you might as well go ahead, huh?"

He shrugged. "I am the commander. That's what they call me. No, they really call me that. The commander."

He gave me Carol's phone number. Having nothing else to do, I went upstairs and used a public phone.

It became apparent from the careful way Carol phrased her sentences that somebody else was at her end. I was able to get her to admit in yes-and-no answers that she'd been with Bruno two or three times during each of the last two weeks, though she could not swear to the Friday in question. It was incredible that she would confess an extramarital affair to a stranger on the telephone, but she did.

Downstairs at the party, I threaded through the masses until I spotted Burt Roberson and Kathy conversing with two other couples. I watched for a while as Roberson downed free booze and barked out dirty jokes.

Juanita Raykovich, in heels that made her almost tall enough to look me in the eye, worked her way through the crowd touching shoulders, introducing guests, and smiling. She approached Kathy's group and spoke to each member, including Roberson, whispering something in Roberson's ear that made him laugh and leer. I doubted he had any idea who she was. But then, in her low-cut dress and pearls, her hair done up, I hardly recognized her myself, and I didn't have the eighteen-year gap to bridge.

After schmoozing with Kathy's group, Juanita walked me across the room to a relatively quiet corner.

"Thanks for coming," she said, kissing my cheek. Roberson and Kathy were both watching. Then, speaking through clenched teeth: "Did you see him? Did you see the son of a bitch? I thought he was going to put his hand down Kathy's dress to see where his eyes had disappeared."

"He's a work of art, all right."

"He's an insect."

"How did you get him here?"

"Two weeks ago when he was in town, we arranged for Kathy to bump into him and invite him."

"Must've been fun for her."

"Yes. Well, don't worry about the rest of the evening. Bruno's handling it."

"I thought you were going to dress him down on the public address system."

"I thought of something better."

For over an hour Juanita cruised the party with me on her arm, touching everybody and laughing gaily. Around nine-thirty I located Susie Scudder talking to three men in front of the windows. One of them was Abdul Sarwar, the father of her

four-year-old. It was hard to tell from Sarwar's body language if
he realized who she was. She, however, gazed on him with a
strange mixture of curiosity and bereavement. It was a sad
business to watch, but I kept with it for a good many minutes
before Nigel approached me with a pair of martinis in his
hands. He wore his threadbare sport coat and a stained tie.
"Pick your poison."

"Thanks, but you know I don't drink."

"That's okay. I don't have anything against nondrinkers." He
gave me a look. "How are things going with Kathy?"

"Kathy?"

"Don't play dumb on me, Tommy. I got you two together,
but I can't do everything. What are your plans?"

"My plans?"

"Marry her."

"Pardon me?"

"The trouble with you is you don't see the garden for the
roses. She's over there with another gentleman, and here you
stand. Marry her. Can you do that for me? Promise me?"

"When I get married, Nigel, it won't be because I promised you."

"What does that mean? Earth to Thomas. Earth to Thomas.
You all there, boy?" He sipped from his drink, then downed the
second one and headed off for another.

"Nigel," I said. "I want to thank you for arranging that dinner with Kathy and then not showing up."

"I took the wrong bus."

"I figured you did. Thanks."

"No. I took the wrong bus."

People had different notions of what the party was about.
People from Juanita's company thought it was a work party.
The lawyers all thought it was a lawyers' party. The mayor was
there, and he seemed to think it was in his honor. One woman
who worked with Susie Scudder at the bank told me it was a
pig party.

"A what?"

"Pig party," she said, before she realized what she was saying and scampered away.

I cornered Susie Scudder a minute later as she came away from one of the banquet tables. "How are you doing?"

As she glanced around the crowd to see who might eavesdrop, her eyes began to water. Her hair was loose and hanging about her shoulders, giving her a softer, prettier look. "He's here. Marian found him for me."

"I saw you talking to him."

"You know Abdul?"

"Met him yesterday. What do you think?"

"He's different than I remember. I guess I was younger."

"We all were. He changed his name. Took up religion. Got married."

"I just want to see the look on his face when we serve the papers. Did you know Marian invited him here before she died?"

"I'm surprised he came."

"Bruno called him and twisted his arm at the last minute. It's so strange for these events she set up to be happening and for her to be dead. Any minute I expect to see her burst through the door."

"Susie. Did you ever know anybody named Deanna Ayers?"

"Not that I recall."

"She's the person who apparently gave the AIDS virus to Chuck Wright, and thus to Marian. Ayers gave Marian a list of everyone she'd had sex with in her life. Abdul was on the list."

"He's got AIDS?"

"I don't know."

"But he might?"

"He might."

"He could have given me a baby that was going to die of AIDS. He could have given me AIDS. Oh, God. We have to get tested. I feel sick."

After a while I was surprised to see Randolph Vanderhoef mixing in the crowd. I kept an eye on him for a few minutes and eventually saw him talking to Kathy. He appeared to have arrived alone.

A few minutes later I found Elmer Slezak at the bar. He was a friend, a small man who normally wore cowboy duds. He squinted at me until he recognized me and said, "You moon-lighting or out catting?"

"A little of both."

He proceeded to tell me a long, involved story about a neighborhood dispute he had gotten into the middle of. He had ended up trading blows with one of the principals. "He was a fag, Thomas."

"Gay, you mean."

"He could have AIDS, man."

"So?"

"So I hit him in the mouth."

"What'd you do that for?"

"I had his blood all over my knuckles. I could have infected myself. What is the world coming to when you can't smack a man in the kisser?"

"It's tough."

At half past ten o'clock a grand prize winner was announced. I didn't even know there had been a contest. I didn't hear the details because I was outside on the balcony watching the lights on the water. From out there I heard applause, laughter, and other announcements as more people were given prizes. After the awards, the party began to crumble the way weeknight parties crumble when most of the participants have to work the next day.

Not far inside the doorway I heard my father telling a group of people about an experience he'd had flying through the Khyber Pass into Pakistan. If genuine, the flight had taken place twenty-five or thirty years ago, because he hadn't piloted a plane, as far as I knew, since he'd been thrown out of the service for popping half the rivets off a P-51 Mustang wing diving it too steeply. When he told the Mustang story, he claimed he had broken the sound barrier before Chuck Yeager, the implication being Nigel had been cheated out of his birthright as a national hero. The inexpert opinions in the family ranged from: (1) he was lying and there had been no infamous dive, (2) the dive had actually been a botched suicide attempt—it had been done a month after the divorce, or (3) so what?

Nigel's point was that contemporary wisdom had dictated

that nobody could go faster than the speed of sound without his craft disintegrating. Had he received the credit he deserved for being the first to break the sound barrier, the implication was, Nigel would have led the happy and successful life he deserved.

Five minutes after the presentations, Roberson, wearing the paper crown he'd received for first prize, came outside to the balcony railing and stood beside me, confetti in his thinning hair. For a moment I pondered why the conquering hero would be out here alone with me, but then he hunched over the railing and barfed. Beneath us the bay water teased the pilings while his vomit slipped into the water.

"You okay?"

He looked up from the railing, smiled, and said, "I don't know whether to shit or go blind. Dear me. Dear me. These women do love me so. You been in that back room yet?"

"Never got invited."

"Maybe when you grow up, son. These women are something. Then there's the brunette. She came up to me out of the blue a couple weeks ago and invited me here. She's the one I can't figure. Acts like some sort of born-again virgin. What's the deal? I gotta be back in Spokane in two days."

"Maybe she doesn't know you're on a tight schedule."

"Naw, she must be a lesbo. Then to top it off, they gave me the grand prize. Know what it is?"

"I guess I didn't hear."

"A Swedish massage." He laughed loudly and large chunks of spittle jetted out of his mouth and shot through the darkness toward the water. "Hey, buddy. I'm going to have to go buy me a bottle of vitamin E just to get the strength to drive back home. What do you think about that? Well, I guess I better head on back in before them heifers scatter."

I looked at the yellow paper crown on his head. "What does that say?"

He took it off and, holding it up to the dim light, tried to focus on the small print on the rim. "Well, what do you know? Lookee here. 'King of the jism.' They love me. I'm telling you, they love me." He handed me the crown and bustled back into the dying party. I held it to the light. The microscopic print said, KING OF THE JERKS.

As I headed outside for my truck, I passed a room in the back of the restaurant and spotted Bruno Collins through the half-open door. Bruno was fiddling with some articles on a table. When I stepped inside and peered over his shoulder, I saw a small TV playing back a camcorder scene of Juanita Raykovich flirting with Burt Roberson.

Juanita was sitting on his lap, nibbling his neck, running her hands over his thighs. In the two minutes of videotape I viewed over Bruno's shoulder, she glanced three times at what was evidently a hidden camera.

"Nice piece of work," I said. Bruno almost knocked the television off the table, he turned around so quickly.

"Oh, you."

Behind him on the videotape, Juanita was saying, "I prefer married men. I prefer a man with experience. Somebody who's not afraid to try new things."

"Well, baby, you come to Papa. I'm married, but I'm still dating. And I'm crazy to try new things."

"What's the chance we can get together in the next few weeks."

"Baby, I wouldn't miss it for the world. Let me give you my number at *work*. Rule numero uno. Never call Papa at home."

"Sure. Here's my number too."

"I thought it'd be jammin'," Bruno said. "But it's better than that. What we got on this tape is the best work I've done. We can ruin this guy. Marriage. Job. The whole shootin' match."

"A good day's work, Bruno. Ruining a man's life. It'll look good on your résumé."

"Yeah, ain't it, though? The plan was to make him look like a pig. I guess we did that."

"Whose phone number did she give him?"

"The North Precinct cops."

CHAPTER 25

When I got into my truck, Kathy was waiting for me. "You're not even going to say hi?"

"I was thinking. Hi. You still have a key to my truck?"

"I still have a key to your everything."

It was nearly midnight when we got to my place. Kathy took her coat off and sat on the sofa in the living room. I took my shoes off, then walked over and sat beside her. She kicked off her shoes too. "You're going to be exhausted at work tomorrow, Sister."

"Taking tomorrow off. So how's the investigation moving along?"

"You really want to know?"

"I guess I do. Yes."

It took half an hour to tell her. She asked all the right questions in all the right places. "How could Susie have slept with a man Dee Ayers slept with, and then end up living in the same building with the ex-wife of a man who slept with Dee, and then become one of that woman's best friends?"

"Exactly what I've been wondering. I've been wracking my brain to figure out how a coincidence like that could be something other than a coincidence. But I can't come up with anything meaningful. They say we're only two people removed from knowing anybody in the world."

"I'd say we're only two people removed from *screwing* anybody in the world. And I heard it was six people."

"Whatever. By the way, what were you talking to Vanderhoef about?"

"He found out I was a lawyer, and we got to talking."

"You mean, he found out you were gorgeous, and you got to talking."

"It wasn't like that. He's got some business we're going to discuss later in the week."

"Juanita invited every villain and buffoon on the planet."

"That's right. You were there. The mayor was there."

"You should stay away from that guy. He pulled a Brock Adams on Dee."

"The mayor did?"

"Vanderhoef did."

"So you don't think I can take care of myself?"

"I know you can take care of yourself. I only want to give you information to do it with."

"I thank you."

"You are welcome."

She picked up my hand, which had been draped over the couch near her bare shoulder, and began rubbing it. "I love your hands."

"That's a line if I ever heard one."

"I *do* love your hands."

"You love my truck too."

"You know I do."

The light reflected off her violet eyes. She held the back of my hand against the soft skin above the top of her dress. "Has it ever occurred to you that not knowing where your father was all those years might have had something to do with you becoming a private investigator?"

"Yeah, it has crossed my mind."

"Just wondering. You know, it's weird. I've been so disoriented and grouchy and punch-drunk. I was helping the man upstairs pull down all the Christmas lights on the house, and I fell off his ladder. I just fell. I didn't hurt myself but it was so weird. I knew it was going to happen and then it was happening and then there I was lying on the ground with my hair in the dirt."

I commiserated with a long sigh. "Kathy, what did Roberson do to Juanita?"

"Can you keep a secret?"

"Is a frog's hankie watertight?"

"Back in college his fraternity gave a party where each member invites the homeliest girl he can find. Then they take a secret vote to see who brought the most unattractive date. Usually, they do something awful to her. Sometimes to all the dates."

"What did they do to Juanita?"

"Shit in her purse. Or is it shat in her purse?"

I took a deep breath and let it out. "No wonder she's still mad."

"She was a freshman. She didn't come out of her dorm room until she was a junior. It was one of the reasons she got such good grades."

"Do you know what she has planned for Roberson?"

"She was going to chew him out in public at the party, but she didn't do it. I don't know what happened. Susie was only going to deliver papers to Abdul, and that got done. But Juanita?"

I told her about the videotape and said, "She's going to need a bodyguard."

"Bruno, I guess. That must be what she's planned." In the backyard next door a couple of dogs yipped. In a distant part of the city a gunshot sounded. "I'm not happy about this," I said. "It's beginning to sound suspiciously like the beginning of a blackmail plot."

"I'm not so happy myself. But it's not blackmail. Believe me. She'll ruin him, but she won't take any money for it. I feel like I've been suckered."

"I don't much like being taken advantage of myself."

"You don't?" Kathy smiled in the near dark, wrapped her arm around my neck.

"No."

She whispered very close. "Then you're probably not going to like this."

She was wrong. I liked it just fine. She kissed me again, and after a while I began to get the idea and kissed her back. Somewhere in the middle we had the kind of awkward conversation people have these days, where they discuss whether or not they're going to die from what they're about to do, the sort of conversation where you spit out your medical history and love history and list your infections and medications, if any. Neither of us had much to confess, and when we were finished, she pushed my head away from her face so she could focus and said, "It's been three years since you've been with a woman? Three years? What about all those babes you've been seeing?"

"I never saw a babe. Not one."

"Okay. Women."

"I was holding out for the top gun."

"Well, you got her now, pal." After a while I swept her up in my arms and carried her to the bedroom. The house was warm and we were both already hot and we made love on top of a blue suit on my bed that I had decided not to wear. When I woke up there was enough light streaming in from the hallway to illuminate one side of each of us. Kathy was naked and sitting beside me on her knees. "Where did you get these bruises?"

"Some clown jumped me in the backyard the other night."

"Why didn't you tell me?"

"He might have been anybody. Somebody I gave the bird to at a four-way stop."

"How many people have you given the bird to at four-way stops?"

"I lose count."

"It looks like he dropped an engine block on you."

"Since when did you become such an expert?"

"Actually, I was looking to see if I'd left handprints on your back."

"Did you?"

"Not that I can find. I'll have to do better next time."

"And when did you figure next time would be?"

"Pretty soon."

It turned out to be sooner than that. Afterward, she said, "Remember that time you dumped your bike? Not a single bruise."

"I thought you were going to say something about what we just did."

"What? You need reassurance?"

"Me? I'm a mature male. Of course I don't need reassurance."

"It was incredibly wonderful."

"Really?"

"Yes." She laughed. "But you know. I really never have seen you with bruises."

"You've never seen me naked either."

"Of course I have. Until tonight, it was the big thrill of my life. Oooo, baby. So what did he want?"

"Who?"

"The guy in your backyard."

"I don't have any idea. Oooo, baby? It was dark. The police haven't found anybody."

"Randolph Vanderhoef had a black eye tonight."

"I was thinking more along the lines of Bruno Collins."

"Bruno?"

"His car and profile match the car and profile I saw driving away the night of the accident. The guy in my backyard was about his size. Bruno lied to me about where he was that night, and he's been acting funny."

"Acting funny is what Bruno does best. But he's got a good heart."

"I sensed that. About his heart. It doesn't mean he's not involved."

She was quiet for a few moments, running her warm hands

over my body. Thirty minutes later, just before I lost consciousness, Kathy whispered, "That marriage proposal still open?"

"You want me to make an honest woman of you? Is that it?"

"I think I do."

"You name the day and the time."

"How about Friday?"

"Friday is good."

"How about two o'clock?"

"I'll have to check the *TV Guide*."

"You do that."

"I will." I fell asleep two seconds later.

CHAPTER 26

Wednesday morning Kathy got up, fussed around, and before she went out the door said, "I've been thinking. Blaming you for Philip's death when it was an accident, taking it out on you, was my own way of distancing you. I went bananas. And I'm somebody who almost never goes bananas." There was a long silence. "Or didn't you notice?"

"I noticed."

"I know Philip's death wasn't your fault, Thomas. And in all my confusion and grief, I'm sorry I ended up blaming you."

"Thank you for saying that, Kathy. You were scared. Too many things were happening."

After a moment she said, "Don't take this wrong, but did you feel last night was a little bit anticlimactic? Our making love? After being friends for so long."

The mattress retained heat where her body had lain. Lost in the remembrances of last night and sequestered under the covers, my face hidden, I edged toward the warmth like a wounded dog edging toward the side of the road. I was so warm and comfortable and lazy, I thought I'd never get up. "Did you think it was anticlimactic, Kathy?"

"Did I? God, no. Are you kidding? I'll be walking into walls for a week. I was just afraid you did."

"It was great."

"Are you ever coming out from under those covers?"

"Probably not."

"Going to stay under there all day, then?"

"Maybe."

She took the Firebird home. It was the first time she had driven it in over a week.

At eleven o'clock I was still grinning when I drove my truck to a spot a block from Vanderhoef's Sports. I parked on a hill where I could see most of their employee parking lot and used the time to phone the four legitimate respondents to my ad for witnesses.

Pay dirt came in the form of Martha Chin, a woman who stressed the odd word in every sentence and spoke in a voice so weak it sounded like a little girl talking into a tin can with a string. "I was there," she said. "I was there that *night*. I saw something *in* the woods. It looked like a Bigfoot. I was very scared. There were *cars* behind me. I couldn't turn around."

"You were stopped for the accident?"

"I was behaving myself in my car waiting for the truck to be cleared. The hay truck. I heard on the radio a woman was killed. I heard it on the radio. And then I knew, just around the bend, there was a poor dead woman. That was when I saw the man in the woods."

"Could you start from the beginning and tell me everything."

"I was trying to be careful. There was a car on my bumper. The whole trip the car rode my bumper. I was only out because I had been in Monroe taking care of my daughter's baby. They had that flu, Muriel and little Mercedes. When I got to the curve, there was a truck on its side. I didn't know if anybody was hurt or anything. I didn't know if I was supposed to get out and help. The people in front of me never got out, so I didn't too."

"So you didn't actually see the accident happen?"

"Oh, no. I don't think anybody did."

"What did you see?"

"My car fogged up, so I reached across and unrolled the

passenger window a few inches. Just to let some air blow through. I heard something on the hill next to the road. Maybe it was a twig breaking. I don't know. I looked out and there was this . . . very large man. He was standing next to my car, only farther up on the hill. He was standing in the rain watching the accident. At first, I thought he might be somebody from one of the cars behind."

"Go on."

"He went up the hill into the woods. I think he was wearing one of those Air Force parkas. You know. With the hood up and the fur around the face."

"Did he come back?"

"I never saw him again. But there's nothing up there. Where he went. My cousin and I have hiked the area below the falls. There's nothing there."

"Do you have any idea what time this happened?"

"Not long after I got to the accident. Not long."

"Can you describe him?"

"I don't think so. It was quite dark."

It took several phone calls to the insurance company in Tacoma where Abdul Sarwar worked before I lucked into a supervisor who was willing to look up his attendance record and tell me about it. She said he'd been out sick Wednesday, Thursday, and Friday of the week Marian Wright had been killed. "I doubt he was sick," she said. "He's a chronic malingerer." Maybe he was, but he didn't strike me that way when I had visited.

It was possible Deanna had contracted the AIDS virus from Abdul. If such were the case, sooner or later Marian Wright would have found out and begun making life miserable for Abdul: harassment, lawsuits, criminal charges. And Abdul knew it. He might not approve of his life getting derailed by a seventy-one-year-old sideshow.

A friend in one of the credit reporting companies told me Randolph Vanderhoef paid off his credit cards, all eight of them, monthly. He owed only twenty-two thousand on his house. She couldn't tell me what his equity was, but I figured it was two or three hundred grand. He owned six rental units and, in fact, used this same company to check the credit of prospective renters.

I was sitting outside Vanderhoef's building on what was almost a whim. Vanderhoef had been evasive, which could have meant nothing more than that he disliked me, or disliked private investigators, or had disliked Marian Wright. A lot of people had disliked her.

The trouble was, if I had hurt an elderly woman and a week later been approached by a private investigator, I would have feigned oily compliance. Even if I had killed her, I would have feigned oily compliance, yet that was the last thing I was getting from Vanderhoef. And he was not a stupid man.

Long arms swinging, Vanderhoef came out of the building and folded himself into the Mercedes. It was twelve noon. Thirty seconds later a woman with short hair, a broomstick skirt, and brown velvet boots came out and got into a small Chevrolet with rust spots low on the doors. The Chevy followed the Mercedes out of the lot closely.

They ended up under the shadow of the Space Needle at a TraveLodge motel. He went in and got a room while she sat in her car and looked around nervously. Four minutes later she followed.

She was a small woman with narrow hips and narrow shoulders and a slit of a mouth and enough bead strings around her neck to keep a toddler happy for a week. Her black blazer had lint on one shoulder. I thought she was going to break a heel, the way she was walking, like a panicky kid his first time on stilts. Sometime later when they came out together, I noticed the lint was gone from her blazer.

I tailed Vanderhoef back to his building on Rainier Avenue South. By the time I got there, I had used the cellular phone and had the woman's name from her license plate. Irene Golinda. When I thought she'd had time to get back to her desk, I phoned Vanderhoef's Sports.

"Irene Golinda, please."

"Maggie? Just a minute."

It took a few seconds. "This is Maggie. How may I help you?"

"Maggie, I'm a private detective. A few minutes ago I followed you from a downtown TraveLodge. I'd like to talk to you about it."

"Oh, God." Her voice dropped into a whisper. "I knew this was going to happen. Oh, shit. Shit. Shit. Shit! Who hired you? Who are you going to . . . ? Oh, shit!"

"Listen. All I want is a little chat, okay?"

"Oh, shit!"

"Meet me at the Kau Kau in Chinatown in ten minutes? Maggie?"

"I'm at work."

"The Kau Kau. I'll have a red carnation in my lapel."

"God. You've got to be kidding."

"Only about the carnation."

"Where's the Kau Kau?"

"Chinatown. On King Street. On the north side. You can't miss it."

"I'll think about it."

Eighteen minutes later she parked in front of the restaurant, fed the meter, and wandered into the Kau Kau with the feigned nonchalance of a lost tourist. I was standing in the entrance next to the tank containing the hundred-year-old fish. She smiled when I called her by name, and like two old friends we walked to a table in the back. After she sat down, she pulled a cigarette out of her purse and played with it. Her hair was combed into a Liberace swirl that had grown out and loosened up. She wore an overabundance of makeup, probably to cover skin problems from earlier in life. Her ears stuck out as if she were a giant mouse.

"I didn't mean to embarrass you," I said.

"No? What did you mean to do?"

"I only want to know about Vanderhoef."

"Randy? You're after Randy?"

"You tell me about him, I let you alone."

"And suppose I don't tell you about him?"

I shrugged.

She bounced the cigarette on its end on the table like a kid with a pencil. My food came; white rice with chicken and bok choy. She watched me eat. "If you were really following me, you would know I didn't have lunch."

"Room 110. You drove over a curb and ran a yellow light getting there. Besides, you have the look of someone who rarely eats lunch."

"I wasn't fooling anyone, was I? There were probably tour buses following us. Oh, God. I knew something bad was going to happen. I knew it."

I should have reassured her, but it was as ugly as a buzzard on a battlefield and we both knew it. I called the waiter over, and Irene Golinda ordered. Trying to make small talk after he'd left, I told her the waiter had been a colonel in the South Vietnamese army. She said nothing.

"You married, are you?" I asked.

"Sort of. Neil and I are having problems. Why?"

"Nothing. Tell me about Vanderhoef."

"What do you want to know?"

I told her.

"The old woman? He felt sorry for her. She came to his office and made a scene. He mentioned her just that one day when it happened. A couple weeks ago. Otherwise I don't know a thing about it."

"She never contacted you?"

"Me? Why would she contact me?"

"Same reason I did."

"You're the detective from yesterday, aren't you? Randy said you were stupid and had no sense of humor."

"No sense of humor?"

"He said guys like you were so busy worrying about when to take their next dump they never had time to live. He said you had a smart mouth and a worse attitude. And you were sneaky."

"No sense of humor? Couldn't wait to share that with me, could you?"

"I'm only quoting. Give me your phone number. He comes up with anything else, I'll call you." She gave me a long, appraising look. I had ruined her afternoon, if not her month. "His wife hire you?"

"Nobody you know."

"From what I hear, Faith Vanderhoef is a real bitch."

When her food came, she took three or four dainty bites of each dish, sat up, pushed her plate away, and sipped hot tea.

"Listen, whether you believe me or not, Randy and his wife don't get along. I don't know why they stay together. Well, I guess I do. When her old man croaks, they'll inherit the business. She's planning a divorce after that. And believe me, she'll take him to the cleaners."

"Is that what Randy told you, or is that what you've surmised?"

"Randy? He thinks she's afraid of a divorce. But Randy's wrong. See, the old guy's got cancer, and his daughter's turned the whole house into a hospital room. It's disrupted all of their lives. Randy hates the old man because he had to work for him when he was a kid and he never forgot how the old man treated him."

"Why would Vanderhoef's wife be afraid of a divorce?"

"First and foremost, she's a good Catholic. She caught him fooling around once before and threatened to divorce him then, but it never happened. He thinks if she was gonna do it, she would have done it then."

"Are you going to marry Vanderhoef? Is that the scheme?"

"Don't be dense. Randy would never marry me. Except for where his daughter's concerned, he's a totally selfish individual. If he marries again, it will be some sweet young delicacy with a stomach tight enough to knock golf balls off of."

"I hope you used protection."

"God. Who do you think you are?"

"Marian Wright was interested in him because she thought he was HIV-infected and gave it to someone who gave it to someone who gave it to her. If you're sleeping with Vanderhoef and Vanderhoef has AIDS, your husband needs to know."

"HIV? AIDS? My God. Randy's a heterosexual white male. He doesn't have it."

"Let's hope you're right."

"He doesn't. And you can go to hell."

I laid out some of the details of how Marian Wright backtracked the HIV transmission lines to Chuck and then to Deanna and then to Vanderhoef. Irene Golinda remained quiet, her brow furrowed, thin lips pursed. She was right in presuming there were a lot of leaps in logic.

I paid for the meal at the cash register in front, but by the time I got outside, Golinda had driven away. Just as well. She was plenty sick of me, and this case had me frustrated. It was possible Wright had parked at a bad spot on 202 and gotten disoriented without any help. It was possible a stranger had assaulted me in my backyard. It was possible Abdul Sarwar wasn't hiding anything and had never seen Marian Wright again. In fact, it was possible that nothing I'd done in the last week made any sense, including ruining Irene Golinda's afternoon.

Running personal errands took up most of the afternoon. When I got home there was some daylight left, so I pumped the tires hard on my Eddy Merckx, bundled into windproof tights, put on shoe covers, a warm cycling jacket and gloves, and pedaled down through the University of Washington campus. I crossed the Montlake Bridge, went past the Museum of History and Industry, and rode through the Arboretum. Eleven miles later I turned around at Seward Park on Lake Washington. Oddly enough, I was only a half mile from where Houser Fears lived. Oddly, too, on my return ride a large American car, possibly a 1970s vintage Ford, ran me off the road.

It happened next to the lake, so I was able to steer into the grass, across the walking path, and crash on the hillside leading down to the water. I didn't get a good look at either the car or the plates, even though I had my lights on and so did he.

When I got home and inspected my bike in the kitchen, I was still shaky. The car's fender had brushed my hip. Another inch or two and he might have killed me.

Fifteen minutes later as I was stepping out of the bathroom in a robe, I heard a key working the lock on my back door. "I'm home, Ward."

"In here, June."

Kathy came around the corner with an armful of groceries, saw me and said, "A half-naked man. My second favorite kind."

"What's this?"

"Basil and some other basic items you are in dire need of."
I kissed her over the groceries. Her face was cold from being
outside, mine hot and damp from the shower. "So, Thomas,"
she said, draping her coat on a chair. "What's going to happen
with us?"

"Anything you want."

"We get married on Friday?"

"I thought you always wanted a big wedding. The whole
nine yards."

"I did, but—"

"What you want is what we do. This is only going to happen once, so we might as well do it right."

"That's right. It's only going to happen once, so why should
I spoil it for you?"

"I've worn a tux before."

"And you still gripe about it."

"Let's think about it." While I stood in the doorway and
watched, she stashed groceries in the various cupboards and
in the refrigerator, then folded the paper sack. She looked up
at me.

"What?" she said.

"I'm thinking." She grinned, strode across the room, tackled
me around the waist and pushed me backward across the hall
and into the bedroom, across the rug and onto the bed. "Kathy.
There's just one thing I need to know."

"What would that be?"

"Do you want to marry me for my mind?"

"What do you mean by that?"

"Well, I'd hate to think you're marrying me just for
my body."

She gave me a long look and said, "First things first."

She wrestled me out of the robe and then I wrestled her out
of everything and then a while later we lay on our backs breathing hard. She had a sheen of perspiration on her forehead, a
couple of strands of dark hair stuck to it. After a minute or two
of quiet contemplation, she said, "You did see *Arsenic and Old
Lace* twenty times."

"Cary Grant said 'first things first.'"

"And Priscilla Lane said—"

I kissed her. "Right. She did." I told her about Irene Golinda. I told her about the car on Lake Washington Boulevard.

She mulled this over, then said, "Burt Roberson called the office this afternoon. Apparently Juanita sent a copy of that videotape they made at the party over to his hotel. He was *really* pissed. He threatened Juanita. Bruno. Me. He even threatened you."

"How did I get involved?"

"He picked me up here. Remember? Somehow he found out you were a private investigator. He told me he'd had too much to drink last night and we'd taken advantage of him. He said he doesn't ordinarily act that way. He told me he's never cheated on his wife. He wants the original tape. Juanita was in the office today and I tried to talk her out of it. I don't see the point, myself, of ruining a family."

"Did you know this was going to happen?"

"No."

"But you just happened to think of this Roberson business when I told you somebody tried to kill me?"

"He threatened you. Today. What kind of car was it?"

"It wasn't his Cadillac."

"He could have borrowed a car."

"I know he didn't follow me. Only a local cyclist would know our route down to the lake and back. Chances are it was just some idiot."

"Good point. So. What do you want for dinner?"

"You cooking?"

"Sure."

"How about my normal?"

"What's that?"

"Froot Loops."

"You're so easy."

"We already knew that."

"And Friday?"

"Getting married? Friday might be tough. There's a rerun of *Hawaii Five-O*."

She kissed my bare shoulder and said, "Whatever you want."

"You're no fun."

"Yes I am. We're both fun, and I know it's going to be like this for the rest of our lives."

"Nah. Eventually we'll get over these rough periods and make love like weasels. Then about sixty years down the line, we'll get the rockers."

"Get me a small one so my feet will touch the ground."

"I like it better when they don't."

"I love you."

"Not as much as I love you."

"You're quite pleased with yourself, aren't you?"

"Yep."

CHAPTER 27

A major curse to Northwest skiers, the El Niño ran, more often than not, off the coast in the Pacific Ocean and heated the region, forcing winter rains in the mountains instead of snow. It had lingered off the coast for years, and by Thursday morning it had kicked in with a vengeance. It was now apparent the recent weeks of cold air and snow flurries had been an anomaly and our winter would revert to balmy temperatures, sweaty kids wearing winter coats because their mothers made them, mixed sunshine and rain, golfers in shirtsleeves, camelias blooming early and turning brown at the next freeze.

Shortly after six Thursday morning I drove past Vanderhoef's house on Mercer Island, ascertained he hadn't yet left for work, and parked up the hill just off the road. Like a kid with a new toy, I had been up late again with Kathy and I was beat.

It was a quarter after eight before he passed me in a brand-new four-door Honda, but instead of turning west toward Seattle, the Honda swung onto the ramp for I-90 eastbound.

Several miles down I-90 he took the twisty, two-lane Lake Sammamish Parkway north. Looking between the ritzy houses on my right, I could see Lake Sammamish from time to time, elegant and sublime in the dawn.

Marymoor Park incorporated baseball fields, marshy lands,

and grassy acreage where people flew kites and sent up motorized model planes. It also was haven for an outdoor cycling velodrome where I sometimes attended the Friday night races.

Vanderhoef turned into the park and drove to a public phone in front of the tennis courts in the north parking lot while I coasted to the other side of the lot and shut off my motor. The lot had six cars in it, spaces for a hundred more. At the north end lay a playground and, beside it, a small concrete-block building containing rest rooms. In front of Vanderhoef's Honda were several fenced tennis courts. Beyond the courts lay baseball fields, the only occupants a squadron of strutting gulls.

A macadam path snaked in front of the tennis courts and stretched out past the baseball diamonds, crossed the slough over a small bridge, and traveled north along the Sammamish River. The Burke Gilman Trail looped from here all the way around the north end of Lake Washington and into Seattle, where it terminated at Gas Works Park.

After a while an older Continental prowled through the lot as if the driver were looking for a place to dump off a litter of kittens. Once he'd cruised all the lanes, he backed into the spot beside my truck. An odd choice, I thought, given the plethora of alternatives. The driver, in his late sixties, killed his engine and looked at me as if he were an eagle and I a mouse in the desert. I dug into my glove box and pressed my plastic Vice Squad badge to the glass. The old man in the Continental ground the starter twice, then drove out of the lot almost as carefully as he had driven in.

Thirty yards away a BMW parked, and a man got out and walked to the public rest rooms. Vanderhoef followed. I hiked the width of the lot to the pay phone next to Vanderhoef's car, buffed the chrome on the phone with my sleeve, and watched the concrete block building behind me in the warped reflection. Twenty-two minutes later the young man came out of the rest room, strode purposefully to his BMW and left.

When Vanderhoef exited, I stepped into the empty lot and cut him off. He wore a business suit and tie. "What the hell?" he said, recognizing me after a moment of squinting.

"The police know about this place?"

"Go to hell."

He tried to move around me, but I blocked his path. "Did Marian Wright follow you here?"

"I only saw the bitch once."

"Did she threaten to talk to your wife? Was that it?"

"Listen, jerkoff. Four years ago my wife lost her mother, and now her father is dying. She doesn't need some creep coming around trying to make her life any worse."

"Did Wright talk to your wife or not?"

Clenching and unclenching his fists at his sides, Vanderhoef glowered and his face turned red. He looked like a boy who was trying to fart and couldn't quite squeeze it out. It was almost thirty seconds before he found his voice. "You . . . talk to my wife and I'll kill you."

"Maybe another private investigator showed up?" Vanderhoef stopped moving and looked at me. "This guy would be heavyset. About my height. A black man."

"Fuck you."

"I'll make a deal with you. You tell me what went on between you and Wright, and you won't see me again."

He thought about that. "She came to my office. She accused me of some things. I tossed her out."

"Let me guess. She accused you of passing around the AIDS virus? Of raping Deanna Ayers a few years ago."

"Who?"

"You drugged her drink and had sex with her while she was unconscious. Be pretty hard to forget a thing like that, wouldn't it?"

"Where'd you hear that bullshit?"

"Where do you think? From Deanna Ayers."

"She's lying."

"*Somebody* gave her AIDS."

"Somebody shot Kennedy. It wasn't me. I haven't seen her in years. What are you talking about? AIDS? I never raped anybody in my life. She had some wine. Couldn't handle it. That wasn't my fault. Besides, she was no good."

"What do you mean?"

"What do you think I mean? She was lousy in the sack."

For just an instant he had a glimmer in his eyes, as if we were brothers under the skin talking about conquests and exchanging phone numbers and counting secret marks on our calendars.

"You really take the cake, Randy. You rape some poor young woman and then complain she was lousy in bed. How many people have you had unprotected sex with in the last few years?"

Vanderhoef pushed his tongue around under his lower lip. He pulled at one wing of his mustache. It was possible I had accused him falsely on several, if not all fronts, but I had at least part of it right. I could tell by his eyes. "Get out of my sight."

"You do have the virus, don't you? Or has it grown into AIDS?"

"Get the fuck out of my face. I hear you saying any of this publicly, I'll sue you for slander. I see you around my home, I see you around my wife, I'll kill you."

"You are a piece of work, Randy. You meet strange men in public rest rooms. You do your employees in the local Trave-Lodge. You drug and rape the ones who turn you down."

"TravelLodge? What the hell. You been following me?"

"How do you think I got here?"

"All this because two weeks ago some old woman came into my office for three minutes? You're not only an asshole, you don't have a clue. . . . What kind of detective are you?" He got into the car, slammed the door, and fired up the engine. I stepped up onto the sidewalk and watched him drive away.

Half an hour later in Seattle, I cornered Kathy in her office and kissed her face like a dog lapping a child's cheeks. She suffered it with a big grin. It was amazing how disturbed you could get around someone who hated you as much as Vanderhoef hated me; equally amazing to be a short time later submerged in the presence of love and to bask in the difference.

"Hey, Sister, I need to talk to you. I'm wondering if I've lost perspective."

"Come on, Thomas. People are smacking you with baseball bats. None of this is worth it."

"If Marian wasn't murdered, it's not. If she was, I'll do

just about anything to nail the perp. You forget. I was in that car too."

"You think it was murder now? Right in front of our eyes?"

"Somebody was there on the highway with her. At one point they had her tied up. That's how she got the abrasions on her wrists the medical examiner found. She was either running from them when she ended up in the road, or she was pushed. And if you hadn't been the one to hit her, it would have been the next car and it would have been the perfect murder. You think it was bad luck, but maybe in a way it was something else."

Kathy was staring out the window in a daze. "Quit it, Thomas. Quit the case."

"I wish I could."

I spent the rest of the morning checking records. I went to the U.S. Bankruptcy, the Superior Court records on the sixth floor of the King County Superior Court. I ran Vanderhoef and the others for criminal actions, misdemeanor charges, and divorces. Randolph Vanderhoef had two drunken driving arrests in the past five years. He'd been to Municipal Court for urinating in public, but the charges had been dismissed.

I phoned another investigator in Tacoma and had him check Abdul Sarwar in the Pierce County records. He called me back after lunch. Under the name of Ransom Marbles, Sarwar had obtained a divorce several years ago. He had been arrested on drug charges and traffic violations, including driving without a valid license. He'd been married to his present wife four years and had been clean since this marriage.

It was an interesting morning. Houser Fears, Bain Littrell's bodyguard, had served two sentences in the state, one for manslaughter and a shorter term for vehicular assault. Vehicular assault? The same charge they'd have brought against the driver who'd tried to run me off the road yesterday afternoon.

Roberson was clean as far as I could tell.

Bain Littrell had been arrested twice in King County for prostitution while working for an escort service. I found a record of her marriage to a man named Keith Littrell, who turned out to be vacationing in the state penitentiary in Walla Walla for manslaughter. Houser Fears had been released from Walla

Walla two and a half years ago. They had to have known each
other.

For the hell of it, I searched the criminal records on my
three principals—Juanita Raykovich, Susie Scudder, and Marian Wright—and was surprised to learn that two years out of
college, Raykovich had been arrested for slashing a woman
across the arm with a potato peeler. I had a feeling there was an
interesting story behind it and wondered if I would ever hear it.

That afternoon when Bruno Collins showed up, I was in the
back room in Kathy's law office. Deferential and meek, Bruno
knocked, stepped inside the door, and, with his hands clasped
in front of himself, said, "I hear they're out to kill you."

"What?"

"I hear they're out to kill you."

"Where did you hear that?"

Bruno grinned. He wore his standard double-breasted suit,
his shoes freshly polished. "I got contacts. People. You know."

"Who?"

"I can't say. You know, I been thinking about this. I'm working for Juanita. You're working for Juanita. Why don't we do
this together? Tell me who else you talked to."

"Tell me who said they were out to kill me."

"I might be able to help if you gave me a list of who you
spoke to." He sounded grave, sincere, snoopy, and a little whiny.

"I don't want help."

"Okay. But I'm experienced with death threats."

"Making or receiving?"

Bruno laughed as he closed the door, then reopened it far
enough to poke his head back in. "Sure you don't want help?
You watch my back, I watch yours?"

"Who's after *you*?"

"That Roberson fella 'cause of the video we made. He's hot."

"Thanks, but no. And watch yourself."

"Sure."

After Bruno left, I glanced through my notes. Collins had arrests for carrying a concealed weapon. For suspicion of assault.
For selling stolen telephone equipment. For selling stolen air-

line tickets. For shooting a neighbor's dog off his front porch. And for digging a pit in the yard of an ex-girlfriend.

I drove out to the Salish Lodge at Snoqualmie Falls, and after explaining the situation, was granted access to their dinner reservation book. I could find no record of a reservation under Wright's name, or any name connected with my search. When I went back through the list, I found a Raycoewitz. I asked the attendant if this might not be Raykovich and she said she didn't know either way, since she hadn't been working that night and probably wouldn't have remembered if she had. But why would Marian drive thirty miles in the rain to a one-horse town like Snoqualmie to meet Juanita who lived next door? It made no sense.

I spent forty minutes in Snoqualmie trying to track down a restaurant Wright might have used in the event Wright and whoever she was meeting had been turned away from the Salish. It had been a busy night, and it occurred to me that Wright and companion might have been traveling to or from an alternate restaurant when she stopped on Highway 202.

I drove down the hill to Fall City and checked Martinell's, the Riverside Tavern, Small Fries, the Fall City Grill, the Colonial Inn. I flashed a picture of Wright to everybody I saw, but nobody remembered her, which didn't surprise me in the least. She was a nondescript old woman with no visible tattoos, easy to overlook, and easier to forget.

Driving back toward Seattle on I-90, I took the Mercer Island exit and went to the Vanderhoef home.

I parked in front of their house, marched up a slanting walkway, then up six concrete steps, hoping Randolph Vanderhoef hadn't come home from work early. The house was a three-storied affair with shuttered windows and brass fittings, off-white with pink trim. A paper sign was affixed to the center of their large front door: PATIENT SLEEPING, KNOCK SOFTLY. I did so.

"Yes? May I help you?"

The woman who opened the door was the same blonde I'd seen in the Mercedes the other night. Up close I was astonished at how much she resembled Irene Golinda: the same small head and tense, brittle features, the same mouse ears. Her head next to Vanderhoef's colossal skull would look like an egg next to a bowling ball. I handed her one of my cards, which she read carefully without looking me in the eye. Behind her in the house I could see part of a hospital-style bed and a large cylinder of oxygen standing in a rack.

"Mrs. Vanderhoef, I'm working a case that might affect your family. I wonder if you would mind talking to me for a few moments."

A minute later we were seated on opposite sofas in a small sitting room off the foyer. The furniture was off-white with small, delicate designs of vines and flowers. Everything in the house appeared to be brand-new. If I hadn't known better, I would have thought they'd recently leased the house and the furnishings.

Even though it was cloudy outside and nearly dark inside, Mrs. Vanderhoef had turned on no lights.

Her clothing consisted of an old sweatshirt with paint spatters on one arm, baggy sweatpants, and thick, puckered socks. In the room behind us a man snored loudly and erratically. I assumed he was her ailing father. Faith Vanderhoef coughed and continued coughing for a few moments, then settled down, hands clasped between her knees, waiting for me to ruin her life.

"If you don't mind, would you look at a picture and tell me if you've ever seen this woman?"

CHAPTER 28

Even though it was clear from the outset that she had never seen Wright, Faith Vanderhoef stared at the photo I'd handed her for a long while, unwilling to fail a stranger. She was so utterly humorless it made me want to laugh. I realized her studied fragility was probably hard to be around on a daily basis. Thin as a broomstick dressed up by little girls, she was about my age, extraordinarily careful with her words. I wondered how this soft-boiled woman had gotten hooked up with Vanderhoef.

"I don't believe I do know this woman. I might, but I don't believe I do. Should I?"

"Mrs. Vanderhoef, the woman in the picture was killed in an auto accident two weeks ago."

"How terrible. I had no idea."

"I'm trying to backtrack her last few days. She had a meeting with your husband. Possibly more than one. Does the name Marian Wright mean anything to you?"

"Have you talked to Randolph about this?"

"This morning. Let me explain what this lady was doing. A few weeks ago she learned she was HIV-infected. Her ex-husband had given it to her."

"I don't see what this has to do with me."

"Please hear me out. She tried to trace where her ex-husband got it and came up with the name of a young woman. She found the young woman, and eventually the young woman gave her the names of everybody she might have gotten it from." Faith Vanderhoef's gaze was suddenly transfixed on the wall behind me. "One of those names was your husband's."

"What do you mean, one of those names was my husband's?"

"Marian Wright spoke to your husband because the young woman with AIDS said one of the places she might have contracted it was from your husband."

"You mean they . . ."

"They had sex."

"I don't think so."

"I've spoken to the woman. I believe her story."

"And I believe my husband."

"I have information about your husband that you're not going to like."

"You know, Mr. Black, I have a lot of work to do."

"I'd like you to hear me out."

Faith Vanderhoef let out a sigh, knotted her hands together in her lap, then reached across and snapped on a lamp. The room was suddenly larger and sadder. She had been staring at the wall in the dark, but now she flicked quick looks at me. "I'm not sure what all this has to do with me."

"It should be obvious."

"What are you telling me? To see a doctor?"

"Because Marian Wright had some harsh words with your husband, and because he was evasive with me when I questioned him about her, I followed him. I don't usually follow people . . . well, maybe I do usually follow people. What I found was your husband visiting a public rest room in Marymoor Park. There's not much doubt he had a homosexual liaison with a stranger."

She continued to wring her hands. With the lamp on, she looked bonier, her ponytail waggling from side to side as she shook her head slowly. "I don't think so," she said. "You've made a mistake."

"If Mrs. Wright had found this out and if she were still

alive, she would have come to you. She would have asked you to be tested.... Mrs. Vanderhoef? I guess I'm here as her emissary."

"Did you talk to my husband about this rest-room business?"

"I did."

"And what did he tell you?"

"He threatened to kill me."

"Why would he do that?"

"Maybe because he thought I was coming here."

"Well, you did. Come here."

"Yes."

"And you think . . . I should be tested?"

"Your husband is from a high-risk group displaying high-risk behavior."

"That's why you came here? To warn me about this?"

"And to ask about Marian Wright."

Paler than ever, Faith Vanderhoef got up and walked to the front door, opened it, and said, "Thank you for dropping by, Mr. Black. Do come again."

"Faith—"

"Thank you for dropping by."

"Sure."

"And I appreciate the advice, Mr. Black."

"Goodbye, Faith. God bless."

"Good evening, Mr. Black."

At home I picked up the mail, got the paper, played the messages on my machine, and phoned Kathy's apartment. No answer. I phoned her at work, but everybody was gone for the day. I fixed a snack and dialed Kathy's apartment one more time, then heard a car in front of the house.

He was knocking on the front door before I opened it. When I realized who it was, I stepped outside and let the lock snap shut behind me. "Hello, Burt."

Roberson's face was red, the veins in his neck pulsing. He wore a sport coat, white shirt, and a garish tie that didn't go with his mood. He jutted his chin forward several times trying to make breathing room in the collar. He looked like he was trying to pass a peach pit. "You okay?" I asked.

"You sonofabitch. You going to blackmail me? You and that little twat? Katherine Twinkle Eyes? I get my hands on her—"

"You better think twice about making threats, Burt."

He had a fist in his coat pocket, and I had a feeling there was a gun in the fist. "You're a fucking blackmailer, is who you are."

"Not me, buddy."

"You were all a part of it."

"You know, Burt, I'm glad you came around. I've been meaning to speak with you."

"Fuck you. Give me the tape."

"I don't have anything to do with the tape, Burt. The only reason I even know about it was I walked in on the guy who was editing it."

"Who was that? Bruno Collins?"

"Let me ask you something, Burt. Do you remember college?"

"What are you talking about?"

"College. It's not a trick question. Remember taking a young woman out on a date? Remember—"

"Yeah, yeah, yeah. She told me all about it on the phone. Sure. Maybe I was there. I don't remember. I don't remember any pig party, but I did a lot of drinking in college."

"You do a lot of drinking now."

"What's it to ya, you stupid fruit?"

I caught something out of the side of my eye and glanced toward my driveway. Horace was watching us, a dripping hose in one hand. A dachshund in his arms, my father stood beyond Horace.

"Listen, asshole," Roberson said. "I want that video."

"I don't have it."

"Then get it."

"Burt, I don't have too much control over this, but my guess is if you come here and try to intimidate me, or you visit Kathy or anybody else who's involved, the video will go straight to your wife. And your boss. And probably your boss's wife. And your boss's wife's mother. And—"

"Fuck you."

"See you later, Burt. It's been a hoot."

"Fuck you." He reached out with the hand that wasn't in his jacket pocket and grabbed my arm. "You got that old lady's car back there. What? She your mom?"

"What do you know about Marian Wright? How did you know it was her car?"

"She came to my office. She was part of this, wasn't she? If I had known what was going to happen, I would have slapped her silly."

"Careful what you say, Burt. She died last Friday night. Where were you Friday night?"

"Not anywhere near the falls."

"Who told you it happened near the falls?"

"Listen, asshole. You got one day to get all those copies to me, and then all hell's going to break loose. You got it?" When I said nothing, Roberson reached out and tried to cuff me across the face with an open palm. I blocked it with my forearm. "Got it?"

I was thinking about knocking him off my porch but decided against it. I was pretty sure he had a gun in his pocket, and I didn't need any random shots flying around with Horace and Nigel so close by. "I got it."

"Good." He turned away and picked his way down my front steps.

"I'm very disappointed in you, son." Horace was already wandering toward his backyard shaking his head, but Nigel was boring into me with his hard brown eyes. "If I had raised you, you would have turned out to be a better neighbor. *And* I would have taught you the manly art of self-defense."

"But you didn't raise me, did you?"

"No, and for the last twenty-five years it's been a point of great sadness for me."

"Not so sad you ever sent any support money. Or even a card at Christmas."

He paused, then spoke bitterly. "Your mother was responsible for that."

"She hid the presents and cards and support money, did she?"

I might as well have stuck a knife in his gut. He had so much pride and so little to be proud of. It was as if he'd been born with too many ego genes and they'd conspired to cross-thread his life. He'd lost every job he ever had because he was smarter than the boss and couldn't stand not to let the boss know.

"I feel sorry for you," he said. "It would take weeks to make you understand."

"No, Nigel," I said, striding to my truck. "You couldn't do it. Not if you had forever."

I drove to Marian Wright's condominium on Sixteenth Avenue, rehearsing and rehearsing again the conversation with my father. There had been a certain amount of release in telling him off, but it had also been a lot like kicking a three-legged dog down a flight of stairs.

When I let myself into Wright's condominium, it was dark and the rooms were cold. The curtains were open. The furniture had not been moved. I could smell perfume. The lights of downtown Seattle and the south part of Capitol Hill brightened the rooms, but I wasn't quite up to a search yet, so I stood in the dark and tried to think my way through the case. I had pored over the materials in Wright's briefcase so many times I had them memorized.

As I muttered to myself, I was startled to hear a sound to my right along the bank of windows, the sound of a crying woman. Standing with her back to the corner, she watched me from the darkness. I'd been in the condo more than five minutes but had just noticed her. She wasn't a woman I ever expected to see crying in the dark.

"What are you doing?" she asked. "Trying to pick up vibes?"

"Something like that. What about you, Juanita?"

"Oh, I don't know. I come over here every night. You know, Marian wasn't a particularly good person, I don't think; but she was a friend. And I don't have many friends. I don't think she had *any*, really, except Susie and me. I miss her."

"Some people don't need many friends."

"Everybody needs friends, Black. She simply didn't have any."

"If you say so."

"Bruno talked to me today. He said you refused to work with him. Why?"

"He lied to me. And he did that sleazeball video operation for you."

"You're saying you don't like him because he did the video for me?"

"I like him fine. I just don't want to work with him."

"You realize, I can't continue to pay you both. I'm going to have to cut you off as of today. You might as well tell me what you've found."

"So I'm fired?"

"Let go."

I told her everything I knew.

"Does Bruno know about any of this?"

"Bruno didn't want to work on it, okay, Juanita? Remember that first day in the office? His attitude made me think he knew more than he was telling. When I asked him where he was that Friday night, he lied. After I found out he lied, he tried another alibi, but the second alibi wasn't any more solid than the first."

"Why would Bruno need an alibi? Why even ask the man for an alibi? Why insult him?"

"Because a man fitting Bruno's description was spotted near the scene of the accident. A man fitting Bruno's description was seen driving away in a car that could have been Bruno's. Then, too, six days after the accident, after I'd asked a few questions around town, somebody came at me with a baseball bat. I didn't see who it was, but he was about Bruno's size. By the way. You didn't happen to have an appointment with Marian that night, did you?"

"What are you talking about?"

"I was thinking maybe you had been the original chaperone. That she'd called Kathy because you hadn't shown up. That you felt guilty and didn't want to tell anybody. If that's the case, you might have some information."

"You're starting to piss me off, Black. You're not anywhere closer to solving this puzzle than you were at the beginning, are you?"

"Probably not."

"And you don't approve of what I'm doing to Burt Roberson."

"I think a grudge that's held for eighteen years says more about the holder than the object of the grudge."

We sat on that for a while, both of us looking out the windows. Neither of us had moved from our initial positions. She continued to cry, as she had off and on throughout the conversation. Finally, I said, "I came back here hoping to look around. I can't help feeling I missed something the first time through."

She held out a piece of typing paper, and I walked over and took it from her. In the dim light from the city, I could see it was dated the day Wright died.

To whom it may concern:

When I was but a child, I was cautioned that to cheat life was a mortal sin. I was further taught that life would even itself out, that sooner or later all good would come to those who waited. In the twilight of my stay here I can see that these precepts I have lived by are no longer valid. Life is not fair. Life never was fair. Life never will be fair. And if this is so then cheating life is certainly no mortal sin.

"Where did you find this?"

"In a portable typewriter she kept in the bottom of her closet. Look at the date. The day she died." The sheet was deformed from having been curled around the platen.

"Anybody could have typed this."

"On Marian's typewriter in Marian's closet in Marian's apartment. My my my. We don't trust a soul in the world, do we, Mr. Black?"

"I trust the president."

"It's a suicide note, pure and simple. It can't be anything else. She wrote it and parked along the highway and waited for somebody to come by, and she jumped in front of them."

"I don't think so."

"Why not?"

"She was too strong-willed to kill herself."

"She was too strong-willed not to kill herself."

"What do you mean by that?"

"Marian needed to be in charge. She didn't like feeling help-less." A small flame brightened Juanita's face for a moment as she fired up a cigarette with a lighter. She was attractive and in-telligent, and opinionated, which I liked, even if the opinions didn't match mine.

I drove home, ate dinner, got the materials from Wright's briefcase, flopped on the couch, turned on the television, and zoned out. It had been a bad day. I'd been fired. I had told a woman her husband was cheating on her in public rest rooms. I had been threatened. To top things off, my father had stolen my dog's affections, probably for good now that I'd fed L.C. peanut butter. Every half hour or so I called Kathy without leaving a message on her machine.

It was eleven-ten when I got the call. I picked up the re-ceiver on the second ring and heard the only voice like it in the world, high-pitched, soft, like the fizz in a carbonated drink. "Black?"

"Fears."

"You called it right, babe. Houser Fears, Esquire."

"How you doing, old man?"

"Black, I gotta talk to you. But first, thanks for not telling Bain I was yella. I wouldn'ta blamed you for welching and tell-ing her I was yella."

"We had a deal."

"I'm calling about something else, though. Black, I know Deanna Ayers."

"And?"

"It's more than knowing her. You might say I'm in love with the lady."

"She know about it?"

"Oh, I'm not trying to say anything is retaliated or ever *was* retaliated. It's not a romantic kind of love. Oh, I mean, if things were different, it could be, if she weren't sick and I were youn-ger and had my own place. I mean, it's not the same kind of love you're thinking. She been sick mostly the whole time I known her. Real sick. She's young, and she don't need some old hood hangin' around damagin' her rep. But I spent a lot of time with her, and that got me to hanging around with the old lady too."

"Which old lady?"

"Marian Wright."

"When was this?"

"Started about two, three weeks ago. She'd be visiting Dee and I'd be there and afterward, when Dee'd need to sleep, we'd go have coffee over at the Taco Time on Madison, look out the window, watch the cars drive by, and talk. I met Dee through Bain. In fact . . . well, no. You don't need to know that.

"Here's what I wanted to say. I know a few things you might want to look into. Wright called me the day she died. She called and wanted me to help her. Look, Black. You and I could both get rich off this."

"How do you figure?"

"I just opened a bottle of 151. Why don't you come on over and we'll kick it around?"

"She wanted help with an individual named Vanderhoef, didn't she?"

The line was silent for a few moments. "Naw. The old lady told me about him. He and I got into it a week or so back. I popped him one for what he did to Dee. Gave him a shiner."

"What did he do to Dee?"

"Years ago. Drugged her and sexed her when she was out. He's the one gave her the disease."

"You learn this from Marian?"

There was another long pause. "She wasn't bad. That old dame. I could sympathize with her."

"Who was she meeting that Friday?"

He hesitated. "A black dude and some woman. That's all I can say on the phone. You comin' over?"

"Sure." He gave me the address, the same house on Seward Park Drive South where Bain Littrell had picked him up.

Maybe this would be the end of it. Maybe Houser knew enough to put this fat bullet of abstract facts into a barrel and give it some spin and a direction. On the other hand, as I drove south I began to get nervous. I didn't want any trouble. Not in the middle of the night. Not from Houser Fears. Using the cellular phone, I called him back, got a taped message, and told him to pick up. He knew I was on the way over. He probably knew I was having second thoughts too. He didn't pick up.

CHAPTER 29

Red lights gyrating, Engine Company 33 sat in front of Houser Fears's house, a medic unit behind them. Eight police cars were parked on the street. Two more, blue light racks blazing, sirens silent, had whirred past me on my drive and were now parking on the grass up the street. A group of police officers stood in the driveway behind a raggedy-looking Chrysler.

Hoping for the worst, one rogue cameraman from a local television station began shooting footage.

I asked two officers what had happened but received no reply. One of them grabbed my arm when I tried to walk up the driveway. "Crime scene. You're not going up there."

An elderly couple in bathrobes stood shivering on the front porch of the house. Beside them, a cop grasped a ten-cell flashlight, shining it mindlessly on her own foot. I went up the steps and said, "What happened?"

"Guy got shot around back," said the cop, moving the light to my face.

"Know his name?"

Without taking the light out of my eyes, she shook her head. The old woman on the porch said, "Houser T. Fears." I'd seen prettier faces on iodine bottles. "And we have to find a new renter."

"Chicken today, feathers tomorrow," said the old man, who came over to me smoking a crooked cigarette, then turned to the street as if the two women wouldn't be able to hear. "They blew his head all to pieces. Put about a hundred bullets into it."

"You go down there?"

"After I seen 'em running down the driveway I did. I seen stuff in the war, so it don't bother me. I remember once in Korea I seen a guy sat on a grenade."

"Who'd you see running?"

"Coupla blacks."

"Two?"

"Couple. They busted into Rutherford's over there twice last year. Been breakin' in all over the place. You can't go to the store no more. Leave your place for ten minutes. We'd like to get outta here and go back to South Dakota, but we can't sell this goddamned house for near what it's worth."

After a while the medical examiner's station wagon arrived and two men pushed a gurney up the driveway. The fire department left. Most of the neighbors shuffled back to their beds. A few of the extraneous police officers defected. When the foot traffic had thinned sufficiently, I walked up the driveway between the battered cars and peered into a basement window. It was a tiny living room made tinier by hulking cops in bulletproof vests and by medical examiner's personnel.

Houser was curled on his side in a pool of blood, both eyes open and glassy. He wore a bathrobe, pajamas underneath the robe, and one slipper. The pajamas had come up on one leg, revealing a massive calf, white and bulging. Needles of blood were spattered everywhere. On the floor beyond his outstretched hand lay a Louisville Slugger baseball bat nearly identical to the one I had taken from the assailant in my backyard. A half-empty bottle of 151 proof Bacardi rum sat on a small table.

My guess was he'd been on his knees when shot, that they'd fired at his head and kept firing, had emptied a clip into him, maybe two clips.

After the photos had been taken, after the medical examiner's wagon carted the body off, after the yellow crime scene ribbon had been strung up, after the police cars left, I went to the front door and knocked until the old woman answered.

"We're plum tuckered," she said, looking up at me the way she would have looked up at a redwood. "Unless you're with the media folks. I s'pose we could talk to the media folks. Eh?"

"I'll have to quote you," I said.

"We don't mind. Come inside." Before I could get my bearings, they spelled their names for me. I got out a pad and wrote. They asked if I could get them on TV. I told them to call KIRO tomorrow and ask for Nigel.

Jointly, solemnly, they reiterated the story they'd given the police. Two black men in suits had run from the property moments after the shots had awakened them. Their bedroom, they told me, was on the second floor at the rear of the house, and I knew it had screens over the windows because I'd been staring at the house for three hours. From up there it would not have been impossible to see two men running from the premises in the dark, but it would have been unlikely they could have ascertained their race.

The police, they told me, had found lipstick-smeared cigarettes in the basement, but Fears did not smoke. I said I doubted he wore lipstick either, remembering that I had seen him smoking. As far as they knew, Fears had no regular women callers and had never had a black caller, until tonight. The old man said, "They told us to keep everybody outta there, but I don't think they coulda meant the news."

I could believe neither my good fortune nor my own poor moral judgment in following him meekly down a flight of narrow stairs at the back of the house to the basement apartment. He waited for me while I reconnoitered. It was a bachelor apartment much like the one in my own basement. I touched nothing and was careful where I stepped.

There were three small rooms. The living room with its bloodstained carpet. A kitchenette. And a tidy bedroom, a radio next to the double bed, oddly still tuned to an easy-listening station. It must have been soothing to the cops. His bed appeared to have been slept in, or at least lain in. He had been reading from the complete Sherlock Holmes, a battered volume that, to judge by its condition, had more than once tumbled off his sleeping chest onto the floor.

The old man reported that the only woman in Fears's life was a grown daughter who lived in Shelton with her husband and his five kids from a previous marriage. The bottle of rum and the baseball bat had been taken by the police, as had the cigarette butts. I touched nothing, disturbed nothing, and took nothing with me except a profound sense of grief and a wonderment that I hadn't gotten here ten minutes sooner. I might now be zipped into a dark sack in the back of the medical examiner's buggy next to Houser.

I drove to Beacon Avenue South, took the turnoff at Juneau Street, and parked in front of Bain Littrell's house. The neighborhood was dark and quiet. We were in that part of the night when most of the sleeping had lapsed into a partial coma. The streets were vacant.

It looked as if she wasn't going to answer, then some blinds at the side window jostled—and a moment later a voice came from behind her door, as bland and unfriendly as I remembered. "Go away. I'll call the police."

"Good. You can turn yourself in."

Still on the chain, the door opened. "Turn myself in for what?"

"For questioning in the death of Houser Fears."

"Houser's dead?" Her eyes were awake now, remarkably small and nondescript without makeup.

"You want to hear about it?"

The door swung wide. I stepped in. The house smelled moist and muggy, like the inside of a plastic bag somebody had been breathing into. The only light came from a back hallway. After standing for so long on the porch in the cold, it seemed warm and snug. She snapped on a lamp and sat in a straight-backed chair. She wore a robe, nothing on her feet. Her shoulder-length hair was as neat as a wig she'd taken off a Styrofoam skull. I remained standing. "Are you sure he's dead?"

"Real sure."

"What happened?"

"Somebody shot him."

"Who would do a thing like that?"

"That's what I came to ask you."

"I don't know anything about his business. He drives a potato chip truck. I call him when I need him, which isn't often. We talk business and that's that."

"You don't know any of his associates?"

"He used to be in the mob back East. New Jersey or someplace."

"So when the police ask you to name a suspect, what are you going to say?"

"You." I laughed. "You think I'm kidding?" she asked.

"I'm laughing because I was planning to name you."

"I was here in bed. Alone."

"You sicced Fears on me, didn't you? You asked him to mess me up in my backyard."

"I don't have to talk to you about this."

"No, you don't, but if you answer my questions and if you're straight, I won't tell them a thing. The cops."

She hesitated, picked at the flap of robe covering her knee, looked around the room and then at me. "It was his idea. He was going to put you in a cast so you couldn't get around so hot."

"But you put him up to it."

"I told him the situation. He volunteered."

"Without remuneration?"

"Four hundred dollars."

"That's all it costs to get my legs broken?"

"Houser and I had a special relationship. I paid him with money and . . ."

"So four hundred dollars and some nooky gets a guy's legs broken."

"You've got a dirty mind. I introduce him to people."

"I'm afraid his death has something to do with this business Marian Wright was involved in. The initial report was that a couple of black men were seen running from his apartment. You don't know who that might have been, do you? Not clients of yours?"

"I only have one black trick, and he's quite elderly."

"What about Fears? Did he have any black associates?"

"Not that I know of."

"You know a man named Bruno Collins?"

"He came and asked to work for me once."

"Doing what?"

"Watching out for my best interests."

"He knew what you did?"

"A lot of people know."

"But you never hired him? Bruno?"

"No."

"Seen him lately?"

"What does that mean?"

"There are no deceptive questions here, Bain. The police are the ones with the deceptive questions."

"I saw him about three days ago."

"Where?"

She hesitated. "With Houser. Downtown. I was on the way home from the dentist. For some reason, I'd decided to take the bus. I saw them on the street. I hadn't spoken to Houser since or I would have asked him about it. They were just walking down the street."

"That's all?"

"You're getting a big kick out of this, aren't you? You going to explain what happened to Houser?"

I told her. She sat rigidly on the chair, one bare leg crossed over the other, bobbing her foot, her toenails painted bright red and cut square. She didn't cry, nor had I expected her to. Her grief came in the form of a flat-toned statement that could have come from the time lady on the phone. "Houser was not exactly what you would call a bosom pal, but for some reason I feel awful about what happened."

"I can tell."

"I do."

"Where did you two meet?"

"He was in Walla Walla with my old man. They got to be pretty good friends. Keith sent him over here when he got out.

You know how it is after you've been in awhile. You need to relax."

"So your husband is in the joint?"

"You knew that before, didn't you?"

"Your answering machine. You take collect calls."

"I met Houser two and a half years ago. A couple of girlfriends and me began using him for odd jobs. He's very intimidating when he wants to be. That is, he was."

"And you introduced him to Dee?"

"Houser met her when she tried to get into the life."

"He was protecting her on her first job?"

"He *was* her first job."

"Houser Fears was Dee's first customer?"

"First and last."

"I thought it was some guy from New Jersey or New York."

"Houser was from New Jersey or New York or someplace. Dee didn't care for the experience, but Houser more or less caught a thing for her. I told her she had to try again, but she got sick right after that."

"Was he HIV positive?"

"He got tested and he was clean. I have to hand it to him, though. He stuck by her. He used to finish his route early and spend the rest of the day up there. They had to start kicking him out."

"Tell me about the times you saw Wright and what was said."

She thought about it and told me. There was nothing new. Wright had ended up calling her a whore, then, later, when they were both visiting Dee at the hospice, they came to a grudging truce.

"And what exactly did she do that made you so frightened of me?" I asked.

"Two of my clients. She spoke to them, maybe to their wives too, for all I know."

"And said what?"

"What do you think? That I was a carrier. She was convinced for the longest time that Dee and I had been in the life together and that if Dee had it, then I had it. She wanted to believe in the worst way that her husband had paid Dee. She couldn't accept the fact that this young woman had willingly gone to bed with her husband, who was maybe thirty years older. I don't know if it was a feeling of competition, or what it was."

"Let me see your client list."

"What? Are you kidding me? I don't keep a list. They call me and I set up the appointment. That's all there is."

"The cops could get a warrant tonight. Maybe before you even had time to ditch it."

"You're just a real pleasant person to be around. You know that, Black?"

"I've got dozens of names linked to Wright, but I can't sort them out. I want to see if any of them are on your list."

"If I get up and go get it, I suppose you're going to follow me?"

"I suppose."

"Into my bedroom?"

"Let's go."

She kept the list in a small floor safe under the carpet in her bedroom. I saw thirty or forty wristwatches when she brought the book out, as well as a hefty amount of cash and a small pistol. Her face was red from stooping when she looked up from the floor.

We took it back into the living room. She had over two hundred names, each tagged with various notations and code signs. Oddly, I found my own name in the book.

"You consider me a customer?"

"Maybe someday."

"How many of these others are like me—maybe someday?"

"Just you."

"You put me here in case the police got ahold of this, didn't you? To cause trouble."

She shrugged, but I knew I was right. On her list I found a former city councilman. A professor from the University of Washington. A well-known radio personality, and quite a few sports figures, including a former Seahawk who had been known as a Jesus freak. The only name connected to the case was Burt Roberson.

"Was Fears involved in anything else that might have gotten him killed?"

"I don't know. He sometimes worked for a couple of other girls. I don't know if he had been lately."

"You going to give me their names?"

She did so reluctantly, making me promise not to implicate her if I spoke to them.

"So tell me about Roberson."

"Who?"

"Burt Roberson. On page twenty, right after the quarter-back."

"I saw him two days ago. What was that? Tuesday? No. Yesterday. I saw him yesterday. He was all charged up. He likes a half and half, but he never gets to the second half. He never tips either, and the cheapskate always wants to go again for free. As if he *could* go again. He thinks he's a lady-killer. But there is one piece of business you might want to know."

"What's that?"

"I had to have Houser speak to him."

"When was that?"

"Couple of years ago."

"What was he doing?"

"He likes it rough. I don't do that."

"How long have you known him?"

"Ummm, three, four years. From before Houser."

"Did you know the old woman talked to him?"

"No. I wonder how many more clients she got to that I don't know about."

"I doubt she knew he *was* a client."

I thought about the connections between Marian Wright and Dee and Houser and Chuck Wright and Abdul Sarwar and Susie Scudder and Randolph Vanderhoef. Marian Wright had been infected by Chuck Wright, who had been infected by Dee, who became friends with Marian, but Dee also slept with Houser Fears and Abdul Sarwar, Abdul when he was known as

Marbles, and he had slept with Susie Scudder, one of my clients, also a neighbor of Wright's.

Roberson had dated Juanita Raykovich, then had slept with Bain Littrell, who'd slept with Houser Fears, who'd slept with Deanna Ayers, who could easily have gotten the disease from Fears and given it to Chuck Wright, who in turn gave it to Marian Wright.

It was like tracking a bee in a hive. Even though I had not had an active sex life in some time, I was willing to wager I'd slept with somebody who'd slept with somebody who'd slept with one of these people. Spooky.

I must have been thinking aloud, because Bain said, "Monogamy went out with penicillin. Once you could cure everything, what was the point? And then the pill came along and there was no more problem with babies. Science turned everything around and gave sex back to the people. Now, if they can't come up with an answer to this new plague, we're going to slip back into the dark ages."

"What do you consider the dark ages?"

"You know. Everybody's a virgin when they get married."

"Wouldn't that be a kettle of fish?"

"Why do you say that?"

"Nothing. No reason. Nostalgia, I guess. A real kettle of fish."

CHAPTER 30

"**Y**ou don't think Fears was killed by two burglars?" Kathy asked. "Even though the neighbors say he was?"

"I really don't know. When I talked to him on the phone, he said Marian had been with a black man and some woman. I think maybe he was with a black man and a woman when he told me that, and they killed him. There was lipstick on a cigarette in his apartment."

It was late Friday morning, almost lunchtime. We were in Kathy's office. My left ear was still moist where she had kissed me. Her hair was long and loose and glossy in the sunshine that poured in through her tall office window. She was dressed in ivory; a long-sleeved ribbed blouse that made her look bustier than she was, and a skirt with patch pockets and gold buttons down the front, unbuttoned above the knee so that when she moved the soft muscle on the inside of her thigh was exposed.

"I hope you don't sit like that for your clients."

"Don't get personal. We're talking serious business here." She hitched up her skirt a fraction of an inch and squinted at me.

"I don't know what was going on, but last night Fears was adamant that I see him. He was a little drunk too."

"You say Fears was in his jammies. The radio was on in his

bedroom, the bed turned down. Why call you? I could see turning the bed down and calling a girlfriend ... maybe."

"Sure. Something happened after he got ready for bed that made him think he had to call me. I think he had visitors."

"Or maybe he'd heard tales of your bedside manner. I've been telling absolutely everybody."

"Whatever it was that made Fears call me, he was awful serious about it. He said he loved Deanna Ayers. He told me in a strange tone of voice, as if he were making a painful confession."

"You said he had a funny voice anyway."

"Like one of the Seven Dwarfs. Sniffy."

"Sniffy wasn't one of the Dwarfs. Have you talked to the police about the murder?"

"On the way here to see you. I got a pretty good rundown from Crum. They think it was some sort of mob execution. Twenty-two-caliber Magnum expandable bullets. No casings. No fingerprints."

"Crum is handling the investigation?"

"A guy named Murphy. So far, they don't know much. Lipstick on some cigarettes. Supposedly he never had female visitors. And they say he didn't smoke. Except he was smoking the first day I saw him. The news is, he had few visitors and no friends. The cops were on their way to visit me when I showed up. I had left a message on his machine. I must have been leaving it at the time the killer was in the apartment, although the cops didn't know that until I told them. His machine didn't have a time notation on the tape. Maybe the killer heard me. Maybe Fears listened too. Maybe he was trying to pick it up when he got shot."

"He might have saved your life. That's scary."

"I heard an interesting tidbit while I was at Homicide. Keith Littrell was sent up seven years ago. He ran over a man with his car. The detectives who did the footwork on the case thought his wife, Bain, had been part of it. At one point they had a witness who swore Bain had been in the car egging him on."

"Let me guess. The witness disappeared?"

"You got it."

Kathy leaned back in her chair, crossed her ankles, and placed her arms under her breasts. "Okay, big boy. Why don't we try to get away this weekend? We can talk and we can be alone and we can—"

"I thought you'd start calling me that sooner or later."

"Which?"

"Big boy."

"Heh."

"What does that mean?"

"Heh."

"You want to get away Friday? I thought we were getting married Friday."

"You had to check your *TV Guide*. I thought you found a *Hawaii Five-O* rerun. Besides, I have to think about how I want to do this. It's going to take some time to figure out. This getting married business."

"Where to this weekend?"

"I've got a place in mind. So, Thomas. Tell me more about Fears."

"He was thinking about Dee when he called me. She was admitted to a hospital yesterday. That's probably what was on his mind. She's in trouble."

"She is the one who gave the acquired immune deficiency syndrome to Marian's husband?"

"Marian thought so. And that's what counts here. Dee had never used needles, had never worked in health care, and had never had a blood transfusion. She had sex with her husband, Abdul Sarwar, Randolph Vanderhoef, and Chuck Wright. And also a man I'd thought was an anonymous john from New Jersey but who turned out to be Houser Fears."

"You're kidding?"

"He was a customer Bain Littrell set up for her when she was trying to talk Dee into the life. I love the way they call it the life, as if the rest of us aren't living. Anyway, Fears more or less fell in love with Dee and has been her watchdog ever since. I wouldn't have put it past Houser to push Marian in front of a car if he thought she was causing Dee any discomfort."

"I thought Dee and Marian got along."

"That's the story, but I don't really know what Houser's take on that was."

"Maybe he thought you and Marian both hastened Dee's illness. Maybe he had people waiting to kill you last night? It could be that while you were driving over they got into a dispute over money or who knows what, and the hired help bumped off Fears instead of you."

"That thought ought to help me sleep better."

"Don't you worry about sleeping. I found out how to put you to sleep." She met my eyes and a very slow smile appeared on her face. "If Houser or Bain hired hit men to get you, they might still be after you."

"Why would a guy like Fears need help bumping me off?"

"Maybe he wasn't the tough guy he pretended to be," Kathy said.

"Okay. It could have gone like this. Bain Littrell is approached by Marian Wright. Now Bain's pissed off. She has Fears try to slow the old woman down. He slows her down. In fact, he gets her killed. Now Bain's upset because I'm coming along trying to figure out what happened. The rest of the world thinks it's an accident, but I'm questioning that.

"So Littrell tells Fears about it, and Fears, having no small interest in the matter himself, decides to put me in traction long enough to discourage me. That doesn't pan out, and I become another Marian Wright, dogging them both. After a week or two, Fears finds somebody to do a job on me. He calls me over. And then—"

"Which means Littrell would still want you out of the way."

"Yes."

"Marian was murdered, wasn't she, Thomas? You really believe that now, don't you?"

"There are too many indicators pointing to it. There was the man I saw driving away. Another witness saw a man, possibly the same man, watching from the woods. There were cigarette butts in Wright's ashtray. So a smoker was in her car. The Salish, where she had planned your meeting, was less than a mile up the hill. It's a dangerous piece of highway, and it was dark and raining. Wright was known to be fearful and cautious of traffic mishaps. She had gas in the car. The car was running. So why was she there?"

"Besides all these other people, there's Burt Roberson. Marian was working on that. And Roberson is *really* pissed."

"But he wasn't pissed two weeks ago when she died, was he? Think about Abdul Sarwar, alias Ransom Marbles. At Bellevue Community College he meets and seduces Dee. A couple of years later he runs into Susie Scudder in Sun Valley and, after telling her he's sterile, gives her a little present. By the way, what's happened with that?"

"He wants to meet Tobey. I'm handling the arrangements."

"Sarwar wants a relationship with the boy?"

"In the worst possible way. Of course, the blood test isn't in yet, but Susie says it's impossible it could have been anybody else. You know, on our drive over to the party, Burt Roberson stopped in front of a motel and tried to get me to go in with him. Said he'd never had a disappointed customer."

"We know at least one."

"By the way, Juanita called first thing this morning and said you were fired."

"Yeah. There's one person we haven't discussed."

"Who?"

"Bruno Collins."

"How do you figure, Thomas?"

"A large man was seen on the hillside the night of the accident. I saw a man driving away from the scene. If I had to guess, I would say he was black. I could be wrong, but that's what I would guess. Two black men were reported to have been running from Fears's apartment after the shooting. Bruno, although he had been working for those three women, refused to investigate Wright's accident."

"Thomas! He was crying right here in this office. I was touched. So were you."

"Wright wanted help. Maybe she called Bruno. That would have put him out at the scene."

"Then why would she call me too?"

"Maybe he didn't show up, and when he didn't, she phoned

you in a last-minute panic. Then he did show up and something went wrong. Maybe she told him to piss off. Maybe he got mad at her. Called out in the rain and then told to get lost. Or maybe he was trying to blackmail somebody Marian had dug up dirt on, and she didn't like that."

"You said yourself you thought Marian had had her wrists tied. You think Bruno would have tied her wrists?"

"Sufficiently provoked, he might."

"But Thomas, think about Houser Fears. He was a big guy. What kind of car did he drive? An older American car like the one you saw speeding away?" I nodded. "You outlined a completely believable scenario when you said Bain Littrell could have put him up to it. We know she sent him to your house. When did you talk to her, anyway?"

"Last night."

"After the murder?"

"Yeah."

"Fears was killed around eleven-thirty?"

"Uh-huh."

"So after the murder would have been about what?"

"Two-thirty, three."

"Three in the morning with a call girl? Where were you?"

"Her house on Beacon Hill."

"What does she look like?"

"You know."

"No, I don't. Is she attractive?"

"Not bad. Why? You jealous?"

"Of course not. Just tell me what she was wearing."

"The usual."

CHAPTER 31

Bruno Collins knocked and then stuck his head inside Kathy's office. "Speak of the devil," Kathy said.

"I been called worse." Collins bunched his cheeks up and tried to pass it off as a smile. "Can we talk, Black? I understand a mutual friend of ours got killed."

"We were just discussing it," Kathy said. "Come in." Bruno Collins closed the door and took a chair. He wore his standard, dark, double-breasted suit, a button now missing from the lowest row. I got up from the edge of Kathy's desk and sat in a chair beside Collins. Kathy tugged her skirt down over her knees.

"I heard it on the news," said Bruno. "Seems like all the people I'm knowing are dead. Mrs. Wright. Fears. Maybe even you, Black."

"What do you mean, maybe even Thomas?" Kathy asked.

"I didn't mean nothin'. It's just everybody is dead."

"How well did you know Fears?" I asked.

"We were gonna work together, him and me. Had this project. But sweet Jesus, who do you think iced him?" Bruno stared at me.

"Witnesses said two black males ran out of the apartment."

"That wasn't on the news."

"It was in the paper this morning."

"I didn't know he hung around with the brothers."

"He hung around with you."

"Not so's anyone could tell. He called the other day and said we should have coffee somewheres. Took me to this dive on First Avenue. It was full of bums pouring wine into their coffee. The counters had dead bugs on them. The waitress looked like an ex-junkie and had these silicone titties that were in the wrong place. She never did look me in the eye. It bothers me when somebody won't look me in the eye."

"What did you talk about?"

"Nothin', really. He kept tellin' me we should work together."

"Where were you last night around eleven-thirty?"

Bruno set his dark eyes on Kathy and then swung them back to me. "Oh, I get it." He grinned, a real grin this time. "You want an alibi, right? You're funny, Black. But I like it. Some brothers wouldn't take that off you, but I like it."

"And?"

"And what?"

"Where were you last night?"

He laughed. "The alibi man. Home in bed. By my lonesome."

"What kind of business was Fears talking to you about, Bruno?"

"Get in a venture together, you know. He had some mob connections from back East. He figured with all the shootings and drugs and stuff in the Central District, we could hire out. You know. Have gun, will travel. I could supply the connections and he could supply the muscle. We were gonna install bullet-proof windows in cars too. We woulda been rich."

"Did he talk to you about Marian Wright?"

"He said one day him and Juanita and her were all at each other like cats in a sack."

"Juanita? Fears knew Juanita?"

"Yeah. It was over that dude Juanita is jamming up."

"Roberson?"

"Roberson. Mrs. Wright found something on him. I don't know what. She wanted to turn him over to the cops. Juanita said no. Roberson got turned over to the cops, she'd have to wait until he got out to fix him."

"Who told you this?" Kathy asked.

"Houser. He claimed Juanita and Mrs. Wright had a knock-down dragout over it. Callin' each other bitches and everythin'."

"Was Fears there?" I asked. "When they were fighting?"

"From the way he told it, he must have been."

"Report him for what?" Kathy asked. "Marian wanted to report Roberson for what?"

"Don't look at me," Bruno said. "I'm clueless."

"Bruno," Kathy said. "Can you think of anybody Marian might have been going to meet that Friday night?"

"Sure. Roberson."

"Roberson's wife tells me he broke his coccyx in Spokane the day before Wright died," I said.

"An alibi," Collins said, grinning. "You checked it?"

"Not yet. But it's probably true. She didn't know there was a death involved when she told me."

"If it was Roberson Friday night," Kathy said, "that quashes the theory that Juanita might have been there. Juanita wouldn't have seen him before the party. She was too afraid she'd be recognized."

"Unless Marian set it up without telling Juanita."

"But her being recognized?" Bruno said. "That was crazy. I saw a picture of her when she was in college. She looked like a completely different human being. She used to have these big old pink cheeks and these big old glasses."

Kathy said, "So maybe you should check out Roberson's alibi for that Friday. Hospital records and all. I believed him when he said he had a broken coccyx. He had to sit on a dough-nut pillow when he was driving. You notice at that party he didn't sit down once."

"He sat down in the video we made," Collins said. "In the back room he sat down and Juanita got on his lap."

"It seems to me," I said, "if you had a broken butt, having a woman as large as Juanita sit on your lap would be excruciating."

"That's right," said Kathy. "So it might *not* have been broken. But if it was, Juanita knew Roberson's wife would realize just how excruciating when she saw the footage. Juanita knew exactly what she was doing."

We thought about that for a few moments. "Bruno," I said, "do you know Abdul Sarwar?"

"I've been knowing him for years. We used to play in the same slow-pitch league. And he's not HIV, if that's what you mean."

"You sure?"

"There's no such thing as a gay brother."

"You don't have to be gay to get it."

"A brother turns gay, he loses his minority status. Sarwar don't have HIV." He gave out a wry smile, so I couldn't tell if he was kidding or not.

When Bruno left, I followed him downstairs and into the street and watched him walk back to his office on Second and Cherry. On the way, he lit a cigarette. He looked tougher on the street, and not nearly so gullible.

After lunch, when it began to quiet down around the office, I pulled out Marian Wright's briefcase and went through the seventeen letters describing the tree of death. Many of the names were recognizable now. Sarwar's ex-wife and two of his ex-girlfriends. Vanderhoef's wife, Faith. Mary Ellen Richardson at Vanderhoef's Sports, who hadn't admitted to me she had had sex with Vanderhoef, but apparently had admitted same to Marian. There was no letter for Irene Golinda. Fears had not been on the list either. Wright was too thorough to have left them out. She hadn't known.

At two-thirty I was summoned to Kathy's office and was surprised to see Faith Vanderhoef sitting meekly on a chair, purse and gloves in her lap, a camel overcoat buttoned to her chin.

"I believe you two have already met," Kathy said.

"Mrs. Vanderhoef. How have you been?"

"I came to see you, Mr. Black. But then I got here and saw Ms. Birchfield's name on the door. My husband has one of her cards."

"Would you like to explain to Thomas what you have in mind?" Kathy said.

Faith Vanderhoef had navy-colored fleece gloves in her lap and used the fingers of one glove to mop her wet eyes. "Maybe you could do it."

Kathy looked over at me. "Mrs. Vanderhoef has found out recently that she is HIV positive. She believes the cause to be her husband's extramarital activities."

"I'm sorry to hear that, Mrs. Vanderhoef. I really am."

"I know you are. I could see that yesterday afternoon, even if I didn't have the common grace to acknowledge it. Or to tell you I'd already been tested."

"You were upset. Besides, I have no right to pry into your personal affairs. I did think I had an obligation to tell you what I had learned, though."

"I hated you when you came. I hated you for what you said. But I knew in my heart it was true. I had a transfusion when Adrianna was born, but that was eleven years ago. The doctors tell me it's much more likely I got the virus someplace else. I've been faithful to my husband, Mr. Black. And I feel so dirty. . . ."

Kathy said, "Would you like to tell Mr. Black the rest of why you're here, Mrs. Vanderhoef?"

"I'm afraid. I've been trying to think of a way to confront my husband ever since Doctor told me, but it's beyond me. I need to have a long talk with Randy, but I need somebody to be there to help me do the talking."

"You want Kathy to represent you in this matter?"

"Ms. Birchfield and you both."

"What would you like us to say to your husband, Mrs. Vanderhoef?"

"I would like . . ." She stared down at her lap for a long minute, her ponytail, because of the position of her head, sitting like a water fountain, and told us what she wanted her husband to hear. Kathy looked at me.

"I'll assist in any way Mrs. Vanderhoef wants," I said.

Faith Vanderhoef had avoided our eyes throughout the conversation. Now she looked directly at me. She had been a pretty woman once, but her frailty had overwhelmed the bloom. "When you visited me last night, it forced me to come to terms with the fact that I was going to have to make some decisions. I guess I've been in denial."

"When would you like to do this?" Kathy asked.

"As soon as possible."

I was already on the office phone, but the receptionist reported Vanderhoef wasn't in and might not be in all afternoon. I relayed the information to Kathy and Faith. I had a fleeting thought she'd killed Vanderhoef and we were part of her alibi, but I dismissed it.

"We could put you and your daughter up somewhere? A hotel, or we could—"

"I'm sorry, but my father is living with us. He's ill and requires round-the-clock care. We have nursing, but I shouldn't even have left him this long."

"We understand," Kathy said. "I'll arrange things and call."

Faith seemed to be stronger and taller when she stood up to leave. "Could I ask you one question, Mr. Black?"

"Be my guest."

"Was he having sex with anybody else? Anybody I might know? A woman?"

I thought about it for a few moments. Kathy's eyes were telling me to take the kindliest path, which would have been easier if I'd known what the kindliest path was. The woman in front of us was about to lose her father to illness. She was giving up her husband. Within a year, maybe two, she would die a lingering death. "He has had relations with others," I said. "I know at least one name, and I have warned that person. If you insist, I'll give you the name, but I'd rather not. I took down the plate number of the car of the man he met in Marymoor Park, and I've already sent him a registered letter explaining the situation."

"I suppose that's . . . the right thing to do."

"I think so."

"I just don't want to cause any trouble," Faith said.

"You haven't caused any trouble," Kathy said.

"Randy and I were close once. We met through the families. Everybody worked at Vanderhoef's Sports at Christmastime, trying to keep up. I was fourteen and he was in college. He used to flirt with me, outrageously, or so I thought. I wasn't allowed to go out with him until I was sixteen, but I was so in love I never even dated another boy. He's the only man, besides my father, I've even kissed." The three of us were standing near the door. Faith was suddenly reluctant to leave without a crust of small talk to sandwich the poisonous meat she was taking with her. "How did you two meet?"

Kathy looked at me with a gleam in her eye and began explaining. We were in U.S. History together at the University of Washington, both of us studying pre-law. I was a cop on second shift with the SPD. She was going to be an attorney. It was a small class, and the professor insisted his students sit in alphabetical order, so we sat next to each other; Birchfield—Black. The prof was dreadful, his lectures nothing more than a humdrum parroting of the reading assignments. From the first day, Kathy yearned for the gumption to get up and walk out of the class, but she never quite got up the nerve.

One particularly boring day I got up, swept my books off the desk, and strode out. Kathy came perilously close to following but did not. From that moment, she knew we were soulmates.

I said, "That's how we met?"

"You know it is."

"I didn't think the prof was dreadful."

"You got up and walked out."

"I had a bloody nose."

"What?"

"For some reason I put my finger in my nose and it started bleeding. After the class I came back and apologized. I thought he was great."

"He was dreadful. He just recited from the reading assignments, word for word."

"No wonder I thought he was great. . . ."

"You never read the textbook, did you?"

"Sure I did."

"You never read it, and on top of that you picked your nose."

"No, I didn't either. I just—"

"I fell for a nose-picking slacker. Mother will just love this."

It wasn't until she was leaving that Faith Vanderhoef turned her tearstained eyes back to me and said, "I would like to hear a name. I guess I would."

"Pardon me?"

"The woman he's seeing?"

"Irene Golinda."

"It doesn't ring a bell."

"She goes by Maggie. Maggie Golinda."

"Yes, I see." Faith left, walking in tight little steps, her head held high.

"Maybe you shouldn't have told her," Kathy said.

"She's had enough secrets kept from her. I don't want to be a part of any more."

Maybe I was going crazy, but I had another fleeting image, of Faith Vanderhoef driving to Vanderhoef's Sports, confronting Maggie Golinda, and shooting her. In fact, maybe she had been the one who killed Fears. The cops had found lipstick-smeared cigarette butts in his apartment. I said, "Did you know Bruno smoked?"

"No, he doesn't."

"I watched him light up down there on the street."

"Hmmmm." Kathy stepped close and straightened my lapel even though it didn't need straightening. "My hero. I can't believe I fell in love with you because you were picking your nose."

"Now listen, I was—"

"If I'd known you were a nose picker, I never would have spoken to you."

"Wait a minute. You said you fell in love with me. We were friends. We've been friends all this time and—"

"Don't be silly. Of course I was in love with you."

"When we first met?"

"Yes."

"You've been in love with me all these years?"

"Of course."

"Cool."

CHAPTER 32

I had no idea what time it was when I got home, just that it was dark.

Earlier I had driven to Swedish Hospital, only to learn Deanna Ayers had died during the lunch hour, news that made me feel as if I'd been drenched in a cold shower. I hadn't known her long, but I felt I'd lost a friend. She'd been ill, and my assumption had been there were months left, or at least weeks. None of her relatives or acquaintances were at the hospital when I got there, and after a while I found myself alone in my truck crying over a woman who had been trying to make a go of it in a world designed for other people.

If it were true Vanderhoef had drugged her and forced sex on her, her death was not by illness, but misadventure—or more aptly, murder, assuming he was the one who gave her AIDS. The thought fueled a determination to prove her allegations.

When I got home, I parked and walked around to my front door. Horace's house was dark.

For the first time in months the extra dead bolt on my front door was thrown from the inside. It was a lock I rarely used, and the key for it was lying loose in the glove box of my truck. I couldn't remember locking it, but I had been caught up in ruminations the past couple of days and wasn't remembering a lot of things. I'd been up half the night after Fears's murder and half the night before that with Kathy.

I heard someone inside and said, "Nigel. Nigel, let me in."

After a moment or two the small, square peephole door creaked and opened. I expected a snide comment, but Nigel said nothing. I caught a momentary glimpse of movement.

"Nigel, open the—"

I attempted to step away from the door, but instead I sat slowly on the mat, then slumped onto my side, my face sliding down the side of the door.

A moment later the painted wooden boards of the porch pressed coolly against my left cheek. I had seen movement, yet I couldn't figure out what the movement had been. It had looked like a rectangular box in the peephole. And now the porch had tilted and was pressing against my face.

"Nigel," I mumbled, but my lips were thick and numb against the cold wood, and the way I said it, the word wasn't recognizable even to me.

It wasn't until my heels caught on the weather stripping at the base of my door that I realized I was sliding into the house on my rear end, my hands up over my head. Somebody was dragging me. A shadow hovered over me in the dark, and for a moment my eyes began to focus on the rectangular box again. "Nigel?"

It wasn't a box, the object above me; it was the grainy butt end of a board. The loud sound of wood on wood resounded in my ears. Then again.

At first I couldn't tell whether I was waking from a nap or waking from a long night's sleep. All I knew was that I'd been dreaming at the wrong time, and when you're dreaming at the wrong time, you're generally either sick or in trouble. The pressure of a cold linoleum floor against my chest and face brought me into focus. My head buzzed and my eyes seemed swollen in their sockets. A headache pulsed inside my skull.

I was in my own bathroom. On the floor. On my face. I could smell the odor of cleanser and bath soap and bowl deodorizer. My hands were bound behind me, and my feet too, ankles tied to wrists. A gag had been fastened around my head and a dry washcloth had been stuffed into my mouth.

I listened.

I listened and did not move. It was possible, in fact it was probable, that whoever had done this was in the other room. The house smelled of cigarette smoke. But why burgle a house, assault the owner, and then wait around? Why tie up an unconscious man? Where was the profit? People tied you up for three reasons that I could think of: to make good their escape, to keep you still while they tortured you, or to give them time to return.

The regulator clock ticked away in the other room. The refrigerator clicked and hummed. A car passed in the street outside.

As I waited, I wrestled with the ropes, heedful lest my thighs cramp, always a possibility for a cyclist in this unusual position. The harder I worked, the hotter and sweatier I became, the more my head hurt, the more my eyeballs felt like grapes under a boy's shoe. And the angrier I got. I was so angry I soon grew angry at how angry I was.

After a while I was able to tongue the rag in my mouth into a compact wad and push it out around the gag, now partially dislodged.

Through the heat register, I had been listening to the innocent sounds of life in the basement apartment. Tap water running in a sink. The soft voices coming from a television in the far room. Chester playing with his toys, and the litany of tones and pitches he'd engineered to mimic car noises. I yelled at my unknown assailant and then yelled again, "Hey, you sonofabitch, come and get me." But the house was still. I was alone.

"Chester! Can you hear me?" The play downstairs stopped, then commenced again. I banged the side of my skull on the floor and nearly blacked out. Both eyes felt as if blood vessels had burst in them. "Chester!"

The play ceased once more. "Hey, Buuuuud! Where are you? In the wall?"

"Upstairs."

"In my closet?"

"I'm upstairs. Listen, Chester. Can you get your dad?"

A long pause. "No."

"Why not?"

"He's at work."

"Get Liseea, then."

"Okay." A few moments later he came back and began mak-ing car noises again.

"Chester?"

"Hey, Bud?"

"What about Liseea?"

"I can't wake her up."

"Chester. Call 911."

"We don't have no phone."

"That's right, you don't. Come on upstairs. I think the inside basement door might have a key in it." He didn't reply, and I heard no further sound from below except the distant televi-sion. I called him three more times and was beginning to panic when I sensed somebody in the bathroom with me. The light came on. Half blind from the glare, I rolled my head toward the door.

I could see his feet. He had a sock on one foot. A shoe on the other. "Hey, Buuuud!"

"Chester. Untie me. Quick."

I felt small hands working the knots and ropes. After about a minute he said, "Who tied these, anyway. Dracula?"

"Go get a knife. In the kitchen. A bread knife. You know. With the wavy edges. And walk with it. Don't run, Chester. Carry it with the point away from you. Can you remember that?"

"Are we playing a game?"

"No. This is not a game, Chester."

Cutting me free, he accidentally sliced the heel of my hand. Fortunately, he didn't cut himself. By the time I had uncoiled and stretched and sawed my ankles apart, I had bled across my trousers.

When I pulled the gag off my head, he said, "Ooooo la-la."

The gag, I found, was a black brassiere that had been hang-ing on a hook on the back of my bathroom door for a couple of days. I hadn't told Kathy where it was because I liked it on the door.

I grabbed a clean washcloth out of the hall closet and wrapped it around my hand, holding it in place by making a fist. On the way past the medicine cabinet I caught a glimpse of myself in the mirror, my skull looking as if it had grown three goiters, a smear of blood visible on one cheek, and the look in my fuzzy brown eyes of a demented postal worker carrying an automatic weapon back into the facility he'd been fired from.

When I came out, Chester was in the dining room running a small metal Ferrari across the table. "Rrrrmmm, rrrrrmmm." I knew it was fifteen minutes past seven when I'd been freed, but had little idea what time my ordeal had begun.

"You need to go back downstairs now, Chester."

"Do I have to?"

"Now!"

"Yes, sir."

"When's your dad coming home?"

"I don't know. We're going to Liseea's parents' cabin."

"Good. You ever been there before?" I was moving through the house quickly now, carrying a wrench I'd picked up in the spare bedroom.

"No."

"You'll like it. There's a witch house next door. Now go tell Liseea she has to take you down the street to her house. Okay? Tell her I said there was a burglar here. And hey, thanks, buddy."

Tiny and frail and goofy in his thick glasses and disheveled clothing, Chester scampered down the basement stairs like a comic actor in a silent movie. I noticed he'd left the car on the dining room table. I dropped it into my pocket.

The house had been searched, the phone ripped from the wall. Kathy often said she had to clean house before she could go anywhere—in case a burglar came while she was gone—and now I knew what she was talking about. It was a creepy feeling to know somebody'd been in here mocking my life. At the front door, I'd had Marian Wright's briefcase and my own, yet now I found no trace of either, not in the living room and not on the front porch.

The part that infuriated me more than any of the rest was the insufferable sense of being had. And worst of all, that Kathy might have arrived first. Chester could have been hurt. Or Liseea.

On the living room floor I found a section of two-by-four that I kept on the back porch to prop the storm door open in the summertime. The rope I'd been tied with was a section of clothesline I snapped to L.C.'s collar for walks. It too had been on the back porch. I stuffed the jumble of rope into a pocket.

It was only when I found the gated grille across the porthole on my front door had been unscrewed that I realized how much planning had gone into this. Removing the grille had allowed freedom of movement for the two-by-four, which had then been plunged through the hole like a piston. Had I come through the back door, I suppose he would have broadsided me.

After the initial blow felled me, he must have opened the door, dragged me inside, and smacked me again, using the butt end of the board each time, because there were three knots on the front of my head, the grain of the wood clearly visible in all three.

Though I had lain helpless and unconscious on the floor, he'd trussed me and taken me to the back of the house where, should I regain consciousness, it was unlikely I would be able to draw any attention. Apparently he had not been aware of the basement apartment, an easy mistake to make.

I felt as if I were sitting on a ticking time bomb, but the harder I tried to think of a reason for the attack, or for the feeling, the more nonsense I came up with.

I should have called the police on the cell phone in my truck, but they would take time to get here and then more time to question me, and all the while this time bomb would be ticking away. I had no certainty who'd been in my house. Or why this feeling of impending doom had descended on me.

Liseea and Chester made a fair amount of noise walking around to the front of the house, the way people make noise walking in a forest known to harbor bears.

My laptop computer had been stolen. The tape in my answering machine was missing. Two beers that had been in the refrigerator since Nigel's last visit had been consumed, the cans crushed and left on my table. A cigarette had been stubbed out on the center of my tablecloth. There was no lipstick on it.

I canvassed the locks on the front and back doors, then checked each window. It was hard to tell how he'd gotten in. Nothing was broken; nothing had been forced.

I went next door and knocked until Horace's rotund wife answered. I tried to smile but found I couldn't. "Thomas. You've hurt yourself."

"Nigel here?"

"He was a minute ago." She pivoted around and peered across the basement. "I guess he's out walking the boys."

I jogged through their backyard, vaulted the fence, and unlocked the side door to my garage. After flipping on the light and rummaging through my garden supplies, I found a bag of Weed and Feed and scooped a handful into my right-hand jacket pocket.

When I got into my truck, I backed out of the driveway and circled the neighborhood. Five minutes later I ambushed Nigel on a cracked sidewalk under a leafless maple tree. I still hadn't figured out what the race was about, but I knew it *was* a race. My assailant would return, and I needed details before he did. He could have killed or maimed me or merely left me unconscious, but he'd packed me away in the bathroom, and there had to be a reason.

"I've been thinking," Nigel said as I double-parked and rushed over to him. "You need to be more aggressive in your dealings with people. It wasn't dignified the way that man pushed you around the other day. On your own porch."

"And carrying a dog around town like a loaf of bread is?"

He looked offended. "Stratton tires easily. Briggs doesn't so much."

"He had a gun in his pocket, Nigel."

"Is that why you let him push you around?"

"It seemed to make sense at the time. Now tell me who you let into my house."

Nigel stepped back and, without looking me in the eye, gave off the general aura of having been deeply hurt. He petted the dog in his arms. "What makes you think I let somebody in?"

"I'm asking you who was in my house."

"You're just like your grandfather."

"You let somebody into my house, Nigel. Didn't you?"

"Maybe you don't want a father who does you favors?"

"Who'd you let in?"

"Wasn't he there when you got home?"

"He was there, but I didn't see who it was."

"He said he was your tax man. You don't recognize your own tax man?"

"Only one person? There was no woman?"

"Just the man. What did you do to your head?"

"I got blindsided."

"That's what I've been saying. You shouldn't let yourself get pushed around."

"It would be easier if you weren't letting strangers into my house."

"I wouldn't call it blindsided if he had a gun. You said he had a gun."

"I'm talking about tonight. Less than an hour ago. The man *last* night had a gun. Was this the same man? The man from last night?"

"I didn't pay all that much attention to the gentleman last night. It could have been."

"Describe him."

Nigel gave me a withering look and put the dachshund down, then put his hands into his jacket pockets. "This is why I got out of the service, people talking to me in precisely this manner. This precise manner."

"Who?"

"My sergeant, for one."

"No. Who did you let into my house?"

"He said he didn't want to wait out in the cold. It made sense to me. You're going to make an appointment with somebody, you should have the courtesy to be there to let them in."

"There *was* no appointment."

"He said there was."

"He lied."

"Why would a man say he had an appointment when he didn't?"

"Probably to get into my house, Nigel. So he could blind-side me. Now tell me what he looked like."

"Well-dressed. Well-spoken."

"Was he black?"

"Were you expecting one of those?"

I was fuming. Nigel clipped a leash onto one of the dogs' collars and followed the trotting mutt up the sidewalk, the dachshund straining against the leash until he choked, the second dog following at his leisure. "Nigel. I need to know what this guy looked like. It's important. He's coming back, and I think he wants to kill me."

Nigel waved a hand with a large military ring on one finger. "You're taking all your private investigation baloney far too seriously."

"You idiot, he's coming back. Now tell me what he looked like."

Nigel stopped. "That tears it. That really tears it. I'm return-ing to the coast. And after how hard I've tried to make things work between us."

"Thanks, Nigel," I shouted after him. "This guy gets me be-cause I don't know what he looks like, remember you could have stopped it." As I watched him trot the rest of the block and round the corner, I muttered, "You stupid sonofabitch."

In the truck I used the cellular phone. When I couldn't reach Kathy, I called Beulah and asked where she thought Kathy was. "Up at your neighbors' cabin, isn't she? She was set-ting up that meeting. You know. With the husband and wife. Up in Enumclaw. You were taking the wife on up. I thought you knew about it. She said you two were going to spend the week-end up there. Maybe it was supposed to be a surprise."

"Thanks, Beulah." I called the Vanderhoef house and learned from a nurse that Faith Vanderhoef was in Seattle to meet a man who was to drive her to a meeting. On a hunch, I asked for Faith's cell phone number. She answered on the first ring. "Thomas Black," I said. "Are we supposed to meet somewhere?"

"I'm sitting outside your house right now. I've been here a few minutes. Nobody answered."

"I'm a few blocks away, Faith. Do me a favor? Lock your doors and don't talk to anybody until I get there."

"I already did," she said in a small voice. "And I never do."

CHAPTER 33

I drove three blocks to a run-down brick apartment house on Brooklyn Avenue, got out, and knocked at an apartment on the second floor.

Built like a toadstool, short-legged and large-busted, Priscilla Pinch was a graduate student in mechanical engineering, said to be a genius. She had dark blond hair and a mouth like a longshoreman. In her late twenties, she was active in all the Northwest sports: sailboarding, Rollerblading, mountain climbing, telemark skiing. She had been introduced by a mutual friend as somebody who might be a cycling companion on my easy days.

Wearing socks and a tatty bathrobe, Priscilla plugged the door with her short, top-heavy body.

"Priscilla. Sorry to bother you without calling first, but could you look at these ropes we cut and tell me what you think about the knots?" Face devoid of expression, she inspected the knots.

"What you got here is a couple of fuckin' square knots and a bowline with a Yosemite finish."

"What does that mean?"

"It's something we use to tie a loop that won't come apart. You can put a strain on it but take it apart later. A loop comes apart climbin', you lose all your shit. Over here you got a coupla fuckin' clove hitches."

"Climbers use these?"

"You bet your ass."

"Damn."

In front of my house Faith Vanderhoef got out of her car, locked it, and then climbed into my truck with such agonizing slowness a bird with a broken wing could have done it faster. She said nothing when I moved away from the curb in a haze of burning rubber and squealing tires.

It was hard to calculate what sort of head start he had without knowing how long I'd been unconscious. I had been freed at seven-fifteen, but what time had I gone down? The only advantage was that it was Friday night, so traffic would have been heavier when he came through earlier.

Zigzagging in and out of the lines of cars on I-5, I took advantage of polite drivers, horned in on thoughtless ones, and scared the ones who weren't already lunatics. I was sweating so badly I could hardly grip the hard blue steering wheel.

After a few minutes Faith Vanderhoef said, "Are we in some kind of hurry?"

"Something like that." Faith had a death grip on the door handle. "You planning to bail out?" I asked, grinning.

"No. It's just . . . you seem so intense."

"I guess I want to get this over with."

"Where are we headed?"

"A cabin outside of Enumclaw on the way to Crystal Mountain. One of my neighbors owns it and lets us use it from time to time. Their daughter will be there tonight with friends. I hope they don't beat us in this traffic. It's not a good place to meet. Were they driving out together? Kathy and your husband?"

"I don't know the answer to that."

"And why is the meeting out here, anyway? Did Kathy say?"

"She said she read an article about it that claimed meetings like this should be somewhere the principals have never been and will never go again. It works better."

"Sometimes Kathy's too diligent." My suspicion was Vanderhoef had spent the afternoon hashing out the etiquette of modern sexual relations with Irene Golinda. If so, she could hardly have failed to mention the fact that I was telling people he was passing around HIV. After Kathy contacted him and told him she wanted a four-way meeting, he wouldn't have missed the implication: if she hadn't been told already, Faith was going to hear he was HIV positive. It wouldn't make him happy.

"Maybe I'd better drop you off somewhere and go in alone," I said. "You know, get the idle chitchat over with before you come. There's an old German farmer up the road who's always looking for somebody to palaver with."

"Something's happened, hasn't it?"

"I'll drop you off at this house up the road."

Thinking traffic would be lighter, I took 169 through Renton, but we got gridlocked in the Kent Valley anyway. The pace picked up past Ravensdale and Black Diamond, and then we hit Enumclaw, a quaint little town under the shadow of Mount Rainier, with flat, square blocks and colossal old houses. People out here owned horses and wore cowboy boots and planted vegetable gardens in their back lots and, when the weather cooperated, hung laundry on lines.

It was a clear night, and frost was beginning to salt the valley. The mountain stood out like a small, snow-clad planet that had crashed this side of the horizon. The glaciers glowed dully, stealing light from an almost-full moon and a couple of billion stars. Low whitish clouds scudded overhead sporadically. If I hadn't been so nervous, it would have been peachy.

Liseea's parents owned a ten-acre spread on a rolling, grassy hillside off a forest service road, the grass buried in snow this time of year. The gravel road climbed from the highway, and soon there were dirty, snowplowed drifts along the roadside.

Furnished with cast-offs from their home, their last set of chipped dishware, their former sofa, the cabin was constructed of logs and a metal roof that sounded off like drums when squirrels ran across it. The rain beating on it could lull even the worst insomniac to sleep. A covered porch encircled three sides of the house.

When we got to the fields where a small cluster of houses

stood, everything brightened considerably from the moonlight on the snow, the road a muddy swatch through the white. I dropped Faith off at a small green house set off by itself.

"If there's any trouble, you call the county cops from here. And don't show yourself." I waited until the old man opened his door. I could see her chagrin as she tried to explain her situation, but he shooed her inside and waved happily to me as I drove on.

Casting shadows like a dim sun, the moon coming over the horizon was about as big as I'd ever seen it. The frozen snow on the trees in the foothills around us looked like white lace. The lower slopes of Rainier loomed and seemed to grow huge as I drove the last two hundred yards to the cabin. The treeless property had been in Liseea's family for ninety years, and tonight it was snowy and barren except for the house and, farther across the slope, a weathered structure that had been the original cabin. Kids in the area called it the witch house.

Three vehicles were parked outside the cabin: Kathy's Firebird, a black Mercedes, and a Ford Escort station wagon driven by Hank Torgerson, my downstairs neighbor. Liseea, Hank, and Kathy were on the front porch. Chester was out in the yard with some kids he'd flushed from the neighborhood. They must have been visiting grandparents for the weekend, because I didn't know of any kids who lived up here. Chester ran over to me and said, "Hey, Buuuud! What took ya so long?"

"Kathy! Are you all right?" I said, bounding onto the porch.

"Sure I am. Why wouldn't I be? Where's Faith?" She kissed me and stood back to look me over. "You were supposed to pick her up. What happened to your face? Aren't you going to shut your motor off?"

"He inside?"

"Yes."

"Long time no see, Bud." It was Chester again, tugging on my coat.

"Yeah, Chester. Hi. How you doin'? Look, can you and the other kids stay outside for a while?"

"If we can play at the witch house."

"Okay. But don't go inside." I turned to Kathy. "He try anything?"

"As a matter of fact, he did."

"What?"

"What happened to your face?"

"What'd he try?"

"I swear I saw him slip something into a soda he wanted me to drink. But I wouldn't . . ."

They were large, open rooms with knotty pine walls and hardwood floors. Randolph Vanderhoef, in a suit without the tie, sat on the edge of an overstuffed chair holding his head with one hand, cupping his groin with the other. It was as if he were trying to decide where his brain was.

I strode across the room, jumped into the air, and drop-kicked the side of his shoulder. I had been aiming for his skull.

It barely affected him. His huge head rolled to one side and both hands came away from his body. He looked up at me, then stood up on wobbly legs.

"You sorry sucker," he whispered, clenching his teeth.

One pocket of his jacket was sagging as if there were something heavy in it. He reached for it. Before he could pull his hand out, I flicked a fistful of Weed and Feed into his face.

A pistol flew off to the side of the room and bounced on the hardwood floor as Vanderhoef raised both hands to his face and began clawing at his eyes. He dropped to the floor on his knees and moaned.

"Goddamn!" he said. "God*damn*! I'm blind. You blinded me. Shit! I'm blind."

I stepped to one side and toed the pistol under a piece of furniture.

"What are you doing?" Kathy said. "Thomas, stop it."

"I guess I was just a little tense."

"Oh, you were, were you?"

"A little."

"Should I tell Mr. Vanderhoef you're feeling more relaxed

now and you won't be kicking him until you build up more tension?"

"Don't worry about it. They could use this guy's skull in a Vikings game and not dent it."

Liseea and Hank Torgerson came into the house and then backed partway out the doorway in disbelief. I said, "Get some water. Lots of water. We're going to have to flush his eyes for twenty minutes."

They ended up holding him at the kitchen sink under the spigot.

"Thomas," Kathy said. "What happened to your face?"

"Him."

"In Seattle?"

"A couple of hours ago."

I stooped, pulled the pistol out from under a couch, and dumped the bullets into my pocket with the weed killer. I dropped the empty gun into my other pocket. "How long has he been here?"

"Oh, about two hours."

"The two of you've been here two hours?"

"I know what you're thinking. We got into a little tussle maybe fifteen minutes ago, right before they showed up. I had to knee him in a weak spot. For a while there he could barely stand. He was trying to recover from it when you came in and gave him the business."

"Two hours?" It was nine o'clock. Two hours plus a driving time of an hour meant Vanderhoef couldn't have left Seattle any later than six. Chester had sawed through my ropes at seven-fifteen.

Kathy patted my swollen forehead with a wet cloth. I couldn't figure out where she'd gotten the cloth. I hadn't noticed her leave the room or come back. "Are you all right? This eye over here is beginning to swell."

"This eye over here? You talk like they're on tentacles."

"They look like they are. Are you sure it was him in Seattle? You know what the doctor said. Any head injury could put you back in a hospital bed."

Kathy had followed me into the kitchen. Vanderhoef remained slumped over the sink like a dead man, Liseea on one side, big, blond Hank on the other. The knuckles on Hank's left hand were raw and bloody, but then, he was always getting scraped at his construction job.

"You been timing it?" I said to Hank.

"Eighteen and a half minutes," he replied calmly. I took one of Vanderhoef's wet wrists, snapped a pair of handcuffs on, then pulled his other wrist behind his back and cuffed his hands together.

"What the hell?" Vanderhoef bellowed. "Now what?"

Kathy said, "I hope you're sure. There could be hell to pay."

"You asshole," Vanderhoef blubbered from the sink. He turned around, hair and face sopping, eyes bloodshot and filled with tears. Liseea mopped his head with a dry towel. "I lose my vision, I'm suing your ass. In fact, I'm suing your ass anyway. What the hell did you do that for?"

I went outside, turned my truck engine off, got an empty water bottle from my kit, a large one, filled it with lukewarm water at the sink in the kitchen, and handed it to Liseea. I pushed Vanderhoef down onto a sofa in the living room, where he'd wandered, and told him to put his head back. Liseea put a towel around his neck and helped him flush his eyes some more. Nursing wasn't natural for her, and she looked awkward doing it.

Kathy pulled me back outside by one arm. On the cold porch she said, "Thomas, was there a specific reason you attacked my client's husband?"

"The same reason you attacked him."

"He was coming on to you?"

"No. He had a gun."

"You kicked him and *then* he pulled the gun."

"Kathy, I got hit in the head with a board. My eyeballs feel like raisins in a microwave. I couldn't fight fair. Besides, he put the make on you. It made me nuts."

"It did?"

"Yes."

"It was a mistake to meet a strange man in a situation like

this. I thought you'd be out here as soon as you and his wife got my messages."

"You can't get a message if somebody takes the tape out of your machine."

"What?"

"Somebody came in and hit me and tied me up and was gone by the time I came to." I walked over to the Mercedes, took the keys out of the ignition, and opened the trunk. Marian Wright's briefcase was on top, mine underneath. My laptop computer was there too, as well as the tiny tape from my answering machine. Standing next to me, Kathy said, "Look at the size of this trunk. You could put a picnic table in here."

"Recognize these?" I pointed to the briefcases. Her eyes widened. "He was asking about Wright, wasn't he?"

"He was asking about everything. Your wife says she wants to meet you with a lawyer and a private detective the day after you're caught in flagrante delicto in a public rest room, you'd figure something was up too."

"And he was acting as if we were never going to show?"

"God, Thomas. That's exactly how he was acting. I didn't pay attention because I kept thinking you'd get here any minute. And then Hank and Liseea showed up unexpectedly with Chester. I guess her mom forgot she promised the cabin to us. But you're right. He was such a jerk. He thought he could flatter me by telling me how pretty I was and how I had these wonderful eyes and—"

"You do."

"What?"

"Have wonderful eyes."

"He wasn't even looking at my eyes. He wanted to argue about it, so I covered them and asked him what color. He said 34B."

"A real card."

"Yeah, but how did he know I'm a 34B?"

"Are you?"

"A perky 34B."

"You left a black brassiere at my place. He used it to gag me."

"How very Freudian, given your predilection for boobs."

"What do you mean? I don't have any—"

"He kept suggesting we have something to drink. He even got a Pepsi and opened it for me. But I already told you about that. Then, just before Hank and Liseea got here, he started grabbing at me."

"That's when you kneed him?"

"That class I took—they said if you feel you have to defend yourself, don't mess around."

"I'm glad you're such a good student. He stole my briefcase. Marian's briefcase. He probably had been planning to skip this meeting, but he realized you probably knew too much. So he came to find out."

"He asked a ton of questions."

"He was trying to decide whether he had to kill us both and if he could get away with it."

"Then it was Vanderhoef in your backyard with the baseball bat?"

"Fears. Bain Littrell admitted to that."

"But who killed Fears? Bruno? Abdul Sarwar? Not this guy?"

"I don't think it was two black men. Or even one black man."

"But Fears told you on the phone Marian had been meeting with a black man and a woman."

"I think he had a gun to his head when he told me that. If he'd had a normal voice, I might have heard the stress in it, but his voice sounded so funny ordinarily, I didn't catch it."

"Who had the gun on Fears?"

"Let's go back in and see what he'll tell us."

"Thomas, this citizen's arrest business could get sticky. I mean, I for one saw you kicking him half to death."

"They won't make you testify."

"Why not?"

"You'll be my wife."

"As soon as I find a current *TV Guide* and clear a wedding date."

"Be thankful I don't have cable."

CHAPTER 34

The lights were all on by the time we got back inside. Hank Torgerson leaned against the kitchen doorway, meaty arms folded across his chest. The situation was making him uncomfortable. Liseea continued to trickle water into Randolph Vanderhoef's eyes as he sat on the sofa with his hands cuffed behind his back.

"You were at my house a couple of hours ago, weren't you?"

"I was right here with your tight-ass fiancée. I tried to loosen her up, but she went mental defective on me."

"We'll know more when we have the police analyze that drink you tried to give her." Vanderhoef brushed Liseea's ministering hands away with his head and glanced around quickly for the Pepsi can, but we had stashed it in a high cupboard to keep it from Chester, who would drink anything. "My father let you in. That gives us a witness who can place you at my house. What happened? You think you could search the place before I showed up?"

"What is this? An arrest? You can't arrest me!"

"First, I'm going to bring your wife here and we're going to have a chat, just the four of us."

"Get me a lawyer." As if she'd been sitting next to a fire that was getting too hot, Liseea got up and stood next to Hank.

"You're going to need a bunch of lawyers. My father. Finger-prints in my house. This drink here. You weren't planning ahead, were you?"

"You give the police a drink with Valium in it, how're they going to know who put it there? It won't stand up."

"Who said it was Valium?" The room was silent for a few beats.

"Well, who said I was at your place?"

I pulled the knotted ropes out of my pocket. "A bowline with a Yosemite finish."

"Shit. That's nothing."

"And what we found in the trunk of your car. You took your time out here because you thought nobody else was com-ing. I was tied up, and Faith wouldn't show because I wasn't bringing her."

"Mr. Black," Hank Torgerson said. "I'm only following a lit-tle of this, but I don't think that man should be handcuffed."

Ignoring Hank, I said, "You had something to do with Mar-ian Wright's death. That's the only possible reason for all this."

Vanderhoef chewed his lower lip and said nothing. Kathy and I asked more questions, but he remained silent.

It took only a few minutes to drive up the road and pick up Faith. Paler than when I'd dropped her off, she was clearly ner-vous. Even though we could both see the Mercedes in front of the house, the trunk open, she said, "Is he there?"

"He won't give you any trouble."

"I just don't want . . ."

"What?" We were getting out of my truck now.

"Nothing. I'm just . . . This is the worst night of my life."

"You're probably not the only one." I walked around the front of my Ford and held her shoulders gently. She had pale blue eyes, a fleck of black in the right one. "You're doing the right thing. And you're a brave woman. You're in a terrible pre-dicament most people wouldn't know how to deal with. I ad-mire your courage."

"But I can't even talk to him myself. I feel like such a . . . wimp."

"I doubt anybody'd want to talk to him alone. I wouldn't."

"Really?"

"Really."

By the time we got inside, Hank and Liseea had left the room. Faith took a chair along one wall, almost twenty feet from her husband. I stood in front of Vanderhoef and next to Kathy, who was standing also. Eyes fixed on a lamp across the room, Randolph Vanderhoef sat on the couch in silence. If he'd seen his wife come in, he made no acknowledgment of it.

"Faith has decided to file for divorce," Kathy said. She waited a few moments but there was no response. "Her reasons are obvious. She is HIV-infected and she knows you gave it to her. She wants you out of the house this weekend. She wants you to know she loved you once and she doesn't know how you could have done this to her. She is aware that you've had extra-marital sex. She finds that unconscionable. She wants you to know she cannot forgive you for what you've cost her. And for what you've cost your daughter, Adianna."

"Adianna?" Vanderhoef blurted, coming to life suddenly, eyes bulging. "I didn't cost Adianna a damned thing."

"You cost her a mother," I said.

It wasn't until he sniffled that we realized Vanderhoef was crying. He turned as far away from me as he could get, and his shoulders began heaving. Squatting on the low couch with his hands cuffed behind his back, it was an awkward motion. We let him put on a show, if it was a show. After a bit he said, "What? You think I did it on purpose? I didn't do anything on purpose. I don't even know where I got it. Once I found out I had it, it was too late. By that time, there was no way you didn't have it too, honey. What did I do that was so awful? Allowed you to live a normal life for a few years without the knowledge that you were going to die? Was that so rotten? You had it. I had it. There wasn't anything anybody could do."

In a surprisingly strong voice, Faith Vanderhoef said, "You could have stopped spreading it to half the county."

"I never spread it anywhere."

"Black tells me otherwise."

"That bastard's a damned liar."

"I don't think so."

"Anybody who got it from me was going to get it anyway."

"Like Deanna Ayers," I said. "She was going to get it anyway?"

"I don't even know who you're talking about."

"You drugged her drink and raped her, the same as you were planning for Kathy."

Faith looked down at the floor.

"Don't believe them." Vanderhoef looked entreatingly at his wife, his face puffy and red, eyes bloodshot. "I don't know how I got it. Probably a blood transfusion."

"Probably in a men's rest room," said Faith.

"That's bullshit. I used to beat up queers in the service."

"After the blow job or before?" Faith said bitterly. Clenching her handbag in front of her, she rose. "You never loved me. You never loved anybody but yourself. It was more important to you to get into some stranger's pants than it was to keep your home and your family together. You deserve this. You deserve every bit of it. I'm the one who doesn't."

The room was silent for ten seconds. When Faith walked outside onto the porch, Kathy followed, and a cold gust of wind came through the door off the moonlit snow. Vanderhoef, who had stopped sobbing, glared sullenly at the wall.

It wasn't until after I walked Vanderhoef outside and was pushing him into my truck that the yelling commenced, two children racing across the snowy slope in a panic, slipping and skidding and skiing on one foot and screaming, "Bennie and that dumb kid are in the witch house! Bennie and that dumb kid are in the witch house!"

Kathy, who had been on the porch with her arm around Faith Vanderhoef, turned her head to look past the corner of the house toward the old cabin. "Oh, my Lord," she said.

I stepped away from my truck to get my own clear view past the house and saw smoke creeping out of the dilapidated cabin, crawling along the moonlit snow. I knew instinctively that Bennie was one of the neighbor kids, and the one they referred to as the *dumb kid* was Chester. He wasn't dumb, but with the thick glasses and his mannerisms, other kids generally thought he was.

I pulled a flashlight out of my glove box and sprinted across the slope. As I ran I zipped my coat up and pulled the collar as high as possible. Hank Torgerson was in front of me. I didn't catch Hank, but I quickly passed Liseea, who cradled her huge belly in her arms as she picked her way through the footprints in the snow.

The property was a square, the new cabin in the front, and smack in the center of the field, the old cabin—the kids' so-called witch house.

Plumes of thick smoke were pouring out the front windows on the first floor, smaller puffs issuing from the upper floor. The house was vacant, and I had an idea how fast a vacant house could burn.

Kathy and I arrived at the structure at the same time, but she was in a skirt and a short-sleeved blouse with a light sweater over it. There was no question she would stay outside. Hank was already on his knees, braving torrents of smoke from the front door, calling out to his son, hacking. I could hear children somewhere inside.

As Hank called out, a child, disoriented and spinning in semicircles, stumbled out through the front door, followed by a large bubble of thick, gray smoke. Hank grabbed him before he could stagger back inside. "The dumb kid's lost," he said, coughing. "The dumb kid's lost."

Still on his knees at the front door, Hank handed the boy off to Kathy, then turned back and put his face into the smoke. "Chester!" he shouted, making no move to enter, although at his post in the doorway he was swallowing as much smoke as he would have inside. His skin was already discolored from the soot. Liseea stood below us in the snow, trying to catch her breath.

I knelt next to Hank, clicked the flashlight on, and was readying myself to crawl inside under the heat when Vander-hoef tapped my foot.

"Get these off me," he panted. "Get these off me."

"Hank," I said. "How 'bout you go left and I go right?"

"Chester!" Hank called out without looking at me. "Chester!" We all listened for a moment.

"You go left and I'll go right," I said again, but Hank was staring inside like a tired bird dog who'd lost a duck. "Hank?"

"Come on, we're talking kids here," yelled Vanderhoef. "Don't fuck around, Black! Can't you see he's useless?"

"Hank?" I said. "Hank?"

I reached into my jeans pocket, dug out the tiny key, and unlocked one bracelet on Vanderhoef. As soon as it was loose he leaped off the creaky porch and splashed down into the crunchy snow, heading for the main house at a high gallop. "Shit," I said. I looked down at the two boys who'd given the original alarm, their eyes filled with expectation. "How many kids are missing?"

"Bennie and the dumb kid," they said in unison.

"Who's that?" I nodded at the boy who'd stumbled out of the smoke and who was throwing up into the snow as Kathy held him.

"That's Augie," said the taller of the two boys.

"Do you know where they are in the house?"

They shook their heads. "Augie had Mom's lighter."

Even with the flashlight, it was black inside. I hadn't been prepared for impenetrability or the absoluteness of the dark. I tried not to breathe, but I was still puffing hard from the running, and it was only a few moments before I was forced to gulp great drafts of toxic smoke that seared the small spaces in my lungs. The flashlight beam was visible only when held close. Although I had watched a vacant house burn to the ground six months earlier, I had never in my life been inside a burning building, and I was surprised at how soon I became frightened and at how frightened I remained.

"Chester," I called out, keeping along one wall. "Bennie?" The rooms were empty, the floors windswept and bare. There was nothing left of the structure but bare wood and boarded-over windows. The fire hadn't flamed up yet, but if it got going, I suspected the place would go up like a box of wooden matches.

Finally, in a back room on the first floor, I felt a pair of tiny legs. I grabbed them and they kicked, and then kicked again when I got a solid grip on them. "Chester? Is that you?"

"Hey, Bud," he coughed. I could tell by his voice he was trying to be brave. Given the situation, he seemed impossibly
calm. But then, he'd seemed calm a couple of hours earlier cutting me out of the ropes.

"Is there another kid in here?"

"Augie."

"We got Augie."

"There's one more. I forgot his name. He peed on the wall."

"You know where he is, Chester?"

"I was trying to find him, but I got lost."

It took longer to get him outside than it had to locate him.
We never did approach the seat of the fire, not that we needed
to. Nor did we find traces of the third boy. It didn't seem hot inside, merely smoky and dark, and very, very lonely until I came
across Chester. For a few minutes we were lost together. I
shouted once for Bennie, but it started me coughing too badly
to try it again. We ended up at the back of the house and eventually found a window, kicked the boards off, and crawled out.

We sat in the snow under the stars trying to clear our lungs,
too weak to walk around to the front. We kept spitting, first
Chester and then me. The house still had not burst into flame.
I handed him the toy car I had in my pocket. "Oh, wow," he
said. "I got one just like it at home."

After a while my head started to clear, and I realized there
were voices coming from the other side of the building. When
I stood, my head whirled and my shaky legs had almost no
strength. I was wet all over, whether from perspiration or from
sitting in the snow, I could not tell. When we got to the front
of the house, Chester skidded across the slippery yard and
bounded into his father's arms. Hank looked over his son's
shoulder at me, but there was nothing in his eyes—no relief, no
gratitude, no curiosity. It was as if Chester had saved himself,
or as if he wanted to believe he had.

Kathy, Liseea, Faith, and the three other boys were lined up
in front of the structure. Because the house had a rotting roof
and it had been raining and snowing the past few weeks, heavily up here in the hills, everything was soaked. The structure
was burning like a wet punk. All smoke and no flame.

"Is the other kid out yet? Bennie?" I asked.

"My God, you're safe," Kathy said, hugging me so hard I thought she was going to break a rib. "You were gone so long. How's Chester?"

"He's okay. I gotta go back for the other kid."

"Vanderhoef is getting him."

"Vanderhoef took off."

"Down to his car to get a flashlight and a blanket. He came right back. He went in practically behind you. You didn't see him?"

"I didn't see anything. He really went in?"

"Right after you."

"Damn." Shortly before Vanderhoef blundered from the building, sirens began keening in the distance. The back of the house was orange with flame now. I had never seen a man's face so red. He came out carrying an object wrapped in a long wool blanket. When he unrolled the blanket onto the grass, the object turned out to be the missing boy, conscious, but not looking so hot, although he wasn't nearly so bad off as Vander- hoef, who had run approximately four hundred yards prior to entering the building. My guess was the boy had been lost somewhere in a corner waiting for help, and hadn't been using as much oxygen as his rescuer.

It wasn't until I stooped next to Vanderhoef to thank him that I realized he'd been burned about the face and neck and the back of his head. He must have been in some pain, al- though he showed no sign of it. He sprawled in the snow, knees propped in front of him, fists against his forehead. The shiny handcuffs dangled from one wrist. Faith stood to one side and watched with an extraordinarily curious look on her sad face.

I said, "Thanks, Randolph. For getting the kid."

"My pleasure."

"No, really. Thanks. I thought you were long gone."

"Hell, no. When I was little I saw a fire where some kids died. I never forgot it. I wasn't going to stand by and let it hap- pen again."

"You didn't even know these kids."

"I got a kid. I know kids."

"Well, thanks."

"You want to know something, Black?"

"What?"

"You're still an asshole."

"You too."

"I know."

CHAPTER 35

As I stood up, Vanderhoef said, "Black, you were right."

The burns on his neck extended down along his spine. Most of his suit had been burned off or burned to him, but for now, shock and ignorance of his condition was protecting him. "I was right about what?"

"You got a smoke?"

"I don't smoke. I didn't think you did either."

"Not usually in public." I looked into his eyes. He gave me that charming smile again, as much of it as he could muster around the sooty nostrils and singed mustache. "I couldn't do it. You were lying there, and all I had to do was put my foot on your neck, but I couldn't do it. I thought I was going to, but when it came down to it, I got squeamish."

"So you came here to meet with Kathy?"

"I thought if I had time to think about it, I could go back and do it. But I couldn't have."

"And Kathy?"

"I needed to find out what she knew."

"What were you afraid she knew?"

"That I've got HIV. I couldn't have either of you telling Howard."

"Howard?"

"Faith's father. He still owns fifty-one percent of the company. If he knew I gave Faith AIDS, he would make sure I never got anything out of Vanderhoef Sports. That's a little less than a third of a million a year I could kiss goodbye."

"So you were going to kill Kathy?"

"Hell, no. I was backing out of the whole arrangement when you got here."

"Sure you were. You were backing out of a kick in the nuts."

"I'm telling you, I changed my mind."

"What about Marian Wright? What happened?"

"She found out I have HIV. I don't have any signs of it, you know. I never did. I've had it for years and I feel fine. But she found out, and she was going to Faith. That damned old busybody. I got to drinking one night and called her for a meeting. I parked my car behind the fish hatchery out by Snoqualmie and called her on my cellular phone, told her my Benz broke down. She came out and picked me up, got to screaming at me, and stopped on the highway just a half mile away. Then she got smacked by that passing motorist."

"That's not how it happened, Randolph."

"Yeah, it is."

"The medical examiner said somebody may have tied her hands."

"Well, she started scratching at me. She was gonna hurt herself."

"So, for her own good, you tied her up and then later threw her out in front of that car?"

"I didn't throw her anywhere, man. Listen to me. She was hysterical. She was so afraid of me. The old bitch. We were talking in the rain next to her car—I untied her and everything—and she saw somebody coming up the road and jumped out. There was nothing I could do."

"You pushed her."

"I wrestled with her. But it was to stop her. She said something that didn't make sense about her lawyer and stepped into the roadway."

A couple of fire engines chugged up the hill, but it was too late. The old cabin was crackling in flames, and we could feel the heat beginning to melt the snow around us. The radiation from the fire felt good against my damp back. Mount Rainier sat behind the burning cabin like a painted backdrop in a high school play. A pair of firefighters rushed over to check on Vanderhoef, then grimaced when they realized how badly he'd been burned.

"And what about Houser Fears?" I said as a firefighter began cutting Vanderhoef's shirt off.

"Who?"

"He was murdered last night over by Seward Park."

"Listen, Black. I have a real bad feeling about how hurt I am. I'll deny this later if I make it, but you might as well know, Fears was blackmailing me. Blackmail's illegal."

"You murdered him, didn't you?" Vanderhoef swiveled his gray eyes toward me, and suddenly he looked remarkably sad, almost as sad as his wife.

"Look, Black. I didn't exactly feel like the citizen of the year after that old lady got run down, all right? She claimed she got the virus from me, but I never saw the old bitch before. And then she claimed her husband got it from some woman who got it from somebody who—it was all bullshit. Anyway, it wasn't my fault. What was I supposed to do at the accident? Come out of the woods and tell the cops I was with her? They would have found out what she was doing, and they would have blamed me for her death. The whole world would have found out about me being HIV positive. I would have lost the company. And one more thing, Black. I never did anything in that rest room. You were way off base there."

"Sure, Randolph."

"You *were*. Way off base."

"One thing I don't understand. Why go around knocking off all these people? You could have knocked off your wife and it would have all ended. Or your father-in-law."

"I never knocked off anyone."

"Okay. You never knocked off anyone. Not Marian Wright. Not Fears. But if your wife were to disappear, or your father-in-law . . ."

"Are you crazy? I love my wife."

CHAPTER 36

It was the type of formal ceremony I'd always feared. With the gown that cost enough to send an ape into space and the rented church and the tuxedos and the bridesmaids' outfits and the floral arrangements and the grouchy organist and the team of ill-dressed video people and gawking relatives and months of haggling phone calls to get it all to work. I went along with it for Kathy's sake, but if we'd taken a vote, I would have voted for dual frontal lobotomies.

Kathy didn't have the faintest idea how depressed I could get in a tuxedo in front of four hundred people, yet just seeing her decked out in her gown and exuding that radiant thingamajig brides exude made it an experience I would treasure for the rest of my life. At least, that part of it.

Not once at the wedding or in the months preceding the wedding did Kathy have an inkling of my discomfort, for I was smoother than a life insurance salesman at a high school reunion. Not an inkling. In only one of the official photos did I lose my composure and let loose a jaundiced smile, which I managed to neatly explain away two weeks later while we were pawing through the returned shots.

Nigel didn't make it to the ceremony, partly because I more or less forgot to invite him, and partly because the day after the fire he slipped out of town and flew home to New Jersey. Later I found out he'd wheedled airfare and several hundred bucks in pocket money from my sister, who later pleaded with me to reimburse her. I handed over the airfare but told her to eat the pocket money. She should have known better. If he'd played true to form, he'd blown the wad on martinis before clearing the airport. Nigel flew the two hot dogs home with him, but L.C. he abandoned in my backyard without explanation. Once again I adopted the mongrel, who, now that he'd been spoiled, made a habit of squatting on the front porch waiting for Nigel's return. Marian Wright's two poodles were eventually adopted by Horace's grown son.

I sent Nigel four rolls of photographs we'd taken together in Seattle. He wrote back and asked for three of the pictures to be reproduced again and then mailed to him posthaste. They were the only three of him alone, and as I thought about it, the request became a metaphor for our entire relationship. Seventy pictures of us together, but he wanted the three of himself. A day later he telephoned, and after asking how L.C. was doing—his first concern always being the animals around the people he claimed to love—he asked for the three photos again. He was so eager and so rude and so adamant that I quietly vowed never to send them.

At the reception, my sister confessed that Nigel had been drunk most of the time he'd stayed with her and that she had kicked him out after he called her a Nazi and christened her living room carpet while trying to pee into a vase. That was the night he showed up on my doorstep.

The three boys who'd been in the burning building suffered various degrees of smoke inhalation, though they were up and having snowball fights within days.

Under a court order, Susie Scudder began receiving payments from Abdul Sarwar, who eagerly drove the hundred-mile round trip twice a month to visit her son, Tobey, who in turn bristled with pride at finally having a father. It was an odd spectacle to be on the sidelines of, because I had been four when I *lost* my father and now Tobey was four when he *found* his.

After Burt Roberson's wife saw the video, she filed for divorce and then two weeks later fingered him for stealing trade secrets from the company he worked for, the same crime Marian had stumbled onto. Rumor had it Roberson fled to Utah, which was the same place my father had fled to prospect for uranium after our divorce.

For reasons I could never fathom, Bain Littrell called one night sounding slightly bombed and told me she'd had a serious problem with a customer a couple of weeks previous and had decided to retire from the life. She said she thought it might make a puritanical type like me happy to hear about it. I told her that, in fact, it did.

We had a chemist test the Pepsi Vanderhoef had been trying to get Kathy to drink and found it contained enough Valium to drop a cow. I didn't believe any of his good intentions speech, although he seemed to have believed part of it while he gave it.

For thirty-eight days Vanderhoef remained in critical condition in the burn ward at Harborview Hospital. A day after the staff predicted recovery, his heart sucked in a blood clot and stopped, oddly, the same malady that had killed Chuck Wright. Upon Vanderhoef's death, the local newspapers turned him into a hero, lauding his actions that night in Enumclaw. Two television stations did segments for their five o'clock news, paeans of praise. What nobody knew was that Homicide had gathered enough evidence to charge him for murder, discovering, among other items, the weapon that killed Houser Fears in a bag of pitons and carabiners in his office.

It was late spring, the middle of the week, with only a handful of tourists on the Washington coast, and we were walking north along the tide line toward Pacific Beach and the bluffs of the Quinault Indian Reservation. It was our belated honeymoon. Waves raced across the flats and splashed our bare feet. Farther up the seashore a stern wind whipped the ocean and blew sprays of dry sand into the weeds like segmented ghosts. We had checked into a place called the Sandpiper and had, carrying our shoes, walked to the shore from our room. Kathy's hair was in a ponytail, frizzed around her temples. The pockets of her yellow raincoat clanked with shells and agates. The pockets of my windbreaker were empty.

Eventually our conversation got around to three months earlier, and we hashed over the facts once more. Contrary to how things had looked, Bruno had had no connection with the murder of Fears. Houser Fears had been obsessed with Dee, blaming her illness on Vanderhoef, the way Marian blamed it on Vanderhoef, the way I blamed it on him. Later, the police uncovered evidence to indicate Fears was blackmailing Vanderhoef. Wanting Fears off his back, Vanderhoef had gone to him that Thursday night and forced him to phone me. He must have got the drop on him fairly easily and decided he could get me too.

My guess was he had been planning to make it look as if Fears and I had killed each other. It would have been a neat trick. Only something happened before I arrived that caused him to shoot Fears and flee. Not the type of man who was likely to sit around quietly and wait to be executed, Houser probably had jumped him. And the cigarette with lipstick on it? Fears's daughter had left it during a visit earlier that day.

The next night, Vanderhoef went to my house and tried again. He told me why he'd tied me up instead of simply killing me, but it had taken me a while to believe it. He'd killed Houser the night before, and he didn't much like it. He'd killed Marian and didn't much like that either. He had been entertaining second thoughts. Also, he'd wanted to see what Kathy knew before finishing me off. It followed a certain kind of logic. Had I not escaped, had Hank and Liseea not shown up, he would have killed Kathy at the cabin and come back for me.

And the black males the landlord saw running away from Fears's place? A product of racial paranoia.

The man I saw driving away from the accident scene the night we hit Marian wasn't Bruno. Nor was he Vanderhoef. He was a man who'd come upon the accident by chance and left the same way. The witness, Martha Chin, saw Vanderhoef on foot, but he'd parked over the hill by the fish hatchery.

"You know what, Thomas?" Kathy said. "You went into a

burning building to rescue those boys and didn't get any recognition. The newspapers wrote up Vanderhoef and never even mentioned you. Weren't you peeved?"

"I'd just as soon they didn't mention me. All I need to ruin my job is my picture in the paper."

"Were you scared in there?"

"Not really," I lied.

"Why not?" She knew I'd been scared. And she knew I knew she knew.

"Too dumb."

"You're not dumb."

"Well, I wasn't scared."

She kissed me. "Hmmmm. Then maybe you are dumb. Hank never thanked you, did he?"

"He's still too busy ignoring the fact that he froze up in the doorway. By the way, they're moving out in a week. They found a place closer to his work. So we need a new renter downstairs."

"He's only ten minutes away from work now! I know why they're moving. It's because he can't stand to face you every day. You give him a place to live, you save his kid's life, and he can't get away too soon."

"I already wrote the ad for a new tenant. Wanted: six-foot-tall, blond, blue-eyed Swedish masseuse to rent studio apartment."

"Masseuse?" She shouldered me halfway across the beach toward the waves like an aggressive lineman. I fought, but she pushed me into knee-deep water. For an hour Kathy and I strolled the hard-packed wet beach, then headed back through the dunes to the Sandpiper. I caught her watching me as we hosed the sand off our feet at the side of the building.

"Happy?" I asked.

"Utterly. I know you hated the wedding and everything that went along with it. Thank you for not getting lost in the desert at the last minute." My friend Elmer Slezak had gotten lost in the desert four hours before one of his weddings.

"I didn't hate it."

"Come on, Thomas. Who are you trying to kid?"

"I have pictures to prove I was delighted with the whole affair."

"Like a cadaver is delighted with the velvet liner and the formaldehyde."

"I *was* delighted."

"There's even one picture where you look so miserable you tried to blame it on gas."

"I had a burrito for lunch." She was laughing. "I did. I learned a valuable lesson. My next wedding, no Mexican food at lunch."

She kept laughing. "How many weddings are you planning?"

"Eight, ten. Fifteen if I live long enough. I kind of like this wife business."

"A burrito." She laughed.

"I didn't fool you even a little?"

"You fooled everyone except me and maybe my mother. Thanks. You looked so handsome in that tux, and you were so charming to all our friends. And you made me laugh. All night."

"What do you mean 'all night'?"

"You know what I mean. And you did hate it. Everything except the cake. You pigged down five pieces of cake."

"Three. I pigged down three." I looked down at her pretty eyes and her wind-burned cheeks and kissed her. "You're welcome. You were beautiful. You always are, but you were special that day. I'll never forget it. On the day I die, at the instant I go, that's the image that'll be burned into my brain."

"Now, don't get all sloppy and sentimental on me. As soon as we get the masseuse in the basement, you'll forget. You have a bad history of falling for the babe in the basement."

"The babe in the basement. I like that." We were at the room now. I took the key that was hanging off the little slug of driftwood and opened the door. I gave her a look and said, "Not too tired from all that walking, are you?"

"What? You think you're going to get lucky again?"

I picked her up and carried her into the room, kicking the door closed behind us. "I know I am."

ABOUT THE AUTHOR

EARL EMERSON is a lieutenant in the Seattle Fire Department. He is the Shamus Award–winning author of the Thomas Black detective series, which includes *The Rainy City, Poverty Bay, Nervous Laughter, Fat Tuesday, Deviant Behavior, Yellow Dog Party*, and *The Portland Laugher*. He has also written three books featuring fire chief and acting sheriff Mac Fontana: *Black Hearts and Slow Dancing, Help Wanted: Orphans Preferred*, and *Morons and Madmen*.

Earl Emerson lives in North Bend, Washington.